PLAYING WITH FIRE

THE MONTANA FIRE SERIES:

Where There's Smoke
Playing With Fire
Burnin' For You
Oh, The Weather Outside is Frightful (novella)

MONTANA FIRE
SUMMER OF FIRE TRILOGY 2

PLAYING WITH FIRE

SUSAN MAY
WARREN

sdg

SDG PUBLISHING
A division of Susan May Warren Fiction
Minneapolis, MN

PRAISE FOR PLAYING WITH FIRE BY AMAZON.COM READERS

Playing With Fire

PLAYING WITH FIRE is the second in Ms. Warren's self-published series "Montana Fire" but it easily stands alone. I was anxious to read Connor's story (I fell in love with him in the first book "Where There's Smoke" when he was a secondary character. I didn't remember who exactly Liza was, but as I started to read I recognized her from Ms. Warren's "Deep Haven" series, and I also was glad to see some other familiar characters in this

If you like romantic suspense, heavier on the romance, you will love PLAYING WITH FIRE. It does play in with the ripped parachutes in "Where There's Smoke" and leaves you hanging, wondering who is targeting the Montana Smoke Jumpers and why.

My adrenaline pumped as I realized Connor and Liza were tracked by a bear while they were searching for the missing teens from camp. I anxiously flipped through pages as they hunted the forest for the missing teens, trying to avoid the grizzly. Would they find the teens in time?

You'll have to read PLAYING WITH FIRE to find out.

I highly recommend PLAYING WITH FIRE and the first book "Where There's Smoke" in Ms. Warren's "Montana Fire" series. Don't miss this book -- or any book -- by my favorite author. ~*Lollipops*, Amazon.com reader

The Best Inspirational Action, Suspense, Romance of the Year!

THIS BOOK!!!

It has to be the most exciting, romantic, hold on to your seat, intense adrenaline rush, suspenseful book I've read this year!!!

The overview's in the book description above and I won't give any spoilers, I'll just tell what I loved about the book, and that's EVERYTHING!!!

Playing with Fire is the perfect title that has handsome, tragedy-plagued Conner running from making promises to beautiful, kind, promise-needing Liza. Neither wants to get burned, but as the Robert Frost saying goes, "the best way out is always through". Their attraction is instant and palpable throughout the story. At one point Conner thinks his heart might explode, mine too! The sparks were flying so fast and furious I thought my kindle might catch fire. Be still my racing heart! This story has a swoon factor of 10+. I was in emotional knots for most of the story and

Could. Not. Put. The. Book. Down!!!

On top of a fantastic love story, there's also the overlapping wilderness experience of Conner, Liza and the search and rescue team trying to find lost Shep and Esther before it's too late, providing enough adrenaline rush to keep me turning the pages as fast as I could. I held my breath more than a few times, having to remind myself to take a breath. Yes, it's that good.

I loved book one, Where There's Smoke, and wondered how Susan May Warren could top that story, or at least equal it. But she did! This is my favorite in the summer series so far, actually, my favorite book this year! It's full of everything I love in inspirational fiction, suspense, drama, humor, action, and romance. A reader just can't ask for anything more, Susan May Warren gave it all. She always does a beautiful job of tying life circumstances into spiritual truths. In this case, "Because of the Lord's great love for us we are not consumed, for His compassions never fail, They are new every morning".

I simply cannot wait for book three, Burnin' For You, to see what intrigue awaits Reuben and Gilly, come on August 2nd! (I never thought I'd be wishing a month of summer away, but if that's what it takes! :)

Thanks to Susan May Warren for writing such thrilling inspirational fiction, you're at the top of your game and I applaud you!! This book's a Winner in every way! ! *~Tracey* book corner fan, Amazon.com reader

Susan May Warren Never Disappoints!

Long Awaited Romance!

Afraid to believe in promises, Liza Beaumont and Connor Young have danced around their feelings for one another for nearly three years, depending on phone calls and brief visits to nourish an endearing long distance friendship. Haunted by their pasts, each of them sadly pushes away from the other, until a grizzly bear and two missing teens have Liza speed dialing Connor out of pure desperation.

This beautifully orchestrated romance between an artsy potter and an adrenaline driven firefighter serves as a lovely reminder of our God's promise to love us faithfully and to fiercely guard our future in the hollow of His hands. Liza is going to need every thread of her faith, because "she was so playing with fire" to believe in a happily-ever-after with this man.

Susan May Warren's "Summer of Fire Trilogy" is just as hot as ever! *~Rebecca Maney*, Amazon.com reader

Montana Fire
Summer of Fire Trilogy
Book Two: *Playing with Fire*
ISBN-13: 978-1-943935-14-7
Published by SDG Publishing
15100 Mckenzie Blvd. Minnetonka, MN 55345

This book is a work of fiction. Names, characters, places, and incidents are either products of the author's imagination or used fictitiously. Any similarity to actual people, organizations, and/or events is purely coincidental.

For more information about Susan May Warren, please access the author's website at the following address: www.susanmaywarren.com.

Published in the United States of America.

For Your glory, Lord

PROLOGUE

THIS WAS NOT HOW Liza Beaumont wanted to die.

Not that anyone ever *wanted* to die, but certainly Liza could think of a dozen or more ways that would be preferable to ending up as an early-morning snack for a six-hundred-pound grizzly.

First choice might be tucked into the embrace of Conner Young, their golden years fading into a molten sunset, perhaps drifting off into sleep, to wake up in glory.

There she went again, wishing for things she didn't have. Like bear spray. Or a tranquilizer gun.

Or maybe even better-than-spotty cell service here, high up on a remote trail in the middle of the Cabinet Mountains in western Montana.

She glanced down the trail, back up at the bear now rocking back and forth. What had the camp wildlife expert said about bears? Stop, drop, and roll—no, no—

Drop. Play *dead.* Except her instincts, frankly, were to scream first, then—well, run.

Of course, that was *always* her instinct.

But this time it felt right, because, really, who had the courage to just lie there while a grizzly sniffed her prone body, ready to take a tasty bite out of her neck. Not when she had heaps more life to live, hopes, dreams…

Only, one of those included a six-foot-two blond smoke-jumper with devastating blue eyes, wide sinewed shoulders, and a body honed by the rigors of fighting fire who claimed to love sunrises as much as she did.

But Conner wasn't here. Just her, her sharpened colored graphite pencils and a fresh canvas to paint her artist's view of the sunrise. The perfect place to remind herself—and her fellow camper—that they didn't need men to live happily ever after.

Except said camper hadn't been in her bunk this morning in the high school girls' cabin.

Esther, where are you?

Clearly not here on the overlook.

Liza could hardly believe it when she'd woken this morning to the sight of Esther's rumpled, empty sleeping bag. She'd torn herself out of bed, grabbed coffee from the lodge, and—with the hope that Esther Rogers was already at the overlook, armed with her own sketch pencils, furiously sketching the arch of a new day—Liza had set out to find her.

Remind her that hiking out from camp without her counselor was a colossal no-no, even at Camp Blue Sky, and especially during the annual Ember Community Church family camp.

Even if the poor girl might be nursing a breakup.

Liza could murder heart-breaker Shep Billings with her bare hands. Or at least wound him with a graphite pencil.

Although, in her gut, Liza had a feeling Esther might have dreamed up Shep's attention toward her. The hot boys simply didn't date artsy, introverted, slightly chubby book nerds with plain dark brown hair like Liza—*er*—Esther.

So, when Liza found the fifteen-year-old holed up last

night, face puffy, surrounded in wadded tissues, an early morning, brain-clearing hike up to the Snowshoe Peak overlook to watch the sunrise over the hoary peaks seemed like something a savvy counselor might suggest.

Even as Liza hiked up to the overlook, the sunrise promised inspiration, clouds mottled with lavender and crimson, and gilded with the finest threads of gold feathering the heavens. A breeze tickled the aspen along the trail, the piney scent from the valley redolent with the heady sense of summer and freedom and fresh starts.

The air suggested another scorcher, dust and tinder-dry yellow needles kicked up on the path, settling onto her boots. Three weeks into her stay at Camp Blue Sky and already she'd seen two fires thicken the air above the Kootenai National Forest.

Most likely, the blond smokejumper was fighting some Glacier Park fire, sooty from head to toe, reeking of sweat and ash and wrung out from a week on the fire line.

At least that was how Conner most often came to her in her dreams.

And there she went again, conjuring him up, as if he might swagger into her life, carrying a donut, a cup of coffee, and that languid smile that made her heart lie to her.

Enough.

The overlook hung over a ledge in the Pine Ridge trail, ten feet of cut-away granite edged with a cowboy split-rail fence for a modicum of protection from the two-hundred-foot drop. Further up, the trail banked around the edge of mountain, the land falling more gently into a valley until it tumbled into the north fork of the Bull River.

A roughhewn bench, smoothed out by early morning enthusiasts, perched in the middle of the overlook.

Liza had dearly hoped to spot Esther, with her mousy brown hair held back with a blue bandanna, dressed in her freshly tie-dyed shirt and grubby jeans, seated and drawing the dawnscape.

Empty. "Esther?"

Liza's voice had echoed in the blue-gold of the morning, scattering the shadows that bled through the trees.

Nothing but the shift of the wind in the trees, the scolding of a wood thrush.

Huh.

So maybe Esther hadn't broken the rules. Which meant she was still back at camp, maybe having gotten up early to use the showers. Although Liza had stopped there, too, on her way, and nothing but a few spiders rustled around the long building in the silvery predawn hours. All seventy-five family campers still tucked soundly in their beds.

Except, of course, Esther.

Liza had stood there, finishing off her coffee, debating.

Now that she was here, she could settle down, take out her board, and start a fresh sketch. Or—probably she should head back to camp, just to make sure Esther wasn't really holed up in the chapel, still weeping. Or maybe in the mess hall, loading up on Captain Crunch.

Yeah, she knew teenage girls. Especially the ones who wore their hearts pinned to their sleeves, bait for the first wily teenage boy to take a whack at it.

But that's why they'd hired her—not only to teach art but because she knew the kind of trouble teenagers could conjure up, both real and imagined. And she might not have all the answers, but she had a desire to keep life from feeling so big they gave into the urge to run.

Maybe someday, too, she could teach herself that same

trick.

Liza had walked to the edge of the cliff, breathed in the ethereal impulse to open her arms, take flight. To soar, caught on the currents rising from the valley. To escape the weight of the aloneness that sometimes took her breath away.

"I love the sunrise. It's Lamentations 3:22 over and over—"

Memories of Conner, lurking in her brain again.

Wow, she missed him, his absence a burning hole in her chest that she probably deserved.

She should have realized that Conner Young simply hadn't been that into her.

Which made her exactly the right candidate to counsel poor Esther. Liza had turned to leave when her gaze caught on something neon blue.

In that second, Liza's heart turned to stone.

A Blue Sky camp jacket. Caught in a gnarled cedar clinging to the rocky edge, as if—blown? Snagged on a fall?

Her breath hiccupped, turned to ash as she peered over the edge—*please, God, no.* Pebbles and the slick loam of old needles and runoff littered the ground of the overlook—easy to slip on should someone lose their footing.

But she saw nothing—no broken branches from the black spruce below, no tumble of boulders evidencing an avalanche.

No broken body of a fifteen-year-old girl crumpled at the base of the cliff.

Liza couldn't help it. She leaned over the edge. "Esther!" Her voice rippled in the air, too much panic in it to deny.

She closed her eyes, listened.

Maybe the jacket didn't belong to Esther. Maybe days ago a camper had shucked it off, left it here. The greedy wind scooped it up, flung it over the cliff, maybe—

It was then that the huffing sound behind her made her stiffen. The wind raked up a smell, earthy, rank, the scent of beast.

Liza held her breath, turned.

Oh—no—

Standing at the head of the trail, forty feet away, his dark eyes rimmed by a ruff of matted brown fur, powerful forearms pawing grooves into the dirt, head swinging—

Grizzly.

Her brain formed around the word even as she moved back against the rail. Glanced down.

Suddenly, the jacket made terrible, gut-wrenching sense.

The bear reared up, pawing at the air.

And sorry, she hadn't a prayer of playing dead with the scream roiling up inside her.

Oh, God, please make me fast.

If she lived, maybe He'd give her the courage to rewind time, past the last thirty minutes, or last night, all the way to last year, to the moment when she'd run away from Conner Young.

And this time she'd stay.

CHAPTER 1

Three years earlier…

THE LAST PLACE CONNER should be right now was fighting a fire in a pinprick of a town in northern Minnesota.

Not when his grandfather had a countdown on his life.

Not when his brother lay unavenged in a dismally marked grave in a meadow in northwestern Montana.

And especially not when Conner hadn't yet dug up any answers.

"Can I help you, mister?"

Conner looked down from where he was unloading his gear from the back of the lime-green, Jude County Hotshot buggy into the innocent blue eyes of a little boy.

The vehicle resembled an ambulance, with two bay doors in the back that opened to supplies and beds. After two days on the road, the box smelled exactly like it should after housing ten cramped, sweaty men and one very tolerant woman. And it wasn't likely to improve anytime soon—not with their immediate debrief at the National Forest Service office that overlooked the tiny hamlet of Deep Haven, Minnesota.

Smoke rose from the forest to the north, the reason why they'd made the trek east from their base in Ember, Montana.

"And who are you, champ?"

"Tiger Christiansen. My daddy is in there." Cute, the kid possessed freckles and a thin red scar over his eye that gave him the look of trouble. To bolster the look, he also nursed a hint of a fat lip and grass stains on his jeans.

Tiger pointed to the NFS building nearby where the rest of the hotshots, starting with Conner's boss, Jed Ransom, would be getting a sit-rep on the lightning strikes that had started a blaze in the tinder-crisp forest of the BWCA—Boundary Waters Canoe Area—along the border to Canada. A blowdown from ten years ago had scattered the carcasses of pine, birch, and poplar like kindling across a million acres of forest, and now with resorts and homes threatened, the NFS had called in the big dogs from the West.

The Jude County Hotshots.

According to Jed, the fire was currently inaccessible by land. They'd have to paddle in, and no doubt Jed was already on the horn to Jock Burns, hoping he could dispatch the rest of the smokejumpers who'd stayed behind to mop up a fire in Montana.

Conner's crew, and he'd be glad to see them.

Especially since the fire had already incinerated over thirteen thousand acres of boreal forest. Despite the ten thousand lakes that populated northern Minnesota, the fire was jumping from island to island. Today's flyover by one of the locals had the flame lengths at over one hundred feet.

"Are you here to help us fight the fire?" Conner asked, grabbing an orange Nomex helmet and fitting it on the boy's head.

"Sure!" Tiger held the helmet on as he jumped up and down, an exuberance in his tone that had Conner smiling. Reminded him of his friend Jim Micah's kid. Four years old now, little Sebastian had the tough hide of his father, a former

Green Beret and one of Conner's best friends.

One of the few people who knew what the little envelope Conner had jammed in his front shirt pocket meant.

Conner had read the letter, oh, roughly eighty-three times since leaving Montana.

Every single time, he wanted to get off the buggy, hop on a plane, and show up in the office of one P. T. Blankenship, lead investigator in his brother's murder.

Maybe offer his off-the-books assistance in a tone of voice he'd left behind in the military, back when he and Jim Micah were operating behind enemy lines in Iraq.

Leave no man behind—apparently the National Security Agency didn't abide by that little golden rule. Because after seven years, certainly they could offer Conner *something* of closure to give his grieving grandfather.

If Conner couldn't hop a plane to DC, then he'd settle for donning his gear and jumping into the dragon's mouth, armed with just his Pulaski and a chain saw.

Anything to burn off the edge of helplessness. It buzzed under his skin, made him irritable. Sweaty. Maybe even a little hungry.

"Okay, buster, carry this," Conner said and handed the kid a backpack of line gear. Nothing heavy—just a fire shelter, a space blanket, an empty canister for water, a couple of candy bars. Tiger pulled on the backpack, nearly as big as he was, and scampered inside the building.

A future hotshot in the making. Conner let a smile tug at his face as he pulled out a large metal box filled with electronics—his remote video surveillance devices, his computer, a few specially designed handheld radios. He opened the door to the NFS office with his hip and carried the box inside.

The once-quiet small-town office hummed with activity,

the radios chattering with flyover reports from spotters. Another squawked weather updates.

The hotshot crew had already filtered in. Graham, from the Blackfeet Nation near Ember, and Pete—"Sarge"—Holt, former military, the dad of a cute two-year-old daughter. Katie Whip, whom they referred to as simply "Whip," was as tough as she was pretty, and smart, too, with her degree in fire management from Boise. She crouched down, offered Tiger her whistle, and he blew it.

Laughter all around, except from the man standing with Jed. Dark hair, his mouth a grim slash, a build that suggested a capability on the fire line, he bent over the map where Jed was outlining the fire and the hotshots' intended assault.

Jed had mentioned his friend Darek Christiansen a dozen times on the trek east. Apparently they'd been greenies together before Darek quit to return home, raise his son. If Conner remembered correctly, the poor guy had lost his wife a few years ago in a horrible car accident.

"Dare, I'd like you to meet Conner Young," Jed said. "He hitched on board with us last year doing some advanced communications work. He developed a program to help us read and predict fire behavior."

Darek met Conner's grip. No preamble, just, "Hard to see a fire from twenty-plus miles away. Better to get close to it, hear it, feel it. Does it work?"

Conner was about to jump in when Jed cut him off.

"We're still testing it, but he's able to upload his data right to the handhelds," Jed said. "Sort of like smartphones but with better service."

Simplified, but okay. Jed wasn't exactly the tech-savvy type.

"Can they survive being dropped in the dirt, kicked, and

burned?"

"Oh, no. We leave that abuse to the hotshots," Conner said. He tried to get a read on Darek, the way he kept checking on Tiger, and with a start, Conner made the connection.

The guy was trying hard to put responsibilities over passion—Conner got that. And the hole it dug into a man when he chose one over the other.

As if in confirmation, Jed asked Darek if he'd like to help them work the fire. Not a bad idea since Darek lived here, worked in these forests.

"I…I'd love to, but—" He glanced at Tiger again. "I can't."

Just then, Tiger jumped up, ran over to his dad, holding himself, doing the potty dance.

Conner hid a grin as Darek steered his son toward the bathroom.

And for a second, seeing the man with his hand on his son's shoulders, the way he guarded the door as Tiger took care of business—it all dug a hole inside Conner that he couldn't place.

An emptiness, an echo of something he'd once wanted long ago.

But, passion versus responsibility. Both had him in a chokehold.

Conner headed back outside and pulled out his cell phone. He took the letter from his pocket, dialed the number at the bottom, and listened to the ringing on the other end.

He stared at the blue of Lake Superior glinting through the pine and birch. A pretty little town, Deep Haven, tucked into the north woods. From his vantage point on the bluff overlooking the town, he made out a pebbled harbor, a few hotels along the rocky edge, a park in the center, a cafe, a tavern, and a coffee shop. And in the air, he smelled the fried crispiness of a donut shop.

The call slipped to voice mail.

"Hey, Grandpa. I thought I'd check in—I'm in Minnesota. Don't know when I'll be back—but when I am, I'll stop by." He ran a hand behind his neck, debating the last part. "I...got a letter from the NSA. Blankenship. They're closing the case, putting it in the cold files."

He swallowed, hated the way the words dug in, fisted his chest. "I'm so sorry. I know I promised—" And he couldn't continue, not with the words turning to acid in his chest.

His promise. It had turned into a noose, cut off his breathing. His life.

"Anyway, I just wanted to see how you're doing."

No, that wasn't what he wanted, but maybe he didn't know what he wanted, really. Absolution? Forgiveness?

Anything to help him close the door on his failures.

"I'll call you later." Conner hung up and heard feet behind him. He turned and spied Tiger running out, still wearing his helmet.

Darek and Jed came out behind him, Jed carrying a map. He took it over to a truck, pulled down the tailgate. Gestured Conner over.

Conner noticed the logo on the side—*Evergreen Outfitter and Cabin Rentals.*

"Darek's found us a place to set up fire camp," Jed said, unrolling the map, and pointing to a clearing north of town. "And he's offered the resort to house the Jude County crew. The rest of the teams will have to fend for themselves in town."

Gravel crunched in the lot, and the three turned as a Jeep pulled in.

A woman got out and pulled out a white box with the

words *World's Best Donuts* imprinted in red on the side.

"Hey, Liza," Darek said.

"Dare. I should have expected you to be hanging out with a group called the hotshots," she said. "Whatever."

Darek laughed.

Conner couldn't take his eyes off her. Tall, shapely, with long, silky sable hair blowing in the wind off the lake., and when she smiled, warmth touched her deep brown eyes. She wore a pair of green fatigues and a pink T-shirt with speckles of lavender paint on the sleeve, hinting that she'd torn herself away from a project to buy them donuts, and flip-flops that showed off blue toenail polish. Sparkly, intriguing, indigo blue.

"I brought donut holes for our local heroes." She opened the box, and inside was a mound of powdered sugar holes. "Especially for my *favorite* hero."

She wasn't talking about him—although for a crazy, split second, when she glanced at him, something caught his attention.

Her eyes. On closer look, they weren't just brown, but the color of rich, freshly pulled espresso, and they had the same effect. A bracing, nourishing jolt that went straight to his bones.

For a second, it jerked him out of the dark funk he'd dragged with him from Montana.

Then she bent and held the box open to Tiger. "You're going to save our little town, right Tig?"

He grinned and grabbed a powdered sugar hole, bit it. It left a ring of white powder around his mouth as the sugar puffed off the pastry. She laughed and handed him a napkin.

Only then did she look up and truly smile at Conner.

She had a sweetness in her smile that matched the donuts, dusting him with a sense of joy. However, not a hint of flirt in it, nothing that carried the hero worship, the adoration that usually accompanied a female welcome committee.

Huh. Finally, a woman he didn't have to dodge.

Even better would be a woman who might share his faith.

Not that it mattered—he didn't look beyond today, couldn't promise anyone a future.

Conner reached for a powdered donut hole before Darek lifted the box away from Liza to carry inside.

"I'm Conner Young," he said. He popped the hole in his mouth then grabbed a napkin. "I'm with the Jude County Hotshots—actually, I'm a smokejumper, but we're helping out the crew."

"Liza Beaumont," she responded. "I'm with the Deep Haven Donut Brigade—actually, I'm a local artist, but I'm helping out the volunteers. I've been sent on a peacekeeping mission by the chamber of commerce to make sure you feel appreciated."

She said it in the most innocent of ways, nothing lurid in her tone. Yeah, he liked her. Felt his defenses lower just a little more.

"There are hotels in the area ready to put you up—"

"We're staying up at the Evergreen Resort," Conner said.

"Perfect. Ingrid and John will take good care of you," Liza said. "And I know you're here to fight the fire, but we're having an art festival this weekend in town. There's a street dance on one of the nights, and although the fireworks display has been canceled, there's crafts and homemade ice cream and... well, if you want, you could stop by my booth. I'm giving demonstrations."

Still nothing of a come-on in her voice.

She was safe and sweet, and something about her expression told him that he just might have found someone he could spend time with without stirring up expectations.

"What kind of booth?" he asked, aware that it didn't really matter. She could be giving demonstrations on stacking rocks and he'd be mesmerized.

"I'm a potter."

And she smiled again. For a crazy second, the coil of frustration tightening his chest since Ember loosened. He took a full, clean breath of the fresh lake air.

Maybe he didn't have to jump into a flaming boreal forest to find a way to forget his failures.

~

Despite the orange haze along the horizon to the north, the hint of wood smoke in the breeze, Deep Haven managed to put together its annual art festival. The chamber of commerce blocked off Main Street, artisans erected flimsy booths, and the smell of cotton candy and kettle corn added a festive flair. Liza could almost convince herself that they weren't going to burn to death in the near future.

Probably not with the cadre of firefighters in town—hotshots from Montana, a fresh crew from Arizona, another from Alaska, not to mention volunteers from Minnesota.

Even the local fire department had deployed to the firebase up the trail. Apparently, they'd set up a first-rate camp, including tents, a chow line, showers, and biffies.

Despite their camping accommodations, on their off days, hotshots roamed around town, hung out at the local VFW, and generally boosted the local economy. Everyone from Polly down at World's Best Donuts to Kathy at the Java Cup thanked the heavens for the boon, despite the hover of danger in the air.

And the reports that the fire was only getting bigger.

Liza refused to think about the hotshots who put themselves between the blaze and their tiny town. Heroes, every last one of them.

And yeah, when she thought of heroes, Conner Young tiptoed to the top of her mind. She shouldn't be thinking of him *quite* so much. Shouldn't hope that he'd take her up on her suggestion to stop by her booth.

It wasn't like he'd noticed her, well, not *that* way, and she'd tried not to flirt—not that she knew how, but the last thing she needed was him getting the wrong impression.

Single, happily so. Really. At thirty-five, she was too old for true love. Besides, she was the kind of woman men saw as *Just Friends.* A listener, sometimes with good advice, and easy to walk away from.

And it was her fault, really. The last thing she wanted to do was try to make a man love her. She wasn't desperate. She wasn't even lonely.

She had God, after all. Which meant that she made it painfully easy for a man to enjoy her friendship and never see her as anything more. She simply refused to reach out, to hold on, figuratively, and especially literally.

Even if she wanted to. Like a few days ago, when Conner had looked like he could use a hug, with so much stress on his face. Her heart had gone out to him.

It had nothing at all to do with his painfully good looks, that dark golden hair tucked behind his ears, the bronze whiskers along his jaw, and his eyes—so devastatingly blue, the color of the lake, striated blue, with layers of secrets. She couldn't breathe for a moment when he'd looked up, asked her what kind of booth she had.

She'd mumbled something hopefully coherent, and right

about then, Darek came back out and wrapped them up in conversation.

She'd made her escape.

Not that it mattered. Conner probably hadn't given her another thought.

And she shouldn't give him one, either.

Liza stared out across the park to where the sun turned the water platinum. A breeze off the lake lifted her long hair, held back in a ponytail. She wore a tank top and a broomstick skirt, but despite the shade in her booth, the pavement could bake through her sandals. However, even in the heat, the freshness of the lake cooled her skin.

She wondered about the breezes and how they might affect the firefighters.

She'd read stories about sudden winds trapping firefighters—

Stop.

From across the park, a flautist played from the stage, the music light, refreshing. A nearby tent hosted a rock-painting contest.

Liza was storing her clay in plastic bags when she spied Darek walking with Tiger and Ivy, the new county prosecutor in town and Liza's tenant in her over-the-garage apartment. Ivy was cute, petite, smart, and sweet, and maybe exactly whom Darek needed to start over with.

Interesting. They stopped at her booth.

"Hello," Liza said and leaned down to tousle Tiger's hair. Such a tragedy, Darek losing his wife with their son so young.

Life was scary that way. It would be helpful if one could be assured of a happy ending.

"Hello, Miz B," Tiger said.

Liza grinned at him, then at Darek, Ivy. "Tiger's preschool class came to my studio last year and they all made bowls."

"I painted it, too!"

Ivy was holding a bowl, looking at the bottom. Probably at the fish imprint. "I have a few of these in my apartment."

True, because Liza had furnished it. "Let me know if you need any replacements." She winked. "So, Tiger, they're painting rocks down at the beach. You should head down to the booth."

Darek looked like she'd suggested walking barefoot through live coals, his attempt at a smile wretched.

"Don't look so ill, Darek. It's just watercolors," Liza said. "Maybe you should paint something. Could be good for you. Loosen you up."

"I don't—"

"C'mon, it'll be fun," Ivy said, enthusiasm in her voice.

Poor Ivy. Darek almost looked annoyed.

Liza had the crazy urge to tell the girl to run. Because if a guy wasn't into you, you should cut him loose before he could do serious damage to your heart.

Wise Liza, the romantic guru. Oh, for crying out loud. Ivy would have a better chance at getting romantic advice from Deep Haven's local Dear Abby, Miss Foolish Heart, who actually *had* found true love with the town football coach. Still, Liza had enough history to know that staying stubbornly single had its advantages.

Like never getting her heart broken…

Or…

She watched them walk over to the children's booth, saw Darek lean down, heard Ivy laugh.

See, what did she know about love and happy endings?

Clearly nothing.

She finished packing up the clay, was starting to wrap the remaining pottery, trying to figure out if she had the energy to stick around for the street dance or if she should just go home.

Maybe write her stepbrother Charlie another letter, again offering a place for his daughter, Raina, to live if she needed it. Talk about needing a happy ending. Her poor niece deserved someone to love her, despite her list of mistakes.

Someone, hello, like *Jesus*. The one who'd put Liza back together.

He was enough. Hello and amen.

"So, can you teach me how to, what, make a bowl or something?"

Liza stilled, her back to her now-dismantled display. His voice was low and soft, a little rough perhaps with smoke and the trauma of the fire line, but strong enough to seep under her skin.

Add a little fire to her pulse.

She turned then, painfully aware of the line of sweat across her brow, the pinch of a sunburn on her face and shoulders, and the fact that she hadn't had time this morning to put on makeup.

Not that it mattered. She was just the festival representative.

"Hey," she said, maybe a little too much exuberance in her voice. "You showed up."

And *how*. He had showered, it seemed, because his hair was wet but tied with a red bandanna, the golden ends curling out behind his ears. He hadn't shaved, his whiskers were longer, bronzing as his beard thickened. He wore a black T-shirt, Gore-Tex pants, and a pair of hiking sandals, and had his hands in his pockets, like he might just be moseying by.

Shoot. She'd sort of hoped...

"Of course," Conner said. "Well, I mean—I wanted to, but I wasn't sure I'd get the night off. But we've been on four days straight, and Jed said we could take twenty-four hours off. The Arizona crew is holding the line."

"You can do that—take time off?"

"In a big fire, yes. We rotate in and out. You get too worn out, people get hurt. We work with axes and chain saws, eyes watering, barely able to breathe, and sleep in the dirt most of the time. So, occasionally we surrender to clean sheets and a shower." He winked at her.

And wow, really, she had clearly been trapped in Deep Haven, the land of No Eligible Men for *way* too long, because her entire body heated.

Probably it was just the warm summer evening.

"It looks like I got here too late for the demonstration," he said. "You're all packed up."

"No—I could—"

"Liza, it's okay."

"But I promised."

He raised an eyebrow. "Actually, no, you didn't. And that's good—promises are usually broken."

She frowned, and he held up his hand. "Because I usually can't stick around for them."

Oh. Right.

"But if it makes you feel better, the rate the fire is going, we'll be here for a while. So maybe I can come back."

Really? And oh, *really*?

She just stood there like an idiot, smiling at him. "Sure."

"Perfect." He smiled back. He had such a nice smile,

white teeth, and a genuine warmth in his eyes, like he had stopped by just to see her booth. To see her.

She heard shouting across the park and looked past him to see—seriously? Darek and Jensen Atwood—Darek's former best friend—tangled in a brawl. Right here in the middle of the festival.

Sheesh—she knew Darek blamed the guy for his wife's death, but—

Conner, however, had stiffened. Something crossed his face, his smile dimming, a hard look flashing in his eyes. Almost as if he were debating diving in, pulling the two apart.

And then, "Daddy!"

Even from here, she could hear Tiger's voice shrilling.

It was as if the entire festival crowd froze on Tiger's cry. Darek certainly did.

Not Conner, however. He took a step toward the brawl.

And then Caleb, the football coach, intervened, pulling Darek away from Jensen, who got up and pushed through the crowd, cute Claire Gibson on his heels.

Ivy wasn't faring much better with Darek, and again Liza went back to her previous supposition.

Run.

"What was that about?" Conner asked.

"It's a long story," Liza said. "I don't know most of it, but the short version is that Darek's wife was hit while she was jogging, and Jensen was at the wheel."

"Oh my."

"I know. The entire town took sides, and poor Jensen has been doing community service for the past three years, working off his sentence."

"That's all he got—community service?"

"It was clearly an accident. Some thought he should have been found not guilty."

A muscle pulled in Conner's jaw, and for a second, she saw a story there.

"You okay?" she asked.

When he turned to her, however, nothing remained of his guarded expression. "Starved. If I don't eat soon, I'll probably need hospitalization."

"Clearly you need a pizza from Pierre's then."

"I like how you think. Can I help you pack up? Because I probably also need a tour guide."

And the way he said it, she couldn't agree more.

Oh, Liza. She could hear her own voice in her head. *Run.*

But he wasn't asking her out. He just needed a friend. A tour guide from the Deep Haven Donut Brigade.

He helped her pack up her pottery, taking care to wrap the pieces in Bubble Wrap, secure them in boxes. He had strong, scarred, even wounded hands, blistered, bruised, and reddened from his work in the forest. She noticed burns on the tops, evidence of his profession.

The band on stage had switched to bluegrass by the time they closed the booth and headed to Pierre's pizza stand. Conner bought himself a slice of pepperoni and insisted on buying one for her, too. They wandered the half block down to the park, sat on a bench listening to the band, shooing away the greedy seagulls.

"How long have you lived here?" He folded his pizza in half, like a sandwich.

"About ten years. I moved here with my best friend. I opened my studio, and she started a bookstore and coffee shop and met the man of her dreams, author Joe Michaels."

"Seriously? I used to read his books when I was stationed overseas."

Stationed? "Where were you—"

"In the army. Desert Storm."

"You were in Iraq."

He made a noncommittal sound.

"Not Iraq?"

His mouth tweaked up on one side. "I was a Green Beret. So, yeah, and whatever."

Oh. No wonder he had this edge about him, a sense that he took in everything around him. Like the kids playing on the pebbled beach, throwing rocks in the water, and the teenagers riding their skateboards in the street, and a few adults sitting on the deck at the nearby tavern. And she guessed he'd probably even seen Kyle Hueston walk by in his deputy uniform.

"How did you go from a Green Beret to a hotshot?"

"Smokejumper."

"What's the difference?" She finished off her pizza, wiped her fingers.

"Smokejumpers are normally the first line of defense when a fire is unreachable. We jump in, usually miles from the nearest road, and use axes, shovels, chain saws, and strategy to put out a fire."

"So, superman firefighters."

Oh, that sounded lame. She wanted to cringe, but that side of his mouth tweaked up again, as if pleased.

"Just kidding. But it sounds dangerous."

"It can be. But we have a crew trained by one of the best—Jock Burns. He's the reason I joined up. My dad used to jump for Jock years ago."

"I'll bet your dad gets a kick out of that," she said.

And oops, she said something wrong, because his smile fell and, as he looked away, a muscle pulled in his jaw. "Yeah."

"Did I tread somewhere I shouldn't have gone?"

"No." He finished his pizza. Looked out at the lake. "My parents died when I was seventeen. Auto accident."

Oh. "I'm so sorry."

"Thanks." He wiped his hands on his napkin. "I think I need a drink."

She glanced at the tavern, heard the raucous music lifting from the deck.

He must have followed her gaze, maybe even seen her expression, because he added, "A Coke will do just fine. Or a malt?"

"How about something from Licks and Stuff?"

He nodded, got up, and they headed for ice cream.

Not a date. Better, actually, because he was easy to be with. Especially when he ordered two chocolate malts and handed her one.

They were walking back to the beach when he added, "I do think he'd be proud of me."

Huh? Oh, his father. She'd been busy watching the way his arms filled out that T-shirt, imagining him swinging a Pulaski—that special ax firefighters used, a tidbit she'd discovered while reading John McClean's *Fire on the Mountain,* thank you, Amazon, for that quick download.

She just might be the most pitiful tour guide in the history of Deep Haven.

Not. A. Date.

"I only joined the army because I didn't know what else to do with my life. My brother and I went to live with my grandpa after our parents died. Grandpa fought in World War II. I guess I wanted to be like him. And the military gave me focus. A purpose."

"How long did you serve?"

"Three tours. I got out about seven years ago."

"And since then you've been smokejumping?"

They reached the edge of the beach and he sat on a boulder, facing the sunset. "Not all the time, but yeah. It seemed like something my father would like me to do. And I like it—it's hard, but focused work. Easy to lose yourself in, and there's a brotherhood, not unlike the military."

He had an interesting face. High cheekbones, a tiny scar under his right eye. A strong jaw, a nose with the tiniest of bumps, as if it had been broken once. And the slightest upturn of his lips, as if even in repose he might be harboring a smile.

The kind of face that held secrets in his enigmatic expressions.

And shoot, if it didn't stir up the desire to sit here forever, listening to his voice as the sunset turned the shore golden, his eyes a deep, sapphire blue.

"Why is there a fish on the bottom of your pots?" he asked.

"I'm a Christian. It's my way of imprinting faith into my work."

And slowly, he smiled. A deep, curious, even delighted smile, and with it, a look that settled on her, no, settled *through* her, as if trying to reach inside her, discover her.

She swallowed, her throat thick.

"Really," he said.

She managed a quick nod.

Then, "Me too."

He held out his hand then, and, curious, she took it. Found it strong, yes, and warm, and solid.

He didn't let go, and she looked up, met his gaze.

It contained a softness she didn't understand.

But she had a crazy, almost ethereal urge to cry.

Especially when he said, simply, "It's so nice to meet you, Liza Beaumont."

CHAPTER 2

THEY WERE ALL GOING to die if Conner didn't get his head back in the game. It'd been a couple of days since he'd last slept. He was dog tired, stiff, and felt like he'd been run over with a dozer. His mouth tasted like ash, his eyelids felt like sandpaper, and his bones rattled with the continual buzz of chain saws.

It didn't help that the fire didn't want to go to bed. Somewhere around 2:00 a.m. he'd chugged down four packets of instant coffee, three ibuprofens, and a chocolate bar that now sat in his gut like a rock. It all did nothing for him. He felt surly and caustic and not at all in the mood for the fire to be misbehaving.

And that's exactly when the wind shifted and sent the fire up the flank he'd just spent sixteen hours cutting.

"Get on those spot fires!" he shouted to the group of shots, rookies at the beginning of the summer. Veterans now, after a month of fighting fires in Montana and the last two weeks in Minnesota.

With them were four smokejumpers from the Jude County team, sent out east courtesy of Jock Burns, who'd stayed behind to run a fire in Montana. Conner had nearly cheered when he saw his teammates pull up—Reuben Marshall, Pete Brooks, Nutter Turnquist, and even rookie Tom Browning.

Now everyone resembled a chain gang—wrung out, peeved, and desperate to defend the line they'd given their last ounce of energy digging. They worked on a meager logging road, widening it by a dozen or more feet. They'd worked their way about two hundred yards from the main road.

The crew used their Pulaskis and water canisters to put out the fires, their headlamps almost unnecessary. But one look at their situation and Conner knew they needed a new plan.

They worked in what looked like a graveyard. Once-majestic white pines and spruce, blown down a decade ago, now lay stripped and gray, the ground littered with the debris of the trees, sapwood slabs, limbs, bark, and a crusty scattering of brown pine needles embedded in the forest floor.

Tinder. Just waiting for a spark.

And with the fire in the distance turning the sky an eerie orange, the smoke threading through the forest, the entire scene resembled something out of a horror movie.

Clearly, he needed a shower. Food. A bed. Not necessarily in that order.

But they still had a quarter mile to dig to the gravel pit that served as the left flank line. With the main blaze a little under two miles away and the wind at five miles an hour, they had a day, at least, to establish the rest of the line. To stop the dragon.

Conner had used his video footage, posted at NFS fire stations, to analyze the fire behavior, and after conferring with Jed what seemed like days ago, agreed that cutting a line along the logging road would be their best bet at stopping the fire before it reached Evergreen Resort.

Or Deep Haven.

And there he went again, his mind drawn back to Liza

Beaumont. Who knew an impulsive decision to stop by her booth and say hi would result in an easy, comfortable evening spent listening to music, talking about his life as a firefighter and hers in this small hamlet. They talked movies and books—and she pointed out their resident author Joe Michaels in the crowd of street dancers. Conner had told her what he could about military life and growing up on his grandfather's ranch, and she even listened to his way-too technical description of his brainchild, a firefighting drone, just in the sketching stage.

She'd sat across from him on the shoreline and as the moon rose, she dug a trail into the pebbled beach, occasionally pitching a rock out into the waves softly whispering on shore. He couldn't help notice how the wind played with her silky hair, the stars glowing in her eyes, and for the first time in he didn't know how long, he just relaxed.

He'd nearly heard his relief gusting out in a rush when she said she was a Christian.

Because that meant she didn't expect anything from him but an easy, right-now friendship. He didn't have to worry about the what-ifs simmering between them, the kind that usually made him dodge these short-term, fire-line-induced relationships. He just wasn't into flings, like some of the other guys might be.

But he did enjoy her laughter, the way she leaned into his stories, listened to him. After spending a week with his sweaty, ornery, and occasionally rough-mouthed team, sitting with Liza felt like bathing in light and hope. Nearly intoxicating, and he dearly hoped he might find her again—

"Conner! Watch out for that snag!"

Jed's voice, just down the line, and Conner looked up to see the wind had torched a nearby white pine, dead and dry, fallen at an angle. Flames raked over it, sizzling at the crown that dripped out over the edge of their line.

In the orange haze of night obscured by the smoke drifting over their line, they might have lost track of how the fire had grown.

Conner stepped away from the snag, jogging down the line. They'd cut in nearly half a mile. Another quarter mile away the road ended in a gravel quarry where the logging trucks turned around.

A big, bare area suitable for a safety zone. But to get to it, they'd have to run through uncut forest.

The snag lit another tree nearby, and fire blazed up the trunk, out through the woodpecker holes, and along the deadened branches.

"We need to get out of here," Jed said, meeting Conner. "I've called in for a tanker, but it's ten minutes or more out."

"We might have ten minutes," Conner said. "But—"

"We don't want to take the chance. Let's get moving."

"To the gravel pit or—"

"Back along the trail. I don't like how the fire is blowing up down the line. We'll tell them to drop retardant on the trail, come back with a dozer."

The trail made for a decent path as Conner rounded up his crew and headed out with Jed.

It only took a matter of minutes for him to realize how right Jed had been to call them off the line. The fire seemed to be creating its own weather, the smoke rushing over them, thick, hot, burning his throat. He pulled up his bandanna, stretched out into a jog.

Not too fast—he didn't want to turn an ankle. But not slow enough for the ash and char to catch him.

Firebrands—pine cones, sticks, needles—swirled in the air, stinging his face.

And then he heard it—the locomotive roar of the fire, whipped to frenzy by the wind. He wanted to turn, to gauge the flame lengths, but out of the corner of his eye he could see it—the fire advancing through the forest, brilliant, hot, red-orange, bright yellow.

Angry.

He kicked up his pace and heard the heavy breathing of his crew behind him.

He heard a shout then—Jed, twenty yards ahead of him, also running hard, half obscured by smoke.

He rounded the bend and Jed caught him by the shoulders. "Stop—the fire's jumped the line."

Sure enough, maybe twenty yards ahead, the fire had spurred over the dirt road, torching an overhanging snag.

"We're cut off—the others are past it," Jed said, surveying the trail behind Conner.

The crew had caught up. Reuben pulled the chainsaw off his shoulder. A big man, even he was breathing hard from the exertion. A red line on his neck betrayed where the saw teeth had bit into his skin.

"We need another escape route. Cascade River is southwest, through the forest, about three hundred yards from here—"

"You're kidding me. Through the forest?" This from Pete Brooks. "We can't outrun the fire."

"We're going to have to," Jed said. "Go!"

And Conner, who hadn't panicked yet, ignored the claws in his chest, turned, and barreled into the twisted debris of forest.

"Don't fall!" Jed's voice, but it could have been Conner's as he fled, slapping through brush, his feet landing on jutted, rocky soil barely illuminated with his headlamp.

He heard Jed's voice on the radio, screaming for the retardant drop.

Conner thrashed ahead, burst into a small clearing. His breath turned to fire in his lungs.

He could hear it.

Either the rush of a river or the fire closing in.

Pete Brooks raced past him; Reuben right behind, thundering through the forest, his saw in his grip.

The other hotshots had abandoned their Pulaskis. Graham ran just a few feet behind Whip, probably making sure that she didn't stumble. They passed Jed without slowing, heading for the forest on the other side.

"We got about forty-five seconds before this thing blows up," Jed yelled as he raced past Conner. "C'mon!"

Conner turned to follow when he saw Tom Browning, ten yards behind, in the woods.

He was limping badly.

And, to Conner's horror, when the kid hit the meadow, he tripped on a rock, and went flying.

Conner stifled a word and ran to him.

Tom's helmet lay on the ground a few feet away. Grime and soot streaked his face, his expression a grimace of pain as he grabbed his ankle and howled.

"Get up—"

Tom rolled to his feet. Swore. Conner grabbed him by the shirt, flung his arm around his shoulder. "Let's move."

"Sorry—"

"Just run!"

The kid fought, his teeth clenched, as the forest exploded around them.

Training images of fire entrapments burned into Conner's brain. How firefighters cooked under the flimsy tinfoil shelters that were meant to shield them from a flashover.

Hardly.

But even if they didn't burn, the superheated air could sear their lungs. Already his eyes watered, sparks swirled around him, landing in the forest, igniting brush and trees.

However, deploying their fire shelters in this fuel-rich forest would be lethal.

They ran through a gauntlet of fire. Conner held his arm up to his face, fighting the burn, the flames.

Then he saw it—a clearing of the trees—and against it, the yellow fire shirts of his team. Heard Jed yelling at him.

The world narrowed, focused on the pinprick hope of survival.

They broke out of the forest, and Jed caught Conner's arm before they both flew over the edge into a gorge twenty feet below, a frothing, cool river.

"C'mon!" Jed said, and pointed to a wash where boulders and rocks formed a natural slope.

His team was already scrambling down the cliff.

Conner helped Tom over to it, the fire crackling behind him, then scooted down, his heart in his mouth as he nearly jumped into the wet sanctuary of the gorge.

Jed tumbled down right behind him.

They stood there, congregated near the river's edge, gulping in air as the smoke gathered above them, the fire flickering out over the cliff.

Reuben let out a hot breath. "That was close." He pulled off his bandanna and pressed it to the wound on his neck.

Jed hauled out his radio, called in to check on the other hotshots.

Conner closed his eyes with near tangible relief when Sarge, the crew boss, called in.

Only then did Conner hear the roar of the drop plane, soaring in to bathe the forest in retardant.

Tom sagged down in the river, grimacing.

No one spoke then, just watched the fire throw cinder and ash into the river, the forest sizzling, popping, choking around them.

The silence stayed with them as they hiked upstream, as they found a place to climb out, as they called in their position and hiked another two miles to a forest service road.

Miles DaFoe, who'd flown in to help as Incident Commander, picked them up in the buggy. They crammed into it, gulping water, staring out the windows.

And this was exactly why he needed friendships with no strings, no promises.

But he needed them all the same.

~

Liza wasn't usually rousted out of bed before dawn, but something nudged her spirit, a darkness that tunneled through her, twisted her through her bedsheets.

She couldn't get Conner off her mind.

She didn't want to attribute her thoughts to the way he'd turned an hour of touring the Deep Haven festival into six delicious hours of conversation, cumulating with them sitting on the beach, listening to the waves comb the shore while he told her about his life in Montana. And a few near misses during his military service that he'd probably completely played down.

He was a quiet man, with a self-deprecating sense of humor, and when he talked, he picked up things, like a rock, rubbing it with his thumb, or folding his napkin, or even sorting through the pebbles, looking for an agate. Like he always had to be moving, thinking, even as he let his thoughts slow down. Unravel.

With their conversation, any sort of weirdness between them, the kind that might accompany a stir of desire, of hope, also settled into a comfortable warmth.

Friends.

Liza couldn't exactly ignore the way that he looked at her with those amazing blue eyes, her heart gave a rebellious leap, but she'd managed to tame it into a soft smile. She'd had good-looking, just-friends before. Most of her life, actually. And sure, nothing like the way Conner made her feel, but it didn't matter.

He was in town for only a few weeks. And during that time, she'd do her best to be his friend.

Especially when God nudged her out of bed at o-dark-hundred to pray.

Although she didn't know the specifics, Liza stood at her window, staring out at the darkened harbor, the tiniest hint of sunrise along the far edge of the horizon, pressed her hand to the window, and asked God to save him.

Save all of them.

Because of Your great love, do not let them be consumed. Do not let Your compassions fail, Lord.

She got dressed and headed out to the harbor, the sunrise beckoning as it filled the eastern horizon with layers of rose, magenta, and gold, gilding the pebbles on the beach, turning the water in the harbor a burnt orange.

She sat on the beach, not too far from where she'd sat with Conner, her tray of graphite pencils sharpened, a fresh board on her lap. Began to sketch.

Not her usual medium, but to Liza, an old habit, one that filled her soul.

She started with the hard line of the water, then the circle of light just lipping the horizon, kept her movements whisper soft. She didn't look at the paper, but drew by gestures, the flow of what she saw as the morning exploded around her.

When she looked down, she'd drawn the outline of the ribbons of color. She switched to her darker B pencils, began to add the layers of color.

The sunrise took life, and she didn't hear footsteps until pebbles shifted beside her, a few trickling down to the water's edge.

She looked up and her heart stopped for a full second when Conner—looking like a medieval hero, complete with sooty face, bloodshot eyes, blond hair in sweaty tangles, and smelling like he'd fought a dragon—smiled down at her. "Hey, Donut Girl."

She managed to *not* dissolve into a puddle and smiled casually up at him. "Hey, Smokejumper. How are you?"

Oh, stupid question, Liza. He looked like he'd been dragged by a horse through live coals. Especially when he looked up at the sunrise, stared at it a long moment, something vacant in his face. Then he inhaled, long, and gave a small nod.

"What are you—I mean—really, you look like—"

"I just came off the fire line?" He hunkered down next to her, as if he belonged there, and only then did she notice he held his bandanna, pock-marked with burns and ash.

It scared her a little to see him so wrung out. She put down her sketch. "What happened?"

He blew out another breath, a little shaky, and she had the crazy urge to reach out, touch his hand. His muscled arm.

Maybe draw him into a hug.

A just-friends-but-I-prayed-for-you hug.

"We nearly got overrun tonight—or this morning, rather. I just dropped off one of my crew at the hospital—he's got a pretty banged-up ankle."

She wanted to ask how he'd ended up with her on the beach but said nothing as he seemed to be working out his words.

"I saw the sunrise from the hospital parking lot and...I just couldn't go back to the resort. Not quite yet. So, here I am." He looked at her. "With you."

And then he smiled again, something sweet and gentle in it. As if he might be glad, even relieved, to see her.

Huh.

"You do this every morning?" he asked, gesturing to the sketch.

"No. I was...well, this is going to sound crazy, but God sort of woke me up to pray for you. So, I was. I did."

His smile vanished, and he looked almost pained, his eyes closing then. He looked away, back at the lake.

"Conner, are you okay?" Now she did touch him, just a hand, gentle on his shoulder. His shirt was sweaty, grimy, and nearly black with ash.

He blew out another breath. "Now I am."

Liza sat in silence, the waves raking the shore, not so sure.

Then, "We came pretty close to disaster today."

She didn't want to hear that but kept her face unmoving, her emotions locked inside.

"And I just keep remembering..."

His jaw tightened, and Liza just about took his hand. Folded hers instead over her updrawn knees.

"Yeah, well, okay...I told you my parents died in a car crash. But what I didn't mention was that the car flipped, and they were trapped. I got out, and got my brother out, but..." He swallowed, his mouth a tight line. Then, "They burned to death."

Oh. No. "Conner, I'm so sorry."

"Yeah. And it's usually just there, lodged in the back of my brain, but days like this..." He gave a silent chuckle, nothing of humor in it. "Shoot. I didn't mean to come down here and unload on you—I was just trying to clear my head."

"Clear it with me. Maybe that's why God brought me out here."

He looked at her then, a quick frown, then another noise that sounded terribly like amazement. "Maybe."

"For sure, Conner. God's compassion for you never fails. It's new every morning, faithful. Like sunrises." Liza slid her hand down to his. Squeezed. "The Lord is good to those whose hope is in Him."

He was looking at her hand on his. Then, suddenly, he turned his hand, caught her fingers in his, wove them together. "Our last trip as a family was to Mt. Rushmore. My dad loved flying remote control airplanes—probably where I got my drone fever—and we woke up early that last day and flew the plane over the park as the sun rose. It turned the faces of the presidents bronze."

"Like the face of Moses when he looked at God."

"I never thought about that before."

"But it makes sense—we should be changed when we look at the light. God. Sunrises—they bring us out of our darkness."

He was looking at her then, his blue eyes on her, something in them that suddenly made her heart stir in her chest, painfully aware of his hand in hers, strong fingers laced together, work worn but gentle. "You bring me out of my darkness, Liza," he said softly.

She stilled, especially as his gaze roamed her face, dropped to her mouth.

Which went dry.

If she didn't know better, she thought he might kiss her. She'd seen desire a few times in her life, and the way he swallowed, the slight lick of his lips, and something hollow and vulnerable flashing across his face. . .

She didn't know what to do, not sure—

Not sure? She'd lost her mind, right? A handsome, strong, brave Christian man wanted to kiss her and she was debating—

Yes. Because Liza didn't do casual. Didn't do right-now-and-never-again. Didn't give her heart away without promises.

But oh, she could nearly taste his lips against hers, gentle. Or maybe a little hungry.

Suddenly, however, he turned away. Let go of her hand.

Phew. Right?

Yes. Good.

"Sorry—I shouldn't have said that. I'm just tired, and—"

"Conner. Shh. Everyone needs a friend now and then." She kept her voice light. "And you had a rough night."

He looked away, and she watched his profile against the shore, his whiskers slightly singed, his face blackened.

"You need breakfast and a shower and sleep. C'mon. I live across the street. I can at least help with the breakfast part."

She grabbed her sketchbook, a little surprised when he held out his hand to help her up.

She loved her little bungalow just off Main Street, with the long sidewalk, the front porch, the stone-stacked fireplace. She had two bedrooms downstairs, one for guests, the other an office. And upstairs was her master, a cute room with dormer window seats and an angled ceiling.

Out the back, her tenant, Ivy, lived over the garage.

Liza let him inside and, on a whim— "I have a man's T-shirt and a pair of sweatpants here from when Mona's husband, Joe, was working on a project a couple weeks ago. If you want to shower—"

"That would be—yeah," Conner said, and she turned to see him standing in her doorway, a little rattled, looking so tired she wanted to cry for him.

"Bathroom is off the guest room. I'll get the clothes."

The shower was going in the bathroom when she returned with the clothes. Liza set them outside the bathroom door and headed to the kitchen.

Pancakes with nutmeg and cinnamon. And scrambled eggs with peppers, onions, mushrooms. She even thawed a couple of wild-rice-and-pork sausages from the local deli.

But he was taking so long, she thought he might have fallen asleep in the shower. And then what?—she couldn't rightly go in and drag him to safety.

Liza was just trying to figure out if she should call Joe or maybe 9-1-1 when he emerged, a towel around his shoulders, his hair clean and toweled off, still damp. The navy Deep Haven Fire and Rescue shirt clung to his body, his wide, work-sculpted shoulders, his lean torso. He wore the sweatpants low, his feet bare.

"This smells amazing," Conner said to her, standing in the doorway. He pulled the towel off his shoulders, hung it on the chair.

She hadn't realized how dirty he'd been. His beard cleaned up to a shiny gold, his hair sun-streaked white, his eyes bright without the soot on his skin. Yes, he must have scrubbed, because his hands were clean.

Again she noticed the scars on his hands. Conner must have seen her looking as she put the plate of eggs and sausage in front of him. He pulled out the chair, sat down. "They're from the car accident," he said quietly. "Not a wildfire."

The accident. The accident where he'd pulled his brother to safety.

Liza had a feeling that the burns might have occurred while his parents were trapped, while he was trying to free them. But she didn't want to ask. Instead, she set pancakes down next to his plate of eggs, then the syrup. Powdered sugar.

"This is enough food to feed everyone in fire camp."

"And yet, I think you'll manage," she said, sitting down opposite him.

Conner grinned, tiny lines around his eyes crinkling. A dimple in his cheek. She had to look away at another rush of her pulse.

He just needed a friend.

To her surprise, however, he held out his hand. "My grandfather always made sure we prayed before our meals."

Liza took his hand. His thumb dragged over the top of her hand, perhaps absently, as he prayed, his voice soft, earnest.

He mentioned the fire, a guy named Tom, and thanked God for Liza.

Then Conner ate like a man who hadn't seen food for a decade. She had dished up eggs for herself, but played with them, watching.

He finally looked up, reaching for his orange juice.

She grinned.

"I'm a cave man, aren't I?"

"A little," she said.

"These are good eggs." He pulled the plate of pancakes closer to himself. "My grandfather is an amazing flapjack maker. He uses real buttermilk in his batter, lets it rise overnight."

"These aren't that good."

But he'd taken a bite. "Oh yes they are." Then he winked.

Just. Friends.

"He used to put in chocolate chips for my brother, the wimp."

"I have sprinkles..."

Conner grinned. "Thanks. I'm good."

"Is he a smokejumper, too?"

"Justin?" He shook his head, his mouth wry. "He was an NSA agent."

Was?

Oh. No. And she didn't want him to finish, but…

"Justin was murdered in the line of duty about seven years ago."

Oh. Liza stared at him, wanting to weep. "Conner—"

"It's okay—"

"It's not okay. I'm so sorry."

Conner gave her a half smile. "Thanks. It was probably even harder on my grandfather. He and Justin were real close. They never solved the murder. And now, the NSA has decided to relegate it to cold cases. So, I'm afraid we'll never have any answers."

It just got worse. Liza pushed her eggs away, unable to speak.

"Wow, I just killed the mood," he said.

She looked up. "What mood?"

"The one where you were trying to cheer me up, keep me alive."

"Is that what I was doing?"

He smiled then. "I hope so. Because I've been thinking about you all week."

And see, what was she supposed to do when he said things like that? Ignore the spark inside?

Just. *Friends.*

"Coffee?" Liza asked, her voice a little thick.

"No. I need serious sleep, and it'll only start me buzzing."

She had the strangest urge to offer him her guest room. Probably not a good idea.

Conner finished his pancakes. "Those were fantastic." He pressed his hand to his stomach. "It's a good thing I get twenty-four hours off, because if I went back out now, they'd have to roll me onto the fire line."

He smiled again, and apparently she'd done her job, cheering him up. Now, if she could only keep him alive.

"Have you been on a lot of fires this summer?"

"About six so far. This is the biggest, though."

"Six?"

"Yeah—mostly in Montana, a couple in Idaho. The smokejumping team used to deploy out of Boise, but we built a training base in Ember, Montana, which is just west of Glacier National Park. We're stationed there. We mostly put out fires in the Cabinet Mountains and, of course, the park."

"Sounds busy and…exhausting. You look like you're going to drop right here."

Conner smiled. "Maybe. If I do, just shove a pillow under my head. I'm used to sleeping in crazy places. But I do like the work. I like the fact that at the end of the day you walk away tired, having kept a promise to yourself that you won't quit. And"—his smile dimmed—"it's the closest thing to being a part of a family a guy like me is going to get."

A guy like him?

She might have let his words flicker in her eyes but said nothing. Still, he answered her.

"I live in a trailer, moving from one fire to the next. And like I said, there's a lot of sleeping on the ground. We never know when we need to deploy—we get about a two-hour notice. Sometimes they take us right off one fire, fly us into another. So it's hard to put down roots or make friends."

Probably his way of telling her that if he left, he wouldn't be able to say good-bye. But if that was meant to scare her off, he had nothing to worry about.

"Some of us are just destined to spend our lives alone," she said and lifted a shoulder. "Doesn't mean you can't have a friend along the way, even temporarily."

She felt Conner's enigmatic look all the way to her bones, turning her world a little off-kilter.

Liza cleared her throat, found her footing. "How *is* the fire going?"

"Not great. Jed called in for more tankers, but if we don't get a handle on it, it's going to start destroying some of the resorts. Like Evergreen. And something called the Garden? Darek mentioned it at a briefing we had a few days ago at the resort."

"The Garden—oh no. That's where Joe's brother Gabriel lives. It's a group home. I should call Mona."

"I think the fire department is already on it," Conner said and finished off his juice.

Then silence fell, awkward between them.

"I should go." He got up. "Thank you for breakfast. And for the clothes. If I don't get a chance to bring them back, I'll leave them at Evergreen."

Liza managed a smile, hating how her heart suddenly hurt.

And she might not be the only one, because he just stared at her, a half smile on his face, as if sorry to leave. "I'm glad you were on the beach, Liza. Thanks for this morning. You've been..."

Just. Friends.

"Amazing."

Oh.

"And easy to talk to, and yeah, I think God used you today to help jar me out of my funk. I know I would have perished without breakfast."

She stood, picked up his towel, held it. "I doubt it."

"I *know* it." His eyes met hers, an emotion she couldn't name just below the surface. He opened his mouth to speak, then closed it. "I definitely needed a friend."

Her smile was genuine. "I'm glad I could be your Deep Haven friend."

He stood there a second longer, looked at the towel in her hand, as if stirring up words. Then, "I don't make promises, but if I can get back into town before I leave, I will, okay?"

Huh? Oh. She knew he was leaving, but found her breath caught. She nodded though, her foolish heart tumbling over with his words.

"Stay alive, Conner."

And then she reached out her hand to him.

He took it. Then quickly pulled her close. Wrapped her in a hug.

A warm, *just-friends* kind of embrace that she probably enjoyed way too much. Because his chest was solid against her cheek, his waist trim and toned, and he smelled freshly showered, the hint of soap on his skin.

"Keep praying," he said, then let her go.

And if that didn't help her tuck her heart back into her chest, then she didn't know what would.

Liza watched him leave, carrying his bundle of smoky, charred clothing, and wished that she wasn't so easy to walk away from.

CHAPTER 3

CONNER COULDN'T BELIEVE Evergreen Resort had actually burned to the ground.

It still seemed surreal to remember standing there on the shore of Pine Acres, watching from across Evergreen Lake as the nearly hundred-year-old resort was consumed by the forest fire. The blaze overran all twelve cabins, the trees, the swing set, an A-frame house, even the towering pines from which the resort got its name.

Darek had narrowly missed being burned alive at the neighbor's house, saving his girlfriend Ivy and her friend Claire. They'd floated to safety under a canoe in Evergreen Lake.

Conner still felt a little lightheaded when he thought about the destruction.

Thankfully, it had stopped at the lodge, Jed's voice in near disbelief as they watched the survival of the stately two-story home glistening wet under the spray of hoses from the lake.

The fire had come right up to the edge of the property, clawing, hungry.

And died.

It also stopped in the field behind Pine Acres, a resort owned by Jensen Atwood, who ingeniously had run a sprinkler system into the green meadow that separated the Acres from the forest.

Conner didn't want to guess what it cost Darek to see his family's history burn. He knew that Darek had made a deliberate choice with Jensen to dig a line across the meadow, sacrificing the resort.

Responsibility over passion. He'd chosen saving the town, stopping the fire over his family's legacy.

Life never came with easy choices. And rarely ended well, something Conner should probably keep in mind as he packed the Jude County buggy outside the fire camp, considering the impulse to head into town and see Liza one more time.

The three days of mop-up had felt like eternity as Jed pushed the crew to put out any final hot spots.

Now Jed came up behind him, carrying a box of flares and drip canisters. "I heard that Jock called, assigned you to Idaho to boost the fire down at Seven Devils."

A nasty, dangerous wilderness. The Midnight Sun Jumpers from Alaska had even been brought in to fight the fires in mountains that had the most entrapments of any in the country.

Conner wasn't thrilled.

And yeah, before he left, he wanted to make one last trip into town.

I don't make promises, but if I can get back into town before I leave, I will, okay?

He knew he'd probably put a little too much into his eyes when he said that, looking for a smile from her—but he couldn't stop thinking about Liza.

Or the way she'd simply stepped up into his charred, raw, darkened heart and shined light through it. Healed it just a little with her words. *God's compassion for you never fails. It's new every morning, faithful. Like sunrises.*

He wanted to believe that. But when he saw the truth—like a family's entire livelihood burn to the ground...

Or his brother, a hero, killed.

Or most recently, a letter from his grandfather, delivering such news as a rise in his PSA levels. The cancer was back.

Yeah, Conner could use a little of Liza's sunshine.

Graham came up, added tents to a compartment on the side of the buggy. "We're nearly packed up," he said. "But Jed said we aren't leaving until later tonight."

Conner cast a glance at Jed, who offered him a slight nod.

"Pick me up at the VFW on your way out," he said to Jed and jogged toward a couple of locals pulling out of camp.

He didn't think beyond right now. Just hitching a ride.

You bring me out of my darkness.

He didn't know why he'd said that. Maybe because he'd so desperately wanted to kiss her at that moment. Just reach out, touch her perfect, beautiful skin, rub his work-hewn hand against her cheek, lean in, and brush her lips with his.

Just a taste of all that sweetness, the compassion, the light that was Liza.

Nearly had, the words just a hint of what he was feeling.

And then...

Then he woke up. Realized just how close he'd come to hurting her. And him.

They had no future, and he didn't want to give her anything—especially a kiss—that might promise something he couldn't deliver.

It wasn't like she would uproot her life, come out to Montana. And he spent six months out of the year sleeping in the woods.

They could never be anything more than friends.

But he needed his friend tonight.

Two local teenagers—Tucker Newman, who had the makings of a smokejumper someday with his go-to attitude, and his buddy Kirby Hueston—dropped Conner off outside Liza's bungalow.

The house was dark, but he knocked anyway. Waited, tried not to let his hopes fall.

Just as he was turning— "Conner."

Liza stood on that path the led from the porch to the back of the house. She wore a pair of baggy overalls, a T-shirt, and an apron covered in paint. But her eyes lit, and she smiled, and something warm and dangerous crested through his body.

"I thought you left town." She held a rag, used it to wipe her hands as she came toward him. "I heard the doorbell and thought it might be the UPS man."

"Sorry—"

"Don't be silly. I'm thrilled to see you."

Thrilled. And for a second, she looked like she might hug him.

He still had memories of that last hug and the feelings it raked up inside him, her curves against his chest, the smell of her as she held him.

He could have held on much, *much* longer.

Maybe that wouldn't have been the best of ideas if he hoped to keep their relationship platonic.

Which, right at this moment... "I'm not leaving for a few hours, so...I thought maybe you'd want to get a bite to eat. I heard the local VFW has amazing hamburgers. I could pay you back for breakfast?"

"You don't have to pay me back, Conner." But she didn't hate the idea, evidenced by the smile, the delight on her face.

"Are you working?" He gestured to the apron. "Can I see your studio?"

"Are you saying you want that demonstration?"

Um. *Sure*. "Yeah."

"C'mon." She led him around back along the trail, past the garage to another house, a shed, really. A stove pipe jutted out from the side of the house. "It's getting a little tight—I probably need to find a new location in the near future. But for now this works."

She opened the door. Conner didn't know what he expected, but not the shelves and shelves of finished, glistening plates, bowls, and pitchers. Liza walked over to a display of dark gray bowls. "These are drying, waiting to be fired."

Liza gestured to two stainless steel ovens on the floor. "I do all my firing here in my electric kilns. I learned on a wood kiln, but these are easier. Then they go here, waiting to be glazed." She walked over to yet another rack, this one filled with more bowls, plates, saucers, cups, all a light bisque color. "I paint each one by hand."

In the center of the room sat what looked like a tub with an electric foot pedal and a metal wheel. "And here's where I throw my bowls."

"You what?"

She laughed. "Do you want to try it?"

He had this sudden image of a *Ghost* replay, her hands on his as they formed a pot, and heat flushed to his face. He shook his head.

"It's fun."

He had no doubt. "You made all these?" He walked over to the painted bowls, picked one off the shelf. Painted orange at the base, a black ribbon ran around the rim, with a white trail etched along the edge. And along it, words. *He can do more than you ask or imagine.*

"What's this?"

"It's a verse. It's my new line. I used to only etch a fish in the bottom. But now I've decided to create each unique piece with its own verse on the rim. I'm basing my new line on John 10:10. 'I have come that they may have life, and have it to the full.'"

Oh, how he liked her. And not just her smile, her beautiful espresso-brown eyes, that long sable hair, but everything inside, how she knew how to say the words that filled him up, softened the raw edges in his life.

Nourished his sometimes fragile faith.

"How did you come to be a potter?"

"After my dad died, my mother went to work as an artist-in-residence at a camp. We did everything from watercolor painting to oils to weaving to papier-mâché—she taught every age and believed that art was the outward expression of the soul. Someday, I'd like to be a teacher too. Maybe work at a camp, try and pass along the idea of God as the source of our creativity. Maybe inspire, like my mom did."

He wanted to comment that maybe she already was.

She walked over to the sink, began to put away the brushes drying there. "I went to an all-girls private high school, and I was a bit...well, different from everyone else. I didn't make friends easily, and I think the art teacher took pity on me. She asked me to work with her in the pottery studio, and something about the quiet, the gentle shaping of a bowl or a plate or a vase gave me focus. My favorite part, however, is the painting. I don't plan out my designs...I just let them happen and wait for God to surprise me. No expectations, just a trust that His grace will show up, make something beautiful."

No expectations. Just trust.

He'd like to live that way, just once.

She finished putting the brushes away, came back to him, put her hand on the bowl he still held. "When I throw a pot, every nuance of it is formed by my hands, the lip, the little grooves, the shape. Even the purpose of it—my design. But you have to be gentle with a pot—too much pressure will cave it in. It takes a deft hand, a deliberate hand."

She took it out of his grip, examining it. "I love the fact that we are clay pots—fragile, yes, but designed perfectly by God to be filled with His good, His heavenly purposes. I like knowing His hands are on my life, shaping me. And that every moment is guided by His love for me."

She took the bowl over to her table, pulled out a long sheet of paper from a roll affixed to the edges. Began to wrap it.

"What are you doing?"

"Giving you this bowl."

"What—no, Liza—"

"Yes, Conner." She taped it up, then wrapped it in Bubble Wrap, put it in a box. Tied it with twine, and handed it to him. "For you."

"Seriously—"

"Yep. And now, when you see this bowl, you can remember that God is in your life. His compassions not only never fail, but He can do more than you can possibly dream."

She smiled at him, and he wanted to simply reach out, taste all that joy radiating from her. Weave his hands into her silky hair, touch her beautiful face.

Taste what it might be like to kiss her.

Oh, his selfishness could knock him right over. Because then what? He couldn't—no, *wouldn't*—make her any promises.

But everything hurt with the thought of saying good-bye.

So he stood there stupidly, holding his box.

But maybe—and before his courage could wane, he said, "Could I call you?"

She just blinked at him, and he thought for a second what a silly—

"I'd love that."

Really? But he tempered his voice, mostly for himself. "I mean, I can't promise anything—I don't get good cell reception when I'm out in the field—"

She stepped closer to him, touched his hand, curling hers around his, meeting his eyes. "Hey. No promises, I know. But call anytime. I mean that."

Good thing there was a box between them full of breakable pottery, because he wanted to drop it and pull her to himself. Instead, he managed a shuddering breath. "Okay."

"But..." She let go and worked her apron over her head. "Can you tell me—why won't you make a promise?"

She was braiding her hair, her fingers deft. He watched, caught in her movements.

"Because they never work out. And it only leads to hurt feelings and eventually failure."

She turned to him, frowning. "Really?"

"I promised my grandfather I would find my brother's murderer. But my grandfather has cancer again and—"

And shoot, he hadn't meant to unload all that right here, right now.

Although he didn't mind so much when she turned to him. "Oh, Conner."

She came up to him, took the box out of his hands, set it on the table.

Then, without a pause, as if she always belonged there, she stepped up and slid her hands around his waist.

And held him. Just pressing her head against his chest. Sweetly. Like a friend might.

Despite the fact that he might have appreciated a different kind of comfort, he needed this. The sweet surrender into her arms. The smell of her hair, something floral, and the feel of her body tight against his, holding him together.

He closed his eyes.

"Conner," she said softly. "Everything is going to be okay. I promise."

And for the first time in years—maybe since he'd sat on the side of a highway watching his life in flames, he believed her words.

Chapter 4

"Aunt Liza, you got a letter. It's from that art colony in Arizona."

Liza didn't need her niece, Raina, to add the sing-song tone for Liza's pulse to jerk, for her to grab a towel, wipe her hands, and leave her lunch dishes in the sink.

Raina came in, dressed in her workout clothes, and dropped the letter onto the antique rolltop desk, along with Liza's other letters and bills. A younger version of Liza with her long dark hair and brown eyes, Raina had come into her life just a couple of months ago, drifting, grieving the loss of her father, alone.

Empty.

And Liza took it as a God-opportunity to fill the girl up with as much love as she could. "I made lunch—egg salad sandwiches and chips."

"Thanks. I woke up feeling a little sick, didn't want to eat breakfast. I should have eaten more last night. And then I had dragon boat practice."

"Are you ready for the festival?"

"Casper has us all practiced up. He thinks the Evergreen boat will take the win this year."

"They've won almost every year with Darek as their coach.

Casper has a lot riding on his shoulders." Liza had to admit that, despite her concerns about Raina making friends with Casper—the middle brother in the Christiansen clan—he'd ended up being good for Raina. Maybe he'd stopped being the town Casanova, although he always possessed, from Liza's view, a love-'em-and-leave-'em personality, off to his next great adventure.

She dearly hoped he didn't break Raina's heart as she was already fragile enough.

Liza knew from experience that one broken heart could derail your entire life.

"Apparently they didn't race last year because of the forest fire," Raina said.

The forest fire. Which only whisked up the memory of meeting Conner.

"A lot of things changed after the fire last year," Liza said. "How is the resort rebuild going?"

"The cabins are nearly finished, but they still have a lot of work to do." Raina went into the kitchen, and Liza picked up the thick envelope from Vitae, the artist commune located in Sedona.

Please.

She slid her thumb under the lip as Raina came out holding a plate, eating her sandwich. "Is that the teaching job?"

"I hope so." Liza took out the folded letter, set the envelope down, and began to read.

We'd be pleased to offer you—

"Yes." She glanced at Raina. "They want me to teach the winter semester. Apparently their only pottery instructor is having a baby. So, if she doesn't come back, I have an option to continue if I want."

"That's great, Auntie. You should totally do it." Raina finished off her sandwich, set down the plate, started crunching on the chips.

Liza read the letter over, the terms, the housing package.

And between the lines, the fact that she would be leaving Deep Haven.

Not forever, of course, but…

She folded the letter back up, put it in the envelope. Tucked it into a chamber inside the desk. Went to retrieve her coffee in the kitchen.

"You don't look as excited as I thought you'd be," Raina said, following her. "Isn't that what you always wanted? To teach, like your mom did?"

Maybe once upon a time. Liza picked up her coffee. "Yeah. Sure. Of course."

"Huh."

Raina slid onto a kitchen chair. "Does this have something to do with Conner? And his random phone calls? You know, you could join the rest of the twenty-first century and get a cell phone. I know they don't work well in Deep Haven, but trust me, the rest of the world is connected. He could call you in Arizona."

Liza offered a laugh, something easy, as if Raina hadn't somehow wheedled through her layers to find that tender spot. "No. This has nothing to do with Conner. Of course not."

Um, yes, absolutely.

Because it had occurred to her that if she left, Conner wouldn't find her…

And now she was breaking every single promise she'd made to herself—to not wrap her future in some man's affection for her.

"Okay. Because if he likes you, he'll find you. At least that's what that book *He's Just Not That Into You* says."

"Raina, you need to stop reading books on dating—"

"I'm not. I'm trying to live in reality, finally." She got up from the table. "And you should, too." She put her plate in the sink. "Conner likes you, otherwise he wouldn't still be calling you. And I'll bet he likes you enough to track you down if you go to Arizona."

Liza leaned over, sprayed water on the plate. "No, honey. Conner and I are just friends."

He'd made that ever so clear over the past year, his phone calls sometimes fun, sometimes dark with stories on the fire line, and yes, he often sounded wrung out and raw, in need of a friend. And that's what she'd been. A friend.

Nothing more.

If she started thinking they'd perhaps, someday, be more, then she was simply setting herself up to get burned.

Besides, he hadn't called in weeks.

"It's not easy for him, being one of the few Christians on the Jude County team—sometimes he just needs someone to help him see truth."

"I think *you* need to see the truth," Raina said, grinning.

"No—that would be wishful thinking—"

"So you *do* like him. I knew it!"

Oh. Liza made a face. "Fine. Yes. He's brave and loyal and a Christian—"

"He must be hot—I'll bet he's hot, with muscles—"

"Raina—"

But Raina had her hands folded across her chest, grinning.

"Fine. Yes. He's handsome. Golden blond hair and blue

eyes—actually, amazing blue eyes. And yes, muscles, not that I noticed—"

"Oh, please. You're not made of stone."

Liza offered a slow smile. "Okay. He filled out his T-shirts pretty well. But he works outside—jumps from airplanes into fire and digs out fire lines—so, yeah, he's pretty fit."

Raina's mouth tweaked up at the tame assessment. But what was Liza going to say? That last time Conner had held her in his arms—actually, she'd started it, but she couldn't help it when he'd simply radiated grief—she sank into him. Smelled the faintest hint of smoke and fire on his skin, the scent of danger and strength, and it all combined to make her want to hold on. Forever.

She'd foolishly hoped he'd kiss her good-bye when his team came to pick him up. They'd eaten dinner at the VFW. Listened to the Blue Monkeys play a set. Talked about the fire and how the lodge at the Evergreen Resort had survived.

All through dinner she'd wondered how *she'd* survive letting him walk out of her life. A foolish thought, because he'd barely been in it.

But while he had, he'd made her feel like she mattered. The fact that he chased *her* down… It made her feel as if she wasn't the one clinging. That she wasn't forcing him to like her...

"Aunt Liza, you're blushing. Which means you're not telling me everything, are you? Did he kiss you?"

Liza pressed a hand to her cheek. "He didn't *really* kiss me."

Sadly. Even though he'd had the chance. They'd stood outside the restaurant in the shadows as the Jude County buggy pulled up, his buddies inside, and right then she hoped he'd turn to her, search her face, and even if just quickly, kiss her.

But, no. Because he hadn't wanted to give her the wrong idea.

A true gentleman.

"I told you, we're just friends."

And if that's all they'd ever be, then that was enough.

Really.

Raina hustled off to her room, and a few minutes later Liza heard the shower. Tried to scrape her thoughts away from the fact that Conner had used that shower nearly a year ago.

Tried to forget the way he came out, towel-drying his wet hair, looking rugged and hungry.

Oh, shoot. She shouldn't let him in to roam around her thoughts. God was enough, hello and amen. She didn't need a man to be complete or happy. And especially not one who couldn't make her any promises to stick around.

Liza finished lunch, stopped by Raina's room to tell her she'd see her at the dragon boat festival parade, watched her leave, and then paid bills at her desk.

Took out the envelope and read the letter again.

She shouldn't put her life on hold for a man.

Liza wrote a response to Vitae. Sealed it. Then she changed for the parade on the harbor—out of her paint-splattered capris into a clean T-shirt, jeans, flip-flops, and a coat.

She picked up the envelope and was just leaving the house when the phone rang. Liza stood on the porch, listening, holding the doorknob.

Aw, shoot.

She answered just before it went over to her machine.

"Liza?"

Her traitorous heart expanded three sizes at the sound of

his voice. Roughened, as if he'd eaten a lot of smoke. Tired.

"Conner. How are you?" She always kept her voice even, a little surprised, but not so much that she put the wrong emotions in it.

"I just got back from three weeks in Arizona. Thought I'd call you..."

She sat down on the sofa, smoothing the envelope on her lap. "You sound tired."

A pause, and she could imagine him as she'd seen him on the beach, sooty, wrung out, maybe a little shaken.

"Please tell me you didn't get hurt or lose anyone." Oh, maybe too much worry, but—

"No. I'm fine. But it was pretty rough. I just..." His voice wavered, and she wanted to reach out, through the phone. "Nothing. How are you?"

Nothing? She wanted to chase that, but instead answered his question, filling him in on Raina and the update on Evergreen Resort and today's dragon boat race, and she hadn't even realized how much she'd been talking until the silence echoed on the other end.

"Conner?"

She'd bored him into slumber.

A pause. "Conner?"

"I'm here. I was just thinking...how nice it would be to be in Deep Haven again. That view of the sunrise over the harbor. And we could grab a burger at the VFW..."

Was he actually missing—no. But, "Our annual Fisherman's Picnic is coming up in a couple of weeks."

She didn't exactly know why she'd said that and hated even the hint of hope in her voice.

"Will you be giving demonstrations?"

She wanted to laugh, but his question reached in, filled her heart with painful hope. "Of course."

She wanted to wince at her breezy, too-high tone.

"That sounds amazing."

Another beat, and maybe he was waiting for her to add a real invitation to their banter.

But that would mean—what? That she wanted to be more than friends? A sure way to send Conner running the opposite direction, if she knew men. And, sad, pitiful her, she'd rather have his friendship than nothing at all.

Still—what if—

"I'd hop a plane in a second if I could."

He would? "Then you should come—"

"But I need to go see my grandfather. He's still fighting cancer and just finished another round of chemo..."

Right. Exactly. "Oh, Conner, I'm sorry. Yes, of course. He needs you."

"It's a nice idea, though. Maybe after the season is over." He said it casually, however, his tone saying *never.*

And that was the confirmation she needed. "I'll be praying for your grandfather." *And for you.* Which she did every day.

Probably, that was part of the problem. She prayed for him, thought about him, yes, even dreamed of him every day.

And he conjured her up only when he was tired, bored, or even just needing a friendly ear.

Exactly how *just friends* behaved. Hello and pay attention.

"Thanks. I appreciate the prayers. It's nice to hear your voice."

"You too. That's what friends are for, right? Be safe."

"Take care, Liza." He clicked off.

She sat there, a shadow over her heart she didn't want to acknowledge. But yes, maybe she needed Vitae just as much as they needed her.

She got up, locked the door behind her, and dropped the letter in the mailbox.

Chapter 5

If Liza was looking to hide from him, she'd picked the most picturesque place on the planet.

And maybe the hottest.

Around Conner, the striated red-rock formations of Sedona rose above the lush green pine and juniper of the valley bordering the city, and especially the Vitae artists' enclave, located just a dozen miles north of Sedona. With adobe buildings clustered around a main house, expansive patios, and decks tucked into the forest, the place looked like a place someone might find healing.

Not that Liza needed healing—after all, she'd come to teach. But maybe *he* did.

Conner ran his hand over his freshly cut hair—it felt strange to have it off his neck—and stepped out of the convertible Camaro he'd rented. A bit of an extravagance, but the entire trip seemed impulsive and over the top. Driven by some errant, rabid emotion he couldn't seem to tame.

Thankfully, Gilly Priest, a pilot for the Jude County Smokejumpers, was a romantic and agreed to fly him down to Arizona.

For the day.

And no, Liza probably wasn't hiding from him. Not

when he'd been the one doing a disappearing act from her life over the past year.

A year where he watched his grandfather dwindle from a robust cowboy to skin and bones, his eyes wracked with pain.

Conner should have called her, but he'd been simply overwhelmed with the daily tasks of medicine and feeding. And then his grandfather's passing simply blew a hole through him.

Thankfully, Grandpa possessed a faith that Conner desperately fought to hang on to.

Romans 8:28. All things work together for good.

It didn't feel like it.

Maybe that's what this trip was about. Finding hope again.

Finding Liza again.

Conner shut the car door, stood in the circular drive, not sure if this was the right place. Her niece on the other end of the phone in Deep Haven had given him the address, reluctantly, he could admit.

Which only confirmed that he should have called. Much earlier.

And, probably, this was a very bad idea. Because friends didn't just drop off the planet…

Oh, who was he kidding? In his mind, Liza had become much more than a friend. Lifeline. Encourager.

Light.

No wonder his world felt so dark.

He shoved his hands in his pockets, headed for the giant double oak doors, the word *Vitae* etched into them. A sign on the door asked visitors to ring the bell.

He heard it chime inside, waited for footsteps.

Nothing.

And probably he deserved that. The man who'd let something good die didn't deserve to show up, have her waiting with open arms.

He turned, put his hands on his hips, surveying the rocks, trying to figure out if he should just go in, or maybe wander around—

"Conner?"

He closed his eyes, just for a second, to mask the sudden rush of relief. Took a breath.

Then turned.

She was just as beautiful as he remembered from that moment he met her two years ago, in Deep Haven—more, probably. She wore white—appropriate, perhaps, for the image she'd conjured in his mind over the past year. A flowy dress with a thick waist and an off-the-shoulder neckline, full sleeves, and a long skirt that dropped to just above her ankles. Sandals on her feet, turquoise beads at her neck, and her long, beautiful mane, shiny like chocolate gold in the sunlight.

He found the courage to meet her eyes. As rich as he remembered, espresso, that warm, delicious jolt that went right through him to his bones.

Fortifying. Then she smiled, nothing of reproach or accusation in her expression.

As if she were genuinely, positively, thrilled to see him.

His raw, fraying heart gave a thump of joy in his chest. Wow, he might need to sit down with the way his legs were giving out.

"I can't believe it. How did you find me?" She walked over to him, and only then did he realize that she was holding a sketch pad and pencils.

His mouth had gone dry, so he swallowed, found his

voice. "I called your house and...I'm so sorry, Liza. I know it's been a while..."

His *a while,* aka a *year* since he'd last talked to her, flickered in her eyes ever so briefly and he braced himself, added, "I missed you."

And if that didn't sound pitiful and make him want to run for his car—

But then she loosened the coil in his chest with a shrug. "I figured you were busy. I kept praying for you..."

Oh, how he didn't deserve that. Deserve her.

"Am I interrupting?"

"Nope. It's the summer session, and I'm artist in residence right now. No classes." She took a step toward him. "How's your grandfather?" She was on the porch, so close he could touch her. Wanted to, especially when he smelled something sweet and floral lifting off her skin.

Needed, really, to feel her arms around him.

"He passed away." About six months ago, but he didn't add that.

More shame, and not a little self-pity, because maybe he could have appreciated her being at the funeral. Or even just in his life as he'd packed up and sold the ranch he'd grown up on. Or even since then, caught in the middle of a brutal fire season.

"Oh, Conner, I'm so sorry." She lifted her hand to reach out to him, then let it fall, as if she didn't want to assume.

Assume. Please.

"Thanks. I should have called you."

"No. You were busy, and I know what he meant to you."

And he had to look away, because, yeah, she did. *Get a hold of yourself.* He hadn't come here for pity.

"So, I was in the area..."

Lie. But if he told her he'd hopped a plane as soon as Raina gave him the information, that would sound *way* too needy.

And, he might have his heart on his sleeve, but Liza had never offered, or even hinted, at anything more than friendship.

So... "And I was thinking about that time you said you wondered what it was like to be a smokejumper. So I thought it would be fun to go skydiving."

She raised an eyebrow.

She had said that, right? Because he knew that he did most of the talking—oh no. What if it was just one of her comments, the kind she didn't mean. Like her comment last summer about him visiting her in Deep Haven.

He'd nearly said yes before his common sense kicked in. Right. The last thing she needed was a guy in her life living moment by moment, not sure what his future would be. Afraid to take a look at it, frankly.

"I mean, I thought—"

"Yes." She smiled at him then, a spark of what he'd seen when he'd first met her. Adventure, warmth.

And he might have missed it before, but her smile also contained a sense of anticipation.

"I'd love to go skydiving with you."

It all broke free then, that darkness that had suffocated him, and in its place, light.

Liza.

"When?"

"Right now, bay-bee." And yeah, he added flirt to his tone. Because he wasn't here just to see his *friend.*

He fully intended on seeing if Liza wanted more, just as much as he did.

~

She didn't want to call it a date—but that's exactly what it felt like. Driving ninety miles to the Grand Canyon, stopping at an airstrip. Meeting Conner's friend Gilly, who apparently was waiting for him—*them.*

As if he'd prearranged his so-called in the neighborhood, whimsical, let's-go-skydiving-or-whatever outing.

It only got more confusing as he gave her a short lesson on what to expect. Then he plopped a helmet on her head, they'd climbed into the belly of Gilly's little red-and-white airplane. He'd strapped on parachute pack, then attached her to him by her tandem harness.

They took off, and Liza felt pretty sure she'd lost her brains.

They'd definitely dislodged an hour ago when she'd spied a man standing on the stoop of Vitae's front entry. It took her a full five seconds for her brain to recognize him.

Conner?

Lean and wide-shouldered, he wore a navy T-shirt and cargo shorts, hiking sandals, his blond hair short and tousled by the wind.

For a second, her heart had hiccupped. But no, it couldn't be.

And then he'd turned to stare at the vista, his hands on his hips, and she knew she'd seen that pose before.

On a beach in Minnesota as he considered the sunrise.

It took her a heartbeat for the realization to emerge. After a year of silence, their last conversation just before she left for Arizona, when she felt sure that their friendship had simply run its course, Conner Young had tracked her down.

She'd probably fallen painfully, irrevocably in love with him somewhere between "*I missed you*" and "*I was thinking about that time...*"

Oh, who was she kidding. It was *long* before that.

But the idea that he thought about her enough to miss her…

She didn't want to consider further than that, or the fact that he'd actually *not* been in the area but had flown down with Gilly from *Montana...*

No. Not for her.

Because that would mean, to use Raina's words, that he was *into* her, too.

Liza should simply hold on and have fun with her adventurous, hot, brave, muscled *just friend.* With beautiful blue eyes and a smile that, when he directed it her way, made her feel beautiful.

Oh, she was so playing with fire to have agreed to be locked in his arms, even if it was to jump from a plane, her life in his hands.

This was really going to hurt.

"You're still flying, aren't you?" Conner said a couple of hours later as he came to the car carrying two coffees. He handed her one. "That happens after a jump—you sort of relive it over and over, experiencing those endorphins."

Oh, those were the source of her endorphins? She wanted to attribute it to the sense of his arms around her, his voice in her ear as they'd drifted down like a cloud, locked together.

"Yeah," she said, sipping the coffee, thankful for the bracing effect that might put her feet back on the ground. "Except

I'll bet it doesn't feel like that when you're jumping into a fire."

He put on his sunglasses, aviators. "No. You're just hoping you don't get blown into the flames, or caught on a tree, or land in a river, or even twist your ankle on the landing. Because then that means you've put your entire team at risk. Someone might have to hike out with you, and for sure, you don't do your job as well."

He put his coffee in the holder, pulled out of the lot.

They stopped in Oak Creek Canyon on the way back, and he found an ice-cream stand, treated her to a double-chocolate mint.

Now, with the afternoon late, the sun heavy on the horizon, she could admit she didn't want their "date" to end. She couldn't remember having so much fun. Laughing at Conner's stories about mishaps on the fire line, the rookie hotshots. "I still can't believe that Tucker Newman joined the team."

"He's working for Jed on the hotshot crew. He has the look of a smokejumper in his eyes. I wouldn't be surprised if he tried out for the team next year."

"Clearly you made an impact on him."

She looked away before he could see it in her eyes—that he'd made an impact on her, too.

"That summer in Deep Haven was...it was impactful for everyone," he said cryptically.

Then, just as she hoped he might elaborate, he fell silent as they closed in on Sedona. He said nothing even as they pulled up to Vitae. He put the car in park, and she didn't know what to say.

Thank you for finding me? For giving me an amazing day?

For being my friend.

Except, that's not what she wanted—not at all. But she

had a code, one that said she wasn't going to read more than there was into a relationship.

She reached for the handle.

His hand on her arm stopped her. "Liza—uh. I have a question."

She looked at him, his sunglasses obscuring his eyes.

"I don't want—I mean." He blew out a breath. "I was going to hike Doe Mountain, catch the sunset. And I was wondering if you would...will you come with me?"

She didn't want to sound too eager, but um, *yes*. "Sure."

"Okay. Good. Do you want to grab a sweater or something? It can get cold."

She felt pretty sure that with Conner around she might never be cold again. But she ducked inside anyway, changed into jeans and grabbed a sweatshirt. He'd zipped the legs back onto his convertible shorts by the time she returned.

Conner grinned at her as she got back into the car, as if he'd been reluctant to say good-bye, too. But that's what friends did spent time together. Enjoyed each other's company.

Liza had always wanted to hike Doe Mountain. The low, flat-topped mesa was famous for its panoramic views of Bear Mountain, the Verde Valley, and of course Chimney Rock.

They parked in the lot, and to her surprise, Conner pulled a backpack out of the trunk. As if yes, he'd intended to hike the mountain, with or without her.

So maybe it wasn't a date—she was simply a tagalong.

She tried not to let it deflate her as they hiked up the switchbacks.

Friends, enjoying the day together. Because he was in the *area*.

Wow, had she overread that.

Still, as they ascended, as the sun began to settle below the far horizon, gilding the tufted clouds overhead with fire—threads of gold, umber, and crimson lighting the red rock ablaze—her disappointment slid away. Standing at the top, the canyon vast and redolent with the smells of the desert—sage, sand, and lime—was a little like flying again.

Not quite. But enough.

And then he took her off the path, walking along the edge of the cliff, along the top.

"Where are we going?"

"To find the best view." Conner reached out his hand.

Huh. She took it, letting his grip enfold her as he picked their way over the reddened clay, around sagebrush, low juniper.

He finally found a niche about four hundred yards off the path, almost obscured from foot traffic, a small enclave in the rocks.

Their own viewing platform about ten feet wide that opened up to the west.

"Box seats," he said. He helped her down to the enclave, then opened his backpack. Pulled out a blanket. He spread it on the ground for her.

Huh.

She hunkered down next to him. "A *day* hike? It looks like you packed for the weekend."

"Just a quick trip up the mountain," he said. "To see something amazing and beautiful."

Her heart just stopped. Because he wasn't looking at the sunset, the layers of magenta and purple, the way it turned the mesa a rich, burnt red.

No, his eyes were on her.

"Liza, I—" He looked away. "I lied to you."

What?

"I wasn't just *in the area.*"

Oh. She let a smile slide free.

"I wanted to see you. I missed you, and I know I should have called, and I know I don't deserve your friendship..."

Oh. Right. She managed to keep her smile.

"But I can't get you out of my head."

Her voice left her, her throat dry as he looked at her again, his eyes thick with emotion. Longing? Sadness? Hope? She couldn't place it, her own emotions a tangle.

He had such beautiful eyes—in the sunset they turned gold at the irises, rich blue at the edges, the kind of eyes that could hold her captive.

Had, actually, for two years.

"I don't know how, but you make me feel like my entire life isn't filled with holes and broken promises." He touched her face, ever so gently, his fingers tracing down her skin.

Lighting it afire.

"Can I...um..."

And then because she couldn't help herself, because suddenly her code of staying just friends seemed stupid and childish in the face of her longings, she leaned forward.

Conner kissed her. Softly, just a brush of his lips against hers, as if testing.

Hoping.

She closed her eyes, savoring.

He nudged his hand around the back of her neck, his thumb on her cheek, caressing, and deepened his kiss, his mouth opening, still gentle.

Still testing.

He tasted of coffee and chocolate ice cream, of a hunger held in check behind the tenderness of his kiss. He smelled of the outdoors, the brilliance of the sunset simmering on the horizon, the exhilaration of the skydive, the courage to jump into a blazing fire.

And he'd tracked her down, all the way to Arizona.

She surrendered, sinking into his embrace, nearly disbelieving this moment.

He put his other hand on her waist, scooted closer to her, curling that arm around her back.

With her hands on his chest, she could feel his heartbeat pulsing against her palm.

As if he were nervous.

Oh. Conner.

Because if she *weren't* dreaming, then it was no use trying to tell herself that she wouldn't be completely shattered, her heart in pieces when he walked away.

Except, maybe, if he could promise her—

What? That he loved her? That he'd never hurt her?

Oh.

What…was…she…*doing*?

Liza pushed on his chest, just a little, enough for his embrace to loosen.

For him to lift his head.

"Are you...is this okay?"

Conner stared down at her, his eyes darkening with the sunset. And she wanted to say yes. That she could stay here all night, pocketed in his embrace.

That it didn't matter that he couldn't give her tomorrow, that he'd vanish from her life.

And she got it—really. Because a guy like Conner, with so many losses, simply couldn't believe in a happy ending.

But she did. Or wanted to.

However, she refused to force him to promise her one.

"Yeah," she said, her eyes filling. "I'm just wondering—" And shoot, she wanted to stop herself, even heard herself screaming, waving semaphores. "What happens next?"

He drew in a breath, swallowed, and she tried not to let it feel like a sledgehammer to her chest. Tried not to let herself die, right there in his arms. Especially when, for a second, a stripped, almost-panicked expression flashed through his eyes.

He attempted to hide it with a smile. Then, "We'll see. We'll just take each day as it comes. I can't make any promises."

Right. Of course. She *knew* that part. "Yeah, okay," she said, her throat thick.

She was right. This was really going to hurt.

And it did. Because she foolishly let him kiss her again. Foolishly stayed there as the sun set, then foolishly let herself relax into his embrace and watch the moon rise, let him wrap the blanket around her, coax her into laughter as she listened to more stories of his life.

Foolishly let him guide her back down the mountain.

And when he asked, she foolishly agreed to meet him early enough to watch the sun rise.

Then, she did the first smart thing she'd done since she met Conner Young.

She packed her bags, slid a letter of resignation under the

door to the Vitae office.

And left town.

Leaving her foolish, broken heart behind.

Chapter 6

Current day…

IT SEEMED TO CONNER that he spent way too long searching for things that just didn't want to be found.

"Seriously, dude. She's gone. Vanished." Reuben urged forward his horse, a beautiful brown-and-white paint, across the meadowland and along the ridge of the gully, muttering his annoyance. In fact, everything out of Reuben's mouth this early in the morning had mostly been just a clearly formed growl.

The sum of the fellow smokejumper and cowboy's words since Conner had rousted him out of bed consisted of *Are you kidding me?* and *Stop talking so loud.*

Not that Reuben had a hangover—Conner suspected the raging headache had to do with his weekend rodeoing at the Ember Hotline Saloon and Grill.

"I have to find her, Reuben. I can't lose her."

"And you wonder why we call this drone-thingie your girlfriend." A modern-day cowboy in a black T-shirt and jeans, except for his requisite cowboy boots and weather-beaten camel-brown Stetson, Reuben bridged two worlds—jumping fire and trying to keep the Marshall family ranch in the black, along with his slew of brothers and sisters still reeling after the death of their father.

Conner didn't care how much Reuben groused. He wasn't throwing in the towel on his piece of mechanical ingenuity.

And yeah, maybe he'd spent way too much time working on the design, testing the improvements, but it wasn't like he had anything else to fill his off time.

Like, say, calling a friend. Or former friend.

Whatever.

"I know it's around here—the map pinpointed the drone's last-known position right over this ridge." Conner held his phone, which he'd imported the drone's tracking system on, and tried to align it with their location.

The town of Ember, four miles ahead to the east, tucked away under the shadow of the Kootenai National Forest. The Cabinet Mountains behind him to the southwest, rising like a dragon, gray spikes pricking the dome of the morning.

To the north, Highway 2 cut through the northwest territory of Montana, running parallel to the Kootenai River. And just below him, the Prairie River, an offshoot of the mighty Kootenai, tumbled over rock, through gullies, and dissected a thousand prime acres of delicious ranch land. Land that was currently dotted with the shaggy, thunderous forms of over five hundred sleeping Montana buffalo.

"I'm not going down there, just in case you were considering it," Reuben, now-former friend and current defector said, shifting in his saddle. "And neither is old Gracie there. When you said you needed a horse, I was picturing a lazy ride into the mountains, not an Old West posse on the hunt for one of your little toys."

And that was... Just. It.

"Not a toy," Conner said tightly, bringing the binoculars up to scan the herd, searching for the blinking tractor beacon.

"A drone. An *expensive* test drone that reads fire and wind and predicts patterns and that just might, someday, save your sorry hide."

He didn't add that maybe it could have saved Jock and the seven other members on their Jude County Smokejumper crew who had perished almost a year ago, trapped in a fire. Instead he skipped to, "So yeah, if I have to ride your old nag down into the middle of that herd of buffalo, that's exactly—"

"Gracie is hardly a nag. She did five years on the rodeo circuit, won three world championships in the Palomino World Show in barrel racing, heeling, and breakaway roping. She's not skittish with dogs, will cross rivers, and stands tied. You couldn't ask for a better horse, and frankly, you don't deserve a gal like Gracie."

Probably that was true. Conner probably didn't deserve *any* gal. "Sorry."

Reuben ran his thumb and finger into his eyes. "Tell me again where you think this life-saving toy plane went down?"

"I don't know. I lost the signal somewhere around here. But even before that, it stopped responding to my commands."

"Even your drones leave you," Reuben said with a smile. "Dude, you have issues."

Conner returned the smile, refusing to flinch at the way Reuben's comment dug into the open wound Liza's unexplained exit—full-out run, really—left in his chest.

"This is the fourth drone that's gone crazy and disappeared off the radar. And I'm the one digging into my wallet to fund these so-called toys, so I've got to find it."

He scanned the field again, the morning shadows still thick enough to detect the orange beacon, should it still be operational.

Reuben shifted in his saddle. "Tell me again why you were flying this at night?"

"Tests. To see how the night vision worked in tracing the terrain. I would have come out last night, but I had to download the flight data and chart it to determine where it went down."

"You missed Kate and Jed's engagement party."

I know. He just nodded, not wanting to give himself away. And yeah, he felt like a chump. But Jed exuded all this messy happiness, and frankly, just a month ago, Jed was nursing his broken heart right alongside Conner.

Now the man had the woman he always loved in his arms, and Conner...well, like the drone, Liza had simply gone crazy and walked out of his radar.

At least that's the best he could figure out, given the data.

He tossed too many of his nights away reliving that last sunset with her tucked in his embrace, her back against his chest as he curled her silky, long brown hair between his fingers.

And when they'd kissed, everything seemed to finally click into place.

Until her question— *What happens next?*—left him dry-mouthed, forming a catch-up reply. *I can't make any promises.*

Yeah, way to charm her.

"I think Jed's hoping he can convince her to elope," Conner said, keeping his voice cool. He even lifted his shoulder in a nonchalant shrug. "No big fuss, you know?"

And that's exactly what he needed to get through his head. It wasn't like he'd made Liza any promises, right?

Her leaving shouldn't cause such a big fuss, then.

Conner put down the binoculars. "Who owns this land?"

"Jim Browning—everyone around here calls him Brownie. Tom was his grandson."

Oh. Conner's hands tightened on the glasses. Twenty-six-year-old Tom had died in the tragic flashover along with the other smokejumpers, including local legend and Kate's father, Jock Burns.

Maybe, hopefully, Brownie would be amenable to letting Conner search through the buffalo pies for his lost drone.

"There's a wash just north of here, maybe we can get down, cut across the field—"

Conner's phone buzzed in his back pocket and he fished it out.

Looked at the caller ID.

Stilled.

What—?

And shoot if his heart didn't nearly take a flying leap out of his body. "Liza?"

"Oh...Conner. *Conner*!"

And his world simply stopped, everything coming to a standstill—his heart, his breath, his thoughts.

All except one.

Finally, *finally,* Liza Beaumont had called him back. After countless messages, a few letters, and even one moment when someone actually picked up the phone and listened in silence.

He felt pretty sure that had been her on the other end of the line.

And while he'd tried, for at least the last six months, to shove her into the dark, hopefully forgotten places in his heart...

Oh, *Thank You*, she'd finally called him back.

And he knew how pitiful he sounded when he said, "I'm

so glad you called."

Then he heard her breath, hiccupping over the line, as if she might be...crying?

And that put a different spin on the call. "Liza—where, what—are you okay?"

"Oh...Yeah, no...I don't know. I didn't know who else to call."

So, she'd called him. He tried not to sing a song of hallelujah, but if she were dating anyone else, then certainly *he* would be on her speed dial.

"You can call me anytime—"

And yes, that sounded even more pitiful, but—

"Are you still in Ember?"

What?

"Not out on a fire?"

"No—I'm in town," Conner said. He had a crazy urge to look around, wondering if he might suddenly see her—what, running through the herd of buffalo?

Wild, crazy hopes, taking him by the throat.

But what was he supposed to do with the relief, the "Oh, thank You, God" on the other end of the line?

His thought exactly.

"I think I outran it, but I'm—"

And now an inhale of quick breath, her voice low, nearly unintelligible.

Outran? The word wrapped a fist around his chest. "Liza, are you in danger?"

"Yes—No—I—"

He couldn't help it. "Breathe, baby. Just, breathe." He simply would ignore the impulsive term of endearment.

"I—there's a...grizzly."

Conner froze.

"I think he's eating my backpack, but I found a tree—"

"What are you talking about? Where are you?"

"I'm here. I mean I'm in Montana and—"

In Montana. And now he did sit up in the saddle, look around.

Reuben regarded him with one eyebrow up.

What are you doing in Montana? Conner wanted to ask it, but his brain wound back, caught her earlier words.

Grizzly. Tree.

She was trying not to cry—he could tell that much from her soft huffs of breath. He cut his voice low, trying to unravel anything of the last minute of conversation that made sense.

She was here, in Montana. She'd outrun a grizzly.

She'd called *him* to save her.

His brain caught up, took charge. "Liza. Breathe. You're up a tree? You know grizzlies can climb trees, right?"

"They can?"

"Yes, they can!" Now *he* needed to breathe. "Where exactly are you, and can you see the bear?"

"I'm...no, I can't see him. I—yeah, I think I outran him—"

"You didn't outrun him, honey. He just wasn't interested."

Please, let it not be interested.

Reuben shifted on his horse, pushing his hat up with one finger.

"Can you tell me exactly where you are? We need to get help to you—"

"That's why I'm calling you! I didn't know what else to do."

And wow, with that, his poor heart just exploded in a sort of painful joy.

So much for relegating her exit in his life to a casual shrug.

He blew out a breath, lowered his voice, keeping it even. "And I want to help you. Where are you, exactly?"

"I'm at Camp Blue Sky, just south of Ember—it's on the Bull River."

Camp Blue Sky.

Yeah, he knew exactly where it was, especially since the Ember Community Church was having its annual family camp up there this week.

What were the odds that she'd come to Montana for *him*?

More explosions inside him—but he schooled his voice to be calm, not eager. "I know where it is. Are you in camp?"

"I hiked up to the overlook to Snowshoe Peak. That's where I saw the bear. I think I ran about half a mile, maybe less. I can probably get to camp—"

"Stay there!" Oops, now his voice added a tremble. He cleared it. "Just...stay put. At least until you know the bear is gone. He could still be rooting around—"

"But—"

"Liza, listen to me. I'm coming for you, okay? I'll be there." He stopped just short of *I promise*, but there it was, aching to emerge. "Just wait for me."

Yes, clearly he was out of his ever-lovin' mind.

"I will, Conner, it's just—"

"Liza—"

"I think the bear—I think he attacked a camper. Or..." And her breaths came over each other again, quick, successive.

"Shh... Just tell me." He hardly heard himself over the voice screaming in his head to hang up and call the rangers.

"She snuck out of camp this morning—and I thought she came up here to watch the sunrise."

He refused to stop and linger on a memory.

"And when I got here, I found her jacket over the side of the cliff. And then the bear was just *there*. I don't know if she went over the cliff, or—" Her voice started to shake again. "I gotta get back to camp."

"Liza—please let me come for you. Stay—"

"I'm going back to camp. I'm just going to—yeah, I think it's okay. I don't see him."

He heard branches snapping, her breath heavy in the phone.

"You have to help me find her, Conner. We have to find her."

"Of course we do—and we will. I gotta call the rangers. But keep calm. I'm on my way."

"Okay. Yeah—Conner. *Hurry*."

The phone clicked off.

Conner stared at it, his hands shaking, tasting his pulse. Trying to untangle his panic to get to the one thought thrumming through him. Liza crying. Liza needing him, turning to him. Trusting him. Liza, perhaps ending up in his arms.

Liza, back in his life.

God, please keep her alive.

Conner hit the number for dispatch.

Reuben leaned on his saddle horn. "Baby? Honey?"

Conner looked at him, not sure where to start. "Cliff—get me the Bull River Ranger Station on the line. We have a grizzly incident up near Snowshoe Peak."

~

No crashing behind her, no grunts, no heated breath.

Maybe she'd outrun the danger. Liza flew down the path, arms pumping, her chest burning as she cut toward camp, her feet stirring up gravel and needles. She tore past the zip line, the horse corral, the art pavilion, the climbing wall, the cabins tucked into the forested grounds, the chapel pit with the giant cross looming in the center. She nearly grabbed the rope in the bell tower but skipped it and headed straight for the mess hall.

"John!"

She slammed open the screen door, screaming the name of the camp director.

A hundred heads swiveled her direction, the reverence for JohnJohn's breakfast prayer a quiet palate for her panic.

Wiry, former military chaplain, current pastor of the Ember Community Church, John Priest put his gimme cap back over his salted, dark hair and advanced toward her from where he stood near the ledge stone fireplace. Dressed in his Gore-Tex camp pants, Keens, and a signature Camp Blue Sky T-shirt, he caught her arms with his wide grip as she collapsed onto the gleaming wood-planked floor.

Gasping and unable to speak, she grabbed his arms, held on as one of the campers came over. "I'm a doctor—what's going on?"

"Is Esther Rogers here? Has anyone seen her?"

Every eye in the room pinned to her, all the diners at the ten-plus picnic tables sat without moving.

Oh, no, this could turn dark, fast. She grabbed Beck's arm, cut her voice low. "Esther Rogers wasn't in her cabin this morning."

Beck's expression creased into concern.

"I thought she might be at the overlook—you know, Snowshoe Peak?"

John nodded. "Why?"

"It's a long story, but we were going to hike up together—and then she wasn't in her bed this morning."

She'd raised her voice just loud enough to ignite a murmur. She stared at Beck, cut her voice low again. "Have you seen her?"

John scanned the room. Then, in his I-am-a-chaplain-don't-worry voice, he said, "Anyone seen Esther Rogers this morning?"

Not a word of response. And Liza's breath unhinged from where she'd held it.

John wore the look she felt as he turned back to her. "Did you check the cabin again? Maybe she went out to the bathhouse—"

"I don't know—yeah, maybe. I will but—"

John gestured to Skye Doyle, one of the nature guides. "Could you check the cabins and the bathhouse?"

Skye nodded and took off, passing Liza with a squeeze to her shoulder.

Yeah. Maybe she was simply—overreacting. Just seeing trouble that wasn't there.

"I think maybe you should sit down," John said, directing her over to his table.

"No, but...I think—" She let him push her down into the seat, clasped her trembling hands together. "No. Beck. You don't understand." She blew out a long breath. "I went up there and..." Her voice started to tremble. "There was a grizzly."

John stilled. A beat passed between them as he appeared to weigh her words. "Where?"

"Snowshoe Peak. And I—I ran. I ran and ran and then I climbed a tree—"

"Grizzlies can climb—"

"I know. But I didn't know what else to do, and I thought, what kind of idiot sticks around to play dead, right? Except maybe, I don't know, but maybe that's what Esther did because—"

She pressed her hands over her face. "Oh, Beck." Her breaths tumbled over each other, her voice rising. "I found her jacket. Or what I think was her jacket—I don't know. It was definitely a Blue Sky jacket."

"Where?" This from the doctor. Doctor Billings. Shep's father.

As in Shep Billings, the boy who had broken Esther's heart.

Liza looked up, met his gaze, saw in his features the same handsome, solid chin, dark-blue eyes, a gleam of authority that he'd probably passed along to his arrogant, charming son.

She'd like to get her hands around Shep's prom-king neck right about now. "Over the edge of the cliff," she said quietly. "The jacket was caught in a bush below the lookout."

The doctor's jaw tightened, and he turned to Beck. "A word?"

John stood up.

The door slammed behind them, and Skye ran back in, breathing hard. "She's not in the cabinsCrocs or the bathhouse. I ran into the chapel but she's not there either."

Something about the way the doctor was leaning toward

Beck... The worry that creased Dr. Billings's face, then Beck's, the quick glance at Liza—

"Shep isn't here," Dr. Billings said quietly.

"Oh. My. You've got to be kidding me." Liza stepped up to their huddle, didn't bother to keep her voice down.

It was the way the doc swallowed, his Adam's apple dipping in his throat, his face whitening. "He wasn't in the cabin this morning."

Liza had a retort cued up and ready when the doc's breath shuddered out, shunted it. "He took his jacket."

The jacket. Liza couldn't move, her brain suddenly fixed on the grizzly, the realization that two might have gone over that cliff.

"Blake, what's going on?" The question came from a petite blonde.

The man glanced at the woman, then took aim, and fired at Liza.

"Shep sneaked out with some girl, and they've disappeared. And apparently, *she* told them to."

Huh?

"I—no, I—"

Another woman arrived, with cropped brown hair, wearing an ill-fitting T-shirt, shorts, and Crocs. "I'm Esther's mom. What's going on?"

"Liza here told my son and your daughter to sneak off—"

"No," Liza said. "Actually—no. I told Esther to meet me, and we'd go—" She shook her head. "It doesn't matter—they're missing. And there's a..." She cut her voice down. "A grizzly out there."

"Oh my—" The petite woman clasped a manicured hand over her mouth. "Oh—Blake." She grabbed his arm.

"It'll be okay, Allison," Dr. Billings said, his expression saying the opposite as he pinned a look on Liza. Liza did the quick math and attached a name to the blonde—Mrs. Billings, Shep's mother.

"Listen, I don't know what happened. We shouldn't jump to any conclusions." Liza took a breath, bitterly aware, however, that she'd led the leaping.

"We need to search the camp," John said. "Let's form groups, and everyone check the cabins, the corrals, the zip lines, and all the outbuildings. But don't leave camp premises."

"But the jacket—" Mrs. Billings started. "My son is out there."

Pastor John held up a hand. "Could be anyone's jacket." But the look he gave Liza suggested he was already over the edge of foregone conclusions and falling into dark consequences. He turned his voice down low, just for their huddle. "We are not going to do anything rash. We don't know if that grizzly is still there, so we'll need to call the rangers before we head back up there."

"I already called for help." Liza's voice matched Beck's. "A friend of mine works at the Ember base as a smokejumper and—"

"This isn't a *fire*, sweetheart," said Dr. Billings. "We need rangers. *Armed* rangers."

Esther's mother's eyes widened. "You don't think—you mean armed, with *guns*?"

"You did hear the word grizzly, right?" Mrs. Billings snapped.

"Everyone, keep calm." Beck's voice rose. "We don't know what to think." He glanced at Dr. Billings. "And by the way, smokejumpers do more than put out fires." He turned to Liza. "Good call."

Really? Because she'd been knocking herself in the head ever since hanging up.

And seriously wondering why her first impulse had been to call a man she had deliberately walked away from.

~

"So who is this girl?"

Reuben rode beside Conner at a gallop, his voice lifting over the exertion of staying on his mount. Except, expert horseman Reuben wasn't wheezing, or frantically grabbing the saddle horn, hoping his horse didn't flip him off.

He should have taken a four-wheeler to search for the drone, but he hadn't known how dense the terrain to scour might be. Having Reuben around meant more questions than Conner wanted to answer.

"Just someone I met during the BWCA fire in Minnesota three years ago."

Understatement of the decade, probably, but he didn't need Reuben's scrutiny.

Conner spotted his fifth-wheel trailer parked at the far edge of the Ember Campground in the last spot, closest to the road. His black Ford 150 was parked beside it in the gravel drive, Reuben's truck and horse trailer behind it.

Conner slowed his horse to a canter once he hit the gravel road.

"She's not just *someone you met,*" Reuben said. "In fact, I think I remember her. Brunette? Didn't you go to Arizona last summer—"

"She's just a friend who's in trouble." He'd tried her number, at least twice, after alerting the rangers at the Bull River

Ranger Station.

Please let them be on their way—although by land, the rangers were nearly an hour out from Liza's location.

"You should call Gilly."

Conner shot him a look, doing the math even as Reuben filled in the answer. "It'll take you two hours or more to get there by car. Gilly can drop you into the camp in twenty minutes."

Easy math, the correct answer. "Good idea. And round up Pete and whoever else is off duty. Liza thinks there's a girl missing—we might need manpower."

Gracie was still breathing hard as he reined her in at his camper. "Thanks, old girl." He patted her heaving withers as he dismounted and headed inside, dialing Gilly's number on his cell. When it went to voice mail, he tried not to panic. "Gilly, call me. I need you."

Rare words, but he didn't care.

Behind him, Reuben had dismounted.

Gracie stood, lathered, waiting.

Conner banged inside his fifth-wheel trailer, already cataloging his supplies. His jump bag of course, a first aid kit, pressure bandages. flare gun. He might leave his Glock locked in his bedside stand.

He startled at the sight of Commander Jed Ransom sitting at his kitchen table. The crew boss wore a grim, dark look, attired in his uniform—black Jude County Smokejumpers T-shirt, green Nomex pants, and boots. He played with his cell phone, turning it like a pack of cards in his grip.

Conner froze and in a moment ticked off a list of everyone he knew who might be in trouble.

Nope, the team wasn't deployed, and the Jude County Hotshots were on the tail end of a cleanup. Which meant the only one left who might leave a gaping hole in his life was the woman who'd just hung up on him. "Jed?"

"Where've you been?"

Conner gaped at him. "On my day off? None of your business." He didn't mean to snap at him, but— "I gotta go, Jed."

He pushed past him, but Jed grabbed his arm.

"I'm here on official business." It was the edge of worry in his voice that kept Conner from yanking his arm away, throwing Jed out of his camper.

"Talk fast."

Conner headed to the back bedroom, grabbed his gear bag.

"We have a problem. There are a couple of arson specialists down at Overhead who seem to think your drones are causing fires."

His drones—? "What—?" Conner glanced at his watch. Fifteen painful minutes since Liza had called. . . *Please, God, don't let her be bleeding to death.*

He returned to the kitchen, searching for his keys. "Listen, Jed. I don't know what they're talking about. My drones aren't flammable, and they haven't been anywhere near any fires—"

"They found one at the Solomon River fire, near the source. And another one at Cherry Creek."

Keys. Another thought about the Glock. "I know I lost one at Cherry Creek, but that fire had been blazing before the drone crashed."

"Not the one you flew in—another one. Again, at what they think is the source."

Jed had his attention now. "They found one of my missing drones?"

"You knew the drone was missing?"

Conner glanced at him. "I lost it over a month ago. Just went crazy, like number four—that's where I was just now. Reuben and I went looking for a drone I lost last night. It went haywire, dropped off the radar."

"You need to come in and answer their questions, get this thing cleared up."

Conner glanced again at his watch. Twenty-one minutes. "I don't have time to answer their questions—listen, I gotta go—there's been a bear mauling—"

Jed froze. "Oh no."

Conner stepped to the door. "I already called the rangers—but I have to get there." He pushed his way outside.

Jed was hot on his tail. "There are investigators headed in from Boise. They want your drones."

Conner threw his bag in the back of the truck. "Absolutely not. I only have one left, and it's a prototype. An expensive, valuable, one-of-a-kind prototype, and if I hand it over, I'll never see it again."

He put his hand on the door handle, but Jed grabbed his arm. "I'm just giving you a heads-up. You take off now, it's going to look like you're running."

"Running from what? I didn't do anything. My drones don't start fires. I don't start fires." He shrugged away from Jed. "Listen—" He blew out a breath. "Liza called. You remember her, right? From Deep Haven..."

It took Jed a second, probably sunk as he was in the ramifications of one of his smokejumpers being hauled in for arson questioning. But he caught up fast. "Liza. Wait—isn't she the one who—"

"Yeah. Walked away from me without a word. I know

what you're going to say, but—"

"So why did she call? Is she in the area?"

"She was in a tree, hiding from a grizzly!"

Jed blinked at him, a frown creasing his face. "Is she hurt?"

"I don't know—maybe. I hope not. But I gotta go."

Jed's mouth tightened. "It'll look like you're guilty of something."

"But I'm not."

"You could get suspended while they sort it out. Maybe be kicked off the team for good."

Conner looked away. Drew in a long breath. Then his voice fell. "Listen, she called me. And she needs me. What would you do if it were Kate?"

Jed's mouth tightened into a grim line of agreement.

"Cover for me. And...give me a plane?"

"A plane?"

"I have to jump in. Liza's at Camp Blue Sky. It'll take me two hours overland to get there, minimum."

"Oh, fantastic. So, lie, cover for you, *and* distract them? Never mind who's going to pay for it."

"And maybe let me have Pete and, I dunno, Rube? Or CJ?"

Jed shook his head, but his expression suggested he'd climbed on board Conner's cause. "Reuben's on call. If you can talk Pete into it—and yeah, I think CJ's got a few days off. But Conner, the minute you're back, you check in with HQ, are we clear?"

Conner's phone buzzed. He glanced at the caller ID. "It's Gilly."

"Tell her to gas up and meet you at the end of the runway. I'll have Pete pick up your gear."

"Thanks." Conner climbed into his truck.

"And lock up your drone. Because if you're not using them to start fires, someone else is."

"It's already secure, somewhere the Feds won't find it."

"Just try and stay out of trouble."

Chapter 7

SHE'D JUST INVITED TROUBLE back into her life.

Liza stood in the middle of the athletic field, where they played soccer and all-camp tag, and braced a hand over her eyes, scanning the blue sky for Conner's drop plane.

I'm on my way with a couple of other guys—we're dropping into the camp. Don't worry, Liza, I'll be there.

She'd replayed Conner's voice mail message three times, finding herself leaning dangerously into his warm, husky baritone.

So, maybe not entirely trouble—because Conner's superpower was dropping in, saving the day. No, trouble arrived in the aftermath, in the dust kicked up by his arrival, the fact that, inevitably, she couldn't stop herself from longing to be in his world.

Which meant that despite her best intentions, she would start holding on, looking for promises, and in short, inadvertently insinuating—*forcing*—herself into his life.

Which would only leave poor Conner to figure out how to disentangle himself from her grip.

We'll see. We'll just take each day as it comes. I can't make any promises.

No promises—in fact, he'd never made her any promises,

something she'd spent nearly her entire adult life telling herself she didn't need.

Until Conner.

However, she had, with general success, spent the last year flushing him out of her system, reminding herself that she didn't need him—or anyone, really. Their kiss had simply been a misunderstanding, caused by the cascade of the glorious rose-gold sunset, making her see something on the horizon that wasn't there. Something he hadn't intended her to conjure up.

The fact that he took her call and was coming to her rescue said that, frankly, he was more of a real friend to her than she'd been to him.

Because she hadn't taken *his* calls since she'd packed her bags and headed back to Minnesota.

"Why are you staring at the sky?" Skye was walking over to her through the grassy athletic field. She wore a running shirt and a pair of water-wicking cargo pants, her long blonde hair pulled back into two Laura-Ingalls braids secured with a bandanna, the quintessential trail guide.

The girl belonged in a magazine, with her slim curves, toned body, and her pretty aqua-gray eyes. A backpack hung over her shoulder, filled with first aid equipment. She was clearly ready to trek out with a search party as soon as the rangers arrived.

Thanks to Liza's grizzly sighting, John refused to let the campers leave the grounds—despite Dr. Billings's outrage—without an armed cadre of rangers.

Never mind that Esther—and Shep—might be bleeding to death on the mountain.

Please, Conner, hurry.

"My friend Conner is jumping in with a couple of buddies to help lead the search."

Skye cupped a hand over her eyes, staring at the same clear blue sky. "Jumping—as in skydiving?"

"Mmmhmm. He's with the Jude County Smokejumpers, out of Ember. I was just lucky to catch him in between fires."

"A firefighter," Skye said, something of curiosity in her voice. "We had a big fire in Colorado when I was thirteen—our church fed a bunch of hotshots who were working in Glenwood Springs."

"I met Conner while he was working a blowup in Minnesota about three years ago."

In fact, it seemed to Liza that she always found herself staring up into the sky, hoping Conner might drop into her life. Not always literally, like now, but at least metaphorically, ever since the moment she'd brought him donuts.

It would behoove her to remember exactly who Conner Young was. Because after she'd patched up her broken heart, she'd finally figured him out. Despite his smile and, frankly, his faith, Conner was like every other man she'd known...here today, gone tomorrow. And, really, hadn't he warned her of that? *A guy like me.*

After they found Esther, she'd stand back, wave good-bye.

Let him walk out of her life without a backwards glance.

And most definitely *not* allow herself to dream up a happy ending with a guy who just wasn't that into her. Didn't have room for her in his nomad life.

Even if he was falling out of the sky like Superman—

"I hear a plane," Skye said, and Liza scanned the sky until she found the small plane, white against the blue vault.

It buzzed high overhead then circled, and she caught her breath when from it dropped a jumper, then two more.

Chutes opened and they began to drift down.

"Cool," Skye said. "I've always wanted to jump out of a plane."

"He took me up once," Liza said, her hand still cupped over her eyes. "I asked him what it was like to jump fire, and he decided to show me. We jumped tandem."

Skye looked at her. "Wow, seriously?"

Liza nodded, easily remembering the way he'd suited her up nearly a year ago, in Arizona. Remembered the feel of him checking her straps, his strong hands fixing her harness. Listen, when we get up there, it'll be too loud to really hear, but I'm going to strap you to the front of me. When we jump, open your arms and legs as if you're flying. We'll fall for about seven seconds, then I'll tap your shoulder, and you'll know to bring your arms in. I'll hang onto your legs and deploy the chute. Then, it's just us, drifting down to earth.

Just us.

She could still sense him behind her, powerful, his arm curled around her waist as they maneuvered toward the open door of the plane, the slipstream whipping against her, trying to pry her from his grip.

Not a chance. She held onto him for dear life.

That high up—four thousand feet, he'd told her later—the earth seemed a canvas, the cars matchbox in size, the houses Lincoln Logs. And, with his hands on her shoulders, the fear dropped away.

"*Ready?*"

She'd heard his voice above the buzz of the plane, the urge to fly swelling inside her.

She pushed out—dove, really—into nothing. Into blue sky and cool air and the sense that she could simply let go.

After all, Superman had her.

"Yeah," Liza said to Skye, watching the trio angle their rectangular chutes toward the field. "It was...well, like flying. Freedom, and of course, I was connected to Conner, so I wasn't afraid."

"Really?"

"Not at all. I knew that he wasn't going to let me drop, and so I just threw my arms out, enjoyed the ride."

Enjoyed the feeling of his strong body pinned to hers, being connected to him as they shared the glorious panorama.

"He hitched a ride with a pilot friend so we could jump near the Grand Canyon, and it was simply glorious to see the layers of earth, the way the canyon carves through the land. It's impressive from the ground, but from the air—it's absolutely breathtaking."

"I wonder what it feels like to jump into a fire," Skye said.

Liza tried not to think about the fact that, most of the time when Conner jumped, it was into flames three-stories high, into a world that could incinerate him with one unlucky gust of wind before he hit the ground.

"Conner says that sometimes they can feel the heat—depending on how big the fire is—from the plane. And of course, there's always the danger of being blown into the fire—"

"Seriously?"

"Yeah, of course. But they have training on how to steer into the wind and—see." She pointed to one of the jumpers. "He's out over the valley but has caught the wind and is using his steering toggles to bring him back in. It doesn't always work, though. Sometimes they can get blown way off course. One of Conner's buddies got caught in a tree one time and broke his leg."

No wonder Conner had started to call her after escaping

the flames. Wrung out, needing to decompress.

He needed that friend she said she'd be.

She didn't blame him, really, for reaching out.

"I didn't know firefighters do search and rescue."

"Not always, but yes, sometimes, if they're needed. Most of the smokejumpers have first-responder skills, and a few are EMTs." Her gaze tracked the closest one coming in. He wore a brown jumpsuit designed with deep leg pockets for his let-down rope, a high collar, and a gridded mask. His gloved hands drove the toggles, steering him to the middle of the field.

He dropped, then rolled, cushioning the landing across his body. Then he popped up and gathered in his chute.

"Wow. That was...smooth," Skye said, appreciation in her voice.

Liza glanced at her, and something pinched in her chest.

Skye, at twenty-one, might be a little young for Conner, but if he was looking for someone who would turn shiny eyes on him, swoon the minute he walked into the room—well, Skye might be the perfect candidate.

Because no way, no how, was Liza going to let herself fall into that place again. Not that she'd meant to the first time—she'd just suddenly found herself there, whispering her fatal words.

What next?

Which, in retrospect, she'd sounded so desperately needy she just wanted to cringe. She had to walk away to save her own shattered pride.

"They practice that landing until they get it perfect," Liza said.

And then, as the two other sky jockeys landed in their

own acrobatic rolls, the first man took off his helmet.

Golden sunshine on his blond hair, longer than before, but tousled, as if he'd been in a hurry to get to her.

Right. Down, girl.

But there stood Conner Young, looking every inch the superhero she'd built in her mind.

Oh boy.

Conner dropped the helmet and unhooked his harness, stepping out of it. Then he unzipped his jumpsuit, peeling it off.

Liza had already started toward him across the field, her heart pounding.

He'd bulked up since she'd last seen him. As he folded up his parachute, his thickened arms stretched out the sleeves of his T-shirt, which smoothed against the sculpted planes of his chest, his washboard torso. A sharp, delicious jolt of memory sluiced through her—the smell of him, cotton and soap and strength, as she'd leaned back against him, her body tucked into his embrace, his powerful legs alongside hers. His voice in her ear, husky, sweet, his arms locked around her as they watched the sunset.

Not unlike skydiving.

He turned, searching, and she felt it the moment he spotted her, a sort of forbidden thrill rocketing through her body as his blue eyes connected with hers.

A beat passed between them, and her heart dropped.

She shouldn't have called him. Because whatever memory she might have, he probably remembered a woman who clung too tightly. Whose imagination shattered their easy, sweet friendship, and who, at the first sign of danger—okay, a big, hairy, grizzly-sized sign of danger, with razor sharp teeth and a feral breath—called him to save her.

Still needy. Forcing herself back into his life.

Liza cleared her throat, scouring up her voice. "Thanks for—"

"Oh, thank God, you're safe." Conner dropped the chute, came toward her, his arms outstretched. "You have no idea how you scared me!"

He pulled her against himself. Hard, holding her—no, clinging to her—and if she wasn't mistaken, he just might be trembling a little.

As if—

She put her arms around his neck and let herself hold on, burying her face into his amazing Superman shoulders.

Because if Conner was good at anything, it was saving the day.

Even if trouble had dropped right out of the sky.

If it had been up to him, Conner might have run toward the grizzly instead of back to the chaos and panic of Camp Blue Sky.

He stood in the middle of the mess hall, surrounded by a knot of angry parents, map spread open on the planks of the picnic table in front of him, listening to the camp pastor, Beck, and Liza speculate on the trails Esther might have taken.

"I told her we would go here up to the overlook," Liza said, pointing out the Pine Ridge trail, a fairly well-traveled path that cut up along the north fork of the Bull River and offered spectacular views of Snowshoe Peak. "There's a path that cuts through camp and hooks into the route here." She traced the path with her pretty finger. Those same fingers that had woven into his as they'd sat watching the sunset in Arizona. Held onto him as they'd kissed, the last time his world felt whole and right.

He should stop right there and get his mind back on the route and the fact that there were not one but two kids lost in the woods.

But his brain still tangled on the way Liza had clung to him out in the field as if she honestly had missed him, and it had his thoughts dissected. Centered on the way that, for a second, she actually looked afraid of him. As if *he'd* done the leaving.

Done the heart breaking.

Left *her* bereft and afraid of letting him too close, back into her life.

Or perhaps she simply reflected the look in his own eyes, the sense that when he saw her standing there, dressed in a pair of cargo pants and a pink T-shirt, she looked exactly like she had the day she'd delivered him donuts, friendship, and a crazy glimpse of a happy ending he'd longed for way too much.

He simply couldn't help himself and gave into the panic, the urge to grab her up and hold her to himself.

Regardless of what it might cost his heart later.

"I still can't believe you would tell a fifteen-year-old girl to sneak off into the woods with a boy!"

This from a woman Liza had identified as Esther's mother, Donna. Conner looked for an accompanying worried father, but no one stepped forward.

"I didn't tell her to sneak off," Liza said quietly. "She was upset over Shep. I told her it would help for her to put him out of her head, find a new perspective, and the plan was to go *together*."

Conner wasn't prepared for the way her words reached

in and grabbed hold of his heart, squeezed. Is that what she'd done? Put him out of her head?

"Shep is a good boy." These words came from a petite blonde. She must have seen the inquiry as to her identity on his face. "Allison Billings, and trust me, Mr.—"

"Conner."

The glance she shot Liza would probably turn a lesser woman to ash. "Trust me, he wasn't interested in Esther. I would have known. They were friends, nothing more."

Liza's jaw tightened. "Right. Well, regardless, they're lost together, so—"

"Are you sure they headed up the path and not down?" Conner asked before he did something crazy like throw both Allison Billings and Donna from the building.

He wasn't a fool, even if Allison and Donna wanted to live in denial.

If Shep had sneaked away with Esther, he was *most certainly* interested in her. "Has anyone ascertained whether the jacket was Shep's or Esther's?"

Liza had briefed him on the details as he'd packed his jump gear, left it in the field with Pete's and CJ's, and hiked to the camp. Pete manned the radio outside, tracking down the rangers who were still en route. Good call to contact Gilly, and he owed Jed for covering for him, even if it did make him feel like a fugitive.

Better a fugitive than locked in some office answering questions he didn't know the answers to.

"It's not Esther's," Donna said. "I checked her belongings—her jacket was in her bag." She put a hand to her mouth. "I hope she won't freeze to death."

"It's nearly eighty degrees and the temp is rising out there, ma'am," CJ said in his Montana drawl. Their token fresh-off-the ranch rookie smokejumper only *looked* like a fireman in his yellow shirt, his green Nomex pants. Under his uniform, he had the hardy common sense and easy get 'er-done spirit of a Montana bull rider. Conner half expected to see a Stetson over his dirty blond hair. Dependable and sturdy, CJ didn't spook easily.

But Conner could have strangled him when CJ smiled and added, "But don't you worry. We'll find her before night settles in, I promise."

The last thing they could give these people were promises.

"I think we need to send a group of searchers down the trail. CJ, you and Skye can head up that group."

Skye, Liza's pretty blonde friend, looked over at CJ, flashing a smile that had warning flares firing. But he didn't have time to lecture CJ on the perils of falling for a woman during fire season.

Or the delights.

Shoot—and there he went again, his mind drifting back to Liza, the memory of her voice on the other end of the phone, sweet laughter or murmurs of empathy deep into the night when he'd crawled back to his trailer, wrung out, lonely.

For a while, dialing her number seemed the only pinprick of light in his dark, overwhelming world.

"I saw the bear here," Liza said, her brown hair caught back in a long ponytail at the nape of her neck. He had the inappropriate urge to loosen it and let her hair run through his fingers, and *for crying out loud, Conner, get your head back in the game.*

"Where was the tree you climbed?" he asked.

"Uh—" She looked up at him, shook her head. "I don't exactly know. Maybe a half mile away?"

"Okay. I'm going to head up the trail, see if I can find

anything. Pete will wait here for the rangers, and as soon as they show up, they'll follow me." He handed John a walkie, CJ another one. "Both of you, keep us informed of your position, and please, if you see the grizzly, back away quietly, stay still if you have to. The last thing you should do is run."

He looked pointedly at Liza.

She narrowed her eyes. "Listen, it worked, okay? And by the way, I'm going with you."

"No—actually, you're not."

Her eyes widened, argument gathering in the deep brown.

"She might not be, but I am."

Conner's gaze locked on the man standing behind Mrs. Billings, his hands on her shoulders. Well groomed, close-cropped dark hair, lean and sturdy, and a spark of fury in his dark eyes.

Oh great. "You're Shep's dad?"

"Dr. Blake Billings, and if anyone is going after my son, it's me. I would have done it earlier, but John demanded we wait."

Conner tried that one on for size and decided to let it go. If Conner's son was lost in the woods, possibly a victim of a grizzly attack, it would take more than an army of Becks, despite the man's seeming sturdiness, to stop him from bringing his boy home.

But maybe this doctor hadn't ever really seen death up close. Heard people you loved dying as you fought to save them. Knew what it felt like to bury your entire family.

So he wasn't buying Dr. Billings's bravado, thanks, but he did understand his frustration, translated into anger.

Conner had been simmering in the same fury for over a decade. You didn't just stand by when something terrible happened to someone you loved.

Still, anger easily turned to desperation, which meant mistakes. And with a bear on the prowl, Conner didn't want to worry about anyone doing something stupid.

No, this was better done alone, at least for now.

"You stay here and come with Pete," he said to Dr. Billings. "The rangers will have weapons. I'll have my radio, and I'll call if I find anything."

Conner grabbed the map, folded it. "I won't go far—just up the trail. Get the lay of the land and see if I can find signs of a grizzly attack." He stuck the map in his pocket and grabbed his pack filled with the first aid supplies he'd envisioned needing for Liza.

He was striding out the door when he realized it hadn't slammed behind him.

Oh, shoot. He turned—

"I'm not kidding you, Conner. And frankly, it's not up to you." Liza stood on the porch of the mess hall, her hands on her hips, shouldering her own backpack. She looked sturdy enough for travel—a jacket knotted around her waist, Gore-Tex pants, and boots—and the look in her eyes suggested this time she might not run from the grizzly.

She tried to stand him down with a look.

"Liza—"

"Those people blame me. You heard them. And the longer we sit here and wait, the angrier they become. And the crazier I will get, I promise you. I'm not asking your permission. I'm going."

He strode over to her, took a chance, and put his hands on her shoulders, lowering his voice. "It's not safe."

She shot him a look that made him release her before she could shove his hands away. "Seriously? I spent the morning in a *tree*. So don't tell me what's safe. Listen, I know that I panicked and called you. And now you're here, and, yeah, I'm grateful. *Super* grateful. And I promise I'm not going to get in your way, but I have to do this."

Get in his— "I'm not worried about you getting in the way, Liza. But I can't promise you that you're not going to get hurt."

"Are you kidding me? Trust me, if I get hurt, it's on me. I know that better than anyone."

He didn't know why, but he had the sudden feeling they were no longer talking about the search.

"Liza, please—"

"Let's just go." She brushed past him, striding up the trail, and he stood there, watching her go.

What was his problem, that his best view of her lately seemed to be her walking *away* from him?

"Liza, come back here!"

"Keep up!"

Shoot—he scrambled up beside her, nearly at a run. Her long legs stretched out, not slowing, her jaw tight.

"This could turn out very badly, you know. Are you ready for that?"

She hooked her hands into her backpack straps, cutting up the path. "I'm very well aware of the trouble we could be walking into, Conner. And I'm truly sorry that I foisted my problems on you, but right now, in this moment, I don't care. I'll do whatever I have to, to find Esther."

Even, apparently, spend time with him.

He didn't know why, but for some reason he reached up and rubbed his chest, a burn there, as if she'd just put her fist into the center of it.

"Fantastic," he said softly and followed her up the trail.

CHAPTER 8

"THE GRIZZLY MADE GOOD work of your backpack," Conner said, picking up Liza's shredded pack from the edge of the overlook. With the sun climbing the sky, slinging long shadows through the forest and across the trail, the sight of the decimated pack sent a shiver through her.

Liza kept her eyes peeled on the trail beyond the overlook, the image of the beast imprinted like a shadow in her head. She simply couldn't blink it away.

"What did you have in it?" Conner asked, peeling the pack open.

"Some cheese, an apple, maybe some jerky." She joined him, sifting through the remains, and picked up a canister, the safety lid still attached.

"Bear spray," Conner said drily.

"Apparently, it's just for ballast," Liza said, but hooked it onto the outside of her new pack.

She tried to ignore the delicious tug of a smile on Conner's face at her lame joke. But it seemed to unscrew the lid on the tension between them.

I'm very well aware of the trouble we could be walking into, Conner.

That had shut down his arguments about her hiking out

with him. It also seemed to curb the way-too-enthusiastic greeting he'd given her.

And her painfully eager response.

Whatever had passed between them on that field, it seemed they'd managed to right themselves, find their footing.

Remember.

Still, it didn't help that every time he looked at her he chipped a little deeper into the wound she'd worked so hard to heal.

Maybe she'd underestimated the danger of hiking out alone with Conner.

Forgotten the damage he could do to her heart.

But he didn't have to know that. He was simply here to rescue Esther, and she'd be grateful for it.

Liza retrieved her lacerated tablet and crushed pencil box.

"Sorry," Conner said.

"They're just drawings."

He touched her arm. "But they're your drawings."

And wasn't that sweet. She shoved the tablet back in the destroyed pack, her hands trembling, suddenly achingly aware of how close she'd come to being mauled along with said pack.

Conner hesitated a moment, as if he wanted to add something, then got up and paced out to the overlook. "It's mostly rock here, but I can make out a few footprints." He squatted, used his hand to measure. "This is a big bear."

"I know," Liza said, scouring the trail and finding a print. She knelt, put her hand next to it. "Can I be seeing this right? A twelve-inch footprint?"

"That's the front print—but yeah. I see some human

traces also. Was Esther wearing Keens? The pattern is fairly distinctive."

"I think so." Liza came over to where he pointed, near the fencing. "They're facing away from the view."

"These aren't," he said, and pointed to another pair, bigger. "These look like Converse."

"Shep wears high tops," she said, mentally trying out the angle. *Oh, Esther.*

Conner stood up. "Clearly he was into her," he muttered.

"What?"

He strode away from her. "Oh, something Shep's mom said about him not liking her. If a guy sneaks away with a girl, he's into her."

"For the moment," Liza said, but thankfully he didn't hear her as he strode over to the trail. *C'mon, Liza, get over it.* Conner obviously cared enough to answer the phone. Just because he didn't want to give her any promises didn't mean that certified him as a jerk.

"There's not much in the way of clean prints beyond these," Conner said. He headed up the trail, past the point where she'd spotted the bear, and around the bend. His voice rose in a shout "I think I got something!"

Liza followed him, a chill running through her as she passed the bear sighting to where Conner stood at a huckleberry bush that was splintered and partially uprooted. He was unwinding a strip of royal blue yarn caught in the brambles. "Is this from a sweater?"

She took it, ran it between her thumb and forefinger "It's from Esther's backpack. It was something she got at the camp store—we have a bunch of consignment crafts, including knitted backpacks."

More yarn caught in the twigs twined in the breeze. Here

the mountain sloped more gently down to the valley, the terrain covered with tangled junipers and prickly wild roses, scattered patches of blueberry bushes until the land fell into a sketchy pine forest below. Overhead, the sun was high, nearly at its apex, the sky a pale blue.

"They must have seen the bear and veered off the trail," Conner said. He had already advanced farther off the trail, through the bramble. "They came through here," he said, pointing to a patch of trampled wildflowers, their yellow petals crushed in the loam, "but..." He stopped, pulled something from the knot of blueberry bushes. "The bear did, too."

Fur, grimy and dark. He met her eyes with a bleak look.

Liza brushed past him, headed down the hillside, tripping over roots, cutting through bushes. "Esther! Shep!"

Nothing answered but the cry of a circling hawk hunting prey.

Liza worked her way down the hillside, pushing past the brambles of golden currant, the white blooms of boulder raspberries, the knee-high shrubbery of cascade bilberry. A regular smorgasbord for a hungry grizzly. The hollow in her stomach grew. "Esther!"

Behind her, Conner called out their names, his boots crunching through the tangle of juniper and scrubby maples.

The bushes caught between lichen-covered boulders, and rocky wash soon gave way to spindly aspen and the red spires of wild dogwood, then towering white-barked birch.

From here, the land sloped precariously down to the north fork of the Bull River. Liza stopped in a patch of blue columbine, noting the delicate blue-and-white flowers torn and scattered on the ground. "They made it this far," she said, glancing over her shoulder at Conner.

He was on his walkie, calling in to Pete, who was still waiting for the rangers back at camp. Pete's voice came through, sketchy and thin. They'd left the ridge trail far behind, the reception choppy.

Conner clipped the walkie to his belt, then came down to her. "I find it hard to believe the bear wouldn't have overtaken them by this point," he said, squatting to pick up a crumpled flower.

"Maybe it gave up—or what if they spooked it and it ran?"

He stood, hands on his lean hips, surveying the area, his mouth in a grim line.

It dredged up a memory, long buried, of his surveying the striated red-rock scenery of Sedona.

So maybe he *had* been into her. For an intoxicating summer moment.

He turned to her, his blue eyes catching hers. "Let's keep going. Maybe they just got lost."

Perhaps. She fell in after him, letting him part the forest, choose the trail.

With the forest thickening as they descended, with towering white spruce, Douglas fir, and shaggy hemlocks clumping together to form a canopy of shadow, they might have kept running, become disoriented.

At least that was the thought Liza reached for, clung to as she lifted her voice, calling. "Esther! Shep!"

A breeze shivered the trees, raking up the scent of cedar and pine as she and Conner cut around boulders the size of buffalo and over jutting limestone, following runs of ledge rock that corrugated the landscape.

She couldn't imagine running through the forest without slipping on loose shale, careening down a gully, wedging her foot into a fissure, or faceplanting into a ravine studded with chert and other jagged remains of mountain runoff.

They could be anywhere in this tangle of Kootenai forest, wounded, dying.

Conner had stopped, pulled out his map, apparently orienting himself.

"The north fork is about half a mile from here. Certainly they couldn't have gotten that far, right?"

"Considering I climbed a tree over half a mile from where I encountered the bear, I'm thinking you cover a lot of ground when you're freaked out."

Conner looked as if he were sifting through her words. Finally, "Yeah, you're right. Maybe, with nothing to stop them, they just kept running."

He folded the map, shoved it in his back pocket, then picked his way down a spree of boulders, grabbing a low-hanging maple branch for support.

Liza scrambled after him, not wanting to lose him.

Under the canopy of forest, the air seemed languid, pockets of cool air lifting the hair off her neck. She pulled out her ponytail, did a quick, loose braid, and let it hang over her shoulder.

They reached a clearing and Conner took out his water bottle, took a drink, again consulted his map. Called Pete and got an update.

"The rangers are on site. They've brought tranquilizer guns and are going to track the bear. But if he's out of the area and hasn't attacked anyone, then they'll let him go. So far there's no evidence of him being a rogue animal—just a guy protecting his territory. It was a male, right? You didn't see any cubs?"

She shook her head.

"Then he probably thought you were simply too close.

He got startled, felt cornered."

Now that made perfect sense, actually.

"He didn't have to roar at me. I had no intention of invading his space."

"He probably did what is called a bluff charge—they aren't intending on attacking, they just want you to know they don't like you in their space. Did it pop its jaw, maybe sway from side to side?"

"In a way."

He frowned.

"He certainly let me know that he wasn't interested in having me hang around."

That seemed to satisfy him. "Hmm. Well, if it was a predatory attack, he would have been stalking you. And, in that case, playing dead doesn't always help. You might have been able to scare him off by throwing something at him or banging a couple of sticks together and making loud noises. Basically making him think that you're a risk if he decided to attack."

"Yeah, I can be scary that way."

This got a return smile. "You have no idea."

And for a second, the world just stopped. Conner's smile dimmed. Her breath caught. And, shoot, but the words felt like bait, the kind she couldn't ignore. "That's what it was, wasn't it? I was too scary?"

He swallowed.

Then he turned and stalked away.

Because, yes, she'd hit on the truth. She was too scary—because she'd fallen too hard, too fast, and when she cornered him, he'd felt trapped.

Thirty feet ahead of her, Conner continued calling, his

voice devoured by the tight canopy, the knot of forest. The breeze thickened into a shiver, and the sound formed around the flow of a waterfall in the distance. She could imagine the couple running through the brush, over logs, tripping on roots, crashing through bushes—

"Liza!"

The tone of Conner's voice alerted her, and she spotted him on a rock, gesturing to her. She cut through low-lying ferns, crunchy brown needles, rotted, downed trees and climbed up beside him, tripping as she reached the top of the rock.

He caught her just before she would've fallen forward into nothing.

Or rather, into the cool breath of the Bull River. Forty feet down, a stair-step waterfall tumbled over cut rock and boulders to drop another thirty feet into a cauldron of foamy, brown water.

And on an outcropping forty feet down, no more than four feet across, crumpled and still, lay the broken form of sixteen-year-old Shep Billings.

"Oh no—" Liza dropped to her knees, barely aware of Conner's hand on her shoulder as she braced herself and leaned forward. "Shep!'

The roar of the falls ate her voice. Below, the body didn't move.

Conner knelt next to her. "We have to find a way down to him."

"Do you see Esther?"

On the other side of the river the forest continued, dark, snarled.

"No," Conner said. He gave her shoulder a tight squeeze as he pulled out his walkie.

~

The Great Bear Escape notwithstanding, it seemed like Liza recovered in a quick minute from seeing Shep crumpled forty feet below, pale, maybe even already deceased.

Her voice betrayed none of her panic as she called down to him. "Shep! We see you. We're on our way."

Well, Conner was at least, although the minute he secured his letdown rope to a nearby aspen, Liza picked up the length as if ready to rappel.

"What are you doing?" he asked.

She appeared to ignore him, looping the rope through her legs, around her left leg, back around and across her chest, over her right shoulder, letting the rope fall behind her, her left hand gripping the slack and riding below her backside for a brake. She leaned into it, testing.

For a long second Conner just gaped at her. "How did you learn to emergency rappel?"

She backed up to the edge. "I live in the boundary waters of Minnesota. It seemed only logical to take a survival course."

Right. And she'd called him because…? "Maybe I should go down first."

"I'm already roped up." Liza leaned back, into her hand. "I just wish I had gloves—this is going to hurt."

"Wait." He pulled a pair from his pack.

She put on his gloves and reacquired her grip.

"I'm right behind you," he said as she lowered herself over the edge.

As Conner knelt at the edge, his jaw tight, he had the terrible urge to leap all forty feet so he could be on hand to catch her. It had nothing to do with her needing him—which apparently, so far, she didn't, despite her phone call—and everything to do with the fact that he couldn't bear to see her get hurt.

That's what it was, wasn't it? I was too scary?

No. Not at all. But he'd scared himself, if he were to be honest, with how much he'd wanted to do something crazy, like yes, make her promises, be the guy who stopped living with his crazy no-commitment rules and actually lived the life he'd always dreamed of.

Liza reached the rocky ledge, landed next to Shep. "I'll send the gloves up."

She tied them to the rope, and he pulled it up as she knelt next to Shep.

"I'll be right down!"

Shep lay on his side, his bottom leg broken and jutted out beneath him. Blood pooled under the injury, suggesting an open fracture. His shoulder also looked crushed, the way his head sank into it. He wore a T-shirt and jeans, his skin gray, eyes closed.

Conner guessed him about five foot ten, maybe a hundred and eighty pounds, an athletic kid with a lean, toned body. No wonder he thought he could outrun a bear. At sixteen, Conner had thought the same thing, that he was king of his world with no idea how it could drop out beneath him.

At nearly thirty-eight, he was smarter. Knew exactly how fast he could fall.

The ledge was only four feet wide, and they would have been standing on top of each other if Liza hadn't moved toward Shep's head when Conner reached the ledge.

Liza tested for a pulse at the base of Shep's jaw while Conner knelt next to him and lifted his shirt, looking for bruising.

He found a dark splotch down by his lower rib, just above his abdomen.

"His pulse is weak and rapid. His breathing is really shallow," Liza said.

"After a fall like that, he probably has internal bleeding." Conner worked off his pack and reached inside, pulling out a Mylar rescue blanket. He draped it over Shep. "I don't want to move him, but we need to try and slow the bleeding. How's his head?"

Liza felt around his skull, her hands gentle. The boy's eyes didn't open. "He's got a wound just above his ear, but it doesn't feel deep. And his skull isn't soft, so I don't think it's broken." She, too, had taken off her pack and now dug around, pulling out a first aid kit. She pulled out a handful of thick gauze pads and worked them under his head.

"We need to get a look at that leg wound," Conner said. He pulled out his knife, sheathed in his belt, and began to tear at the fabric of the boy's jeans, working his way past the fracture to the knee.

There a bone spur stuck out the back of Shep's leg, tearing the calf.

A tap on his shoulder, and Liza handed him a roll of gauze, a handful of pads. "Cover the wound, and we'll figure out if we can splint it."

He could hardly believe this was the same person who'd called him just six hours ago, frantic.

Reflex? Panic? He was hoping for Good Excuse to Call Conner because if she didn't need him, she certainly wouldn't invite him back into her life after they got Shep—and Esther—back up the mountain.

Conner pressed the pad on the wound, and Liza helped him wrap Shep's leg.

Then he watched as she put her hands on Shep's head and closed her eyes.

Was she—praying?

Yep. And seeing it, his entire body ached.

I kept praying for you...

Did she still think of him, still pray?

He got up and pulled out his walkie.

"Young, Brooks. Pete, come in."

He waited, then the voice kicked in, crackly, but clearer than he would have expected.

"Brooks, Young. What's your position?"

"We found the boy. He's on a ledge overlooking a waterfall on the north fork of Bull River."

Silence, then, "Roger that, Conner. And, uh, what's his... status?"

Conner could picture Pete walking away from the rangers and especially Dr. Billings as he phrased his question.

"Alive. He took a fall, broke his leg, probably has internal injuries, maybe a broken shoulder. He hit his head, too. I think he's in shock."

A beat, then, "Roger that. We're on our way. Can you give us your best position?"

Conner pulled out his map, gave the coordinates.

"We're a good five clicks from you," Pete came back. "Ranger Eric suggests we call in the chopper out of Mercy Falls. PEAK Rescue has a hoist and an EMT team."

"Roger that. Can you get hold of dispatch?"

"Will do. Dr. Billings wants to talk to you."

He shot a look at Liza, but she was still praying.

"How badly injured is he?" Billings asked.

"We're working on getting the bleeding stopped and we're keeping him warm."

"Don't give him any liquids, he might vomit them up."

"Roger that. We'll keep you informed."

Conner clipped the walkie on his belt and crouched down next to the boy, touching his face. Cool, almost clammy. Please, let him not be going into shock.

That's when he saw Liza's hand trembling, her body shaking. Her breath shuddered out.

Oh, no, was she— "Liza, are you crying?"

Whoops, he hadn't meant it quite like that. She looked up at him and, sure enough, tears hung in her beautiful brown eyes, streaked down her face. She wiped her cheeks quickly with the back of her hand.

"No."

"Liza—"

"I'm fine."

He jerked back, more stung than she probably intended, but he couldn't help but feel as if she'd put a hand to his chest and shoved.

Still, as she looked away, her jaw tight as if trying not to cry, he couldn't help it. "He's going to be okay—"

"Are you kidding me?" She rounded on him, her eyes sharp in his. "He's probably going into shock. His pressure is dropping. His leg is busted and he has a head injury—he's hardly going to be okay—"

Beneath her hand, the boy stirred, and something akin to horror filled her expression.

Conner put his hand on hers. "He didn't hear you."

She cut her voice low as she shook her head, pulled her hand away. "You don't know that, either." She wiped her face again, this time sloppily with both hands. "This is all my fault."

He frowned at her words. "Liza, there was a bear—"

But she looked at him, her eyes red, her face streaked with sweat and dirt, and her grief swiped away his words. "She came to me, crying. Said that Shep had told her to get lost, that he didn't want her hanging around him, and she was crushed. So, yeah, I told her that she didn't need him, or any guy, and then I had this oh-so-brilliant idea for her to watch the sunrise, as if that might be a magic elixir for solving a girl's man problems."

"Except she didn't have man problems—"

"That's just it." She looked at him. "Who knows what happened last night that ended with her up here with Shep? And now she's missing and he's dying. She should have listened to me and told Shep to stay out of her life before he crushed her fragile little heart."

"But what if he really likes her? What if he was just, I don't know, confused when he told her to get lost?"

She emitted a sound that bordered on disgust. "Yeah, right." She looked at him, and her expression made him feel a little stupid.

"Upright, healthy, and not broken, Shep is a sixteen-year-old poster child for the hottest boy in class. Tall, strong, blue eyes, a smile that can charm the common sense right out of a girl. Apparently he plays football, is class president, and prom king. Esther is a...well, let's just say that she and I would have hung out together in the art studio."

He sort of liked her art studio.

"Guys like Shep like cheerleaders and dance-line girls, the pretty ones who know how to flirt, not girls like Esther, who wear thrift-store jeans, don't know how to use mascara, and would rather spend Saturday afternoon holed up with a good novel. And if he was chasing her, it wasn't because he was into her—at least not in the way she wanted. It was because he had one thing on his mind. And the minute he got it, he would exit her life so fast she'd get windburn."

Her voice had sharpened, and now her mouth tightened into a bud of frustration. "And I should have told her that raw truth instead telling her that she didn't need a guy to be happy. Or telling her that painting a sunrise might make things okay."

Conner was trying hard to keep up, to read between the words, but he only managed to come up with something lame. "I love sunrises."

She looked away. "I know."

The boy groaned, shifting, and in a second, Liza's hand pressed his cheek. "Shep, don't move. It's going to be okay."

What *he'd* said, hello.

Shep's eyes fluttered open.

Disoriented, he looked at Conner, then Liza. "Where am I?"

"Shh," Liza said in that tone of voice that always made Conner's heartbeat slow, made him feel like everything would be okay. "You fell off a cliff. Help is coming."

Shep winced as he tried to orient himself. "Esther—!" He made to push himself up, then fell back with a cry, whimpering.

"Dude! You're pretty busted up here." Conner put a hand on Shep's chest, testing his breathing, his heart rate, hoping to calm him. "Just breathe."

"She's in...the water." Shep's breathing came erratically, hiccupping out the words. "We were holding hands when we jumped, and then I landed and she—I couldn't hold her.

Oh..." His voice cut in and out with broken sobs. "Oh no, oh... Please, I heard her. She was calling my name..."

"When, Shep?" Liza leaned over him, her hand over his forehead. "Was it after she fell?"

"She was..." Shep seemed to sift through his fractured memories. "Yeah. After she fell. She landed in the water, I think. But she yelled that she was going to find a way back."

Liza looked up at Conner, so much hope in her eyes, Conner wanted to reach out and hug her.

But he had the strangest feeling that her outburst about Shep the Prom King might have been less about Esther and more about the girl in art class, the one with long brown hair and luminous, beautiful brown eyes. And he couldn't quite let go of the rest of her words. *Tall, strong, blue eyes, a smile that can charm the common sense right out of a girl.*

Conner had felt a little sick at her words.

"She's alive," Liza said then, cutting through the dark chatter in his head. "She landed in the river and decided to float downstream until she could climb out."

That was one scenario, sure. Conner managed a smile, not wanting to voice the other options. "Maybe."

"Which means that she could be on her way here or at least hiking back up." Liza looked down at Shep, and this woman Conner recognized. Tender. Kind, despite her doubts about him. "Can you tell us what happened?"

Tears cut down his cheeks. "She was upset—I didn't know why, so I said I'd meet her at the bell tower." He closed his eyes, winced. "She wanted to talk about what happened between her and my mom—they got into a fight." His face darkened. "Mom said something stupid, like I didn't want to hang around her. But it wasn't true. It's *not* true and—" His breath stuttered.

"Shh. We'll find her," Liza said. "Did you see a bear?"

"Yeah. It came up the trail at us. Esther saw it first—I don't think it smelled us or anything, it was just walking up the trail, but we didn't know what to do. She wanted to play dead like they taught us at camp, but I—I pushed her up the trail. The bear started charging, and I freaked out and threw my coat at him and then. . . I don't know. We were off the trail and running, and I think it followed us. I heard branches breaking, but we just kept running—" He was breathing hard now, and again Conner put a hand on his chest.

"Slow down. Just breathe."

Tears ran down into Shep's ears. "We didn't even see the cliff until we'd launched off it. I tried to hold on—she was screaming..."

His entire body shook, and he raised his hand to cover his eyes.

Conner looked away, his throat tight.

"Please...find her."

Shep grabbed Conner's hand, and Conner met his eyes. It was the tremble in the boy's voice, the pleading that made Conner turn his hand into Shep's in a buddy grasp. "I'll find her."

But Shep wasn't done. He tightened his grip. "Promise me."

Aw, shoot…Conner couldn't stop himself. He nodded, fast, sharp. "I promise."

He couldn't look at Liza. But she put her hand over his and held it there.

Chapter 9

I PROMISE.

Conner's words hung in Liza's mind as she stood on the ledge watching the EMT from PEAK Rescue load Shep into the rescue litter. With little room on the outcropping, only the female EMT and Pete remained to worked the litter, both of them attached to the chopper above by the hoist cable.

Liza and Conner had climbed back up to the cliff edge as soon as the chopper arrived. Apparently, Pete knew the folks from PEAK Rescue. He'd introduced the woman as Jess. Liza hadn't gotten a good look at the woman, other than her blonde hair pulled into a tight nub just below her helmet, but she seemed strong and no-nonsense like, taking control from Conner almost immediately.

Conner's smokejumper pal CJ had joined them, along with Skye, and frankly, Liza couldn't figure out why they were all still standing here. Conner had his map open a few feet away, crouched on the rock, holding it down with his knees. Skye held down the other side as he studied the route of the Bull River.

Apparently intent on keeping his promise.

Probably only Liza knew the effort it had taken for Conner to say that.

The chopper hovered some fifty yards above, the rotors whisking the needles from the trees, the wash so loud they couldn't hear the commands the EMTs shouted to each other. Pete used hand signals to respond to Jess's directions.

Just a few feet away, Dr. Billings and the two rangers—a thirty-something woman with short brown hair and her counterpart, a thicker man in his mid-fifties—were engineering a return ride to camp once they hiked back to the ridge.

None of the searchers had seen a trace of the grizzly.

It didn't mean the animal wasn't lurking nearby, however.

Dr. Billings had added nearly nothing to Shep's emergency care—especially when they discovered his specialty was dermatology. But he'd paced, barked orders, and generally behaved like a distraught father, and that had Liza's heart softening.

No one escaped suffering when seeing their child hurt.

She didn't hear Conner step up beside her, what with the spectacle of the chopper hoisting the litter up, Jess affixed to the rig. The EMT climbed into the chopper and pulled the litter in.

"They'll take him to Kalispell Regional Medical Center. Calling the chopper in was the right call," Conner said.

The chopper moved off, ascending as it followed the river east, toward Kalispell.

Pete climbed up the cliff, belayed by CJ.

Dr. Billings stopped as he turned to climb the hill back to the trail above. He ignored Liza but stuck out his hand to Conner. "Thank you."

Conner met his grip, glanced at Liza. "She helped him just as much as I did."

Clearly his words fell on deaf ears, because Billings barely cast a glance at Liza as he moved away.

"He's just upset," Conner said, apparently feeling the need to defend the man. "I remember the first time I broke my arm—I was riding a four-wheeler, took a turn too fast, and down I went. My dad completely lost it—drove to the hospital like a maniac. That's just the way fathers are when their kids are hurt."

"I'm sure. I don't remember, really, but I believe you."

He went silent. She'd told him, of course, of her father dying when she was only five.

"Sorry," he said. "Of course not."

"Let's just get going. We have a promise to keep."

The words simply emerged—she didn't mean to drag up old wounds. Still, Conner's mouth tightened.

"About a quarter mile from here, the river thins. Skye and CJ are going to cross over to the other side, just in case Esther washed up and got stranded on the opposite bank. You and I will hike down the river on this side just in case she's there."

Liza was still watching the chopper, a blue-and-white bird, as it glided down the river. "What I wouldn't give to be able to get a bird's eye view."

Silence beside her, and she looked at Conner. He wore a faraway look, but came back to himself at her glance. Then, a smile curved up his face. "Oh wow—why didn't I think of that earlier?"

Huh?

He turned to Pete, sitting on the rock nearby, winding up the letdown rope between his feet into a perfect loop. "Pete, you gotta do me a solid here."

Pete seemed built for the outdoors, with a lean, tight frame, wide ropy shoulders, a calm agility around danger. He had dark-blond hair tied back with a lanyard, a square chin, blue eyes, and seemed the kind of guy built to get the lost out of trouble. She had no doubt he probably got *into* trouble as well, with his charming smile and easy laughter, the kind that could woo his way too easily into a girl's heart.

"Name it."

"I need you to get back to Ember and pick up my drone." Conner reached into his pocket and fished out a ring of keys.

"Dude, you brought your keys on a jump?"

"I didn't stop off at my locker, remember?"

"Right," Pete said, catching the keys with one hand. "Okay, what am I getting?"

"My last drone. I rent a storage locker just outside town. Listen, you'll also need the remote control—that's in my trailer, locked in my nightstand."

"You lock your bedroom furniture?"

"I keep my gun there, too."

"Right."

Pete got up, handed Conner the rope. "So, do I call Gilly to drop me again?"

"Maybe. Check in, I might have a better jump spot than camp. Unless, hopefully, we find Esther before then."

"It'll take me a few hours—I gotta hike back, then drive back to Ember—it could be nightfall."

"I know. And if we haven't found Esther by dark, you'll have to wait until tomorrow. But by then, we'll definitely need the drone."

"Roger that." Pete glanced at Liza, gave her a tight smile. "If anyone can find Esther, Conner can," he said and nodded as if trying to instilll comfort.

"I know."

Conner had already walked away, but Skye came up, buckling the waist strap of her pack. "A drone?"

Away from them, Conner had folded the map into a square, pulled CJ over for consultation.

"Conner's an inventor," Liza said, watching him. He'd seemed intense before, when they'd hiked down from the ridge. But with the set of his jaw, his gestures and instructions to CJ... He'd taken out a bandanna and tied it over his head to keep the hair out of his face, and now the wind rippled his blue T-shirt across his strong back. Nothing would stop Conner this time from keeping his promise.

"He's sort of a communications wizard—worked as the com guy on his Green Beret team. He's been working on the drones for a while now, hoping to use them to predict fire behavior. But, yeah, it could also be used to find Esther."

Conner had started down the side of the gorge, gesturing for Liza and Skye to follow.

"You did the right thing, calling him," Skye said. "And CJ. He's great."

Liza glanced over at her, couldn't help the smile. Yeah, she'd worn the same silly expression when she'd met Conner. And it had only worsened as the Deep Haven fire ignited their friendship.

Friendship. They *had* been friends—the kind who knew each other's stories. The ones that lurked in the darkness, the ones that still bruised with the telling.

I promise.

Oh, Conner.

See, that's why a gal couldn't escape falling for him—because the man led with his heart, despite what it cost him.

Like making a crazy, ill-advised promise to a sixteen-year-old kid.

Or responding to her panicked phone call with "I'll be there."

And maybe even taking her in his arms as the sun fell behind the red bluffs outside Sedona and kissing her. The kind of kiss that lit her entire body, that sometimes still made her lick her lips, the tingle, the taste of him right there, fresh, alive.

She probably shouldn't blame him for panicking when he realized he'd gone too far—after all, she'd done the same thing when she realized just how much of her heart she'd handed over to him.

And now she'd dragged them right back into trouble.

She glanced at Conner, striding like a force through the woods some thirty yards ahead, followed closely by CJ, a younger, more cowboy version of his mentor.

"Yeah, CJ's great," Liza said. "Dependable, brave. But keep your heart in check, because guys like CJ—and Conner—thrive on saving the day. That's what firefighters do—they're heroes to the core. But you have to be willing to let them walk away. That's their life—jump in, put out the fire, then move on to the next one. They can't make you any promises."

Skye frowned. "That's a little harsh."

It was? Liza shook her head. "I'm just trying to save you needless heartache. Smokejumpers are way too easy to fall for. But entanglements are the last thing they need, even if they are too nice to say it."

Liza tendered a smile, hoping to ease her words, but Skye frowned. "Oh, I get it. CJ said you and Conner used to date. I understand. But I was just saying that CJ's cute. And sweet. I'm not looking to hold onto him. A guy doesn't have to promise me a ring for me to be his friend."

Wow. She hadn't realized she'd turned into such a jerk. But Skye was right. Liza knew she was playing with fire when she'd opened her heart to Conner. Knew that he couldn't offer her more than just friendship. She'd set *herself* up for heartache and walked away from a friendship that he—and frankly, she too—enjoyed.

How many times had she answered the phone, listening to him wind down from a fire? Needing someone to listen, to care.

To let him know he wasn't alone.

She caught up to him, downed branches and dry needles crackling under her boots. He glanced back, over his shoulder, and she gave him a smile.

Most of all, if he could make a promise, so could she—to help him *keep* that promise to save Esther.

Nothing more.

Half a mile from where Shep had fallen, the river flattened out, widening beneath the gorge. The water flowed around boulders jutting out from the rapids enough to serve as stepping-stones. Conner watched as CJ, then Skye rappelled down nearly fifty feet to the river basin, then worked their way across to the far bank.

CJ called in their position from the far side through the walkie. They'd already confirmed a rendezvous point two miles farther downstream should they not find Esther.

Please, let them find Esther. Something about Shep's panicked voice, his pleading for a promise, had settled low in Conner's gut, tightening as the sun sank into the Cabinet Mountains.

Below the cliff, the late hour turned the river to a deep indigo, almost black as it foamed and churned west toward the main river. Liza stood at the edge of the gorge scanning the basin for any sign of the girl.

A call to Pete on the walkie had yielded an update from Beck, who informed him that Pete had left in the camp pickup for Ember. He'd make an update via his cell phone to Beck, who would forward it to Conner.

This kind of wonky communication made Conner want to throw his walkie across the river and let out a scream—another reason to equip his drones with communication relay capabilities. Acting as a transponder in the sky, a communications drone just might save time and lives.

Not cost lives or start fires. Whatever the National Interagency Fire Center suspected, they'd guessed wrong.

But Conner couldn't sit around waiting for them to clear him.

He knew exactly how effective the government could be at finding justice, thank you. The government didn't have a prayer of getting their hands on his last working drone.

"The river only narrows from here, and the cliffs are higher," Liza said, dropping the binoculars to hang around her neck.

"You know Esther. Could she climb out of the gorge?"

Liza lifted her shoulder in a shrug. "She's probably scared and maybe hurt, and that rarely makes for rational thinking. She might have tried and fallen back in..." She caught her lip in her teeth, a shadow crossing her face.

Conner took her hand, the urge too great to stop himself.

"We'll find her." Then, because he didn't want to add anything to it, he turned and tugged her along beside him.

Liza walked for a few feet, her hand tucked in his, and just when he thought she might acquiesce, let him settle into a place where their past didn't jut up between them, she let go.

He clenched his fist before shoving it into his pocket.

Walked out ahead of her.

They walked in silence, dread crawling into his bones as shadows crept from the folds of the forest.

It felt precariously like old times, when he needed the sound of her voice to break through the crusty layer of fatigue, of darkness. "What did you mean, you know I like sunrises?" he asked quietly.

He didn't look at her, and for a long moment he couldn't be sure she heard him.

Then, "Aside from the fact that..." She cleared her throat and spoke again, her voice kind. "You told me you did. That story, about your parents, that last summer they were alive. You took a trip to Mt. Rushmore, remember?"

He glanced over his shoulder, saw her smiling, and it lit a warmth in him he hadn't realized he'd missed. "I can't believe you remember that."

"Of course I do. I remember... Well, maybe not everything, but most of your stories."

His stories. The ones he'd told her as he lay in his bed, exhausted after a fire. Or if he had cell service, sitting by a campfire at a strike camp, sooty and on edge. He'd dredged the stories out of the dark places, just so he could keep her on the line.

"I remember most of yours, too. But..." He stopped, turned, and she nearly plowed into him. "But not the one about a pretty art student and a football player who had *one thing on his mind.*"

His voice had turned solemn, his chest tightening with each word.

Liza's eyes widened. Then she shook her head, made to push past him. "It doesn't matter—"

He grabbed her hand, stopping her. "It matters to me."

She glanced at him, swallowed, and for a second, he saw it again—that expression he'd seen in the field, a crazy flash of what he could only name as fear.

Of him?

Then, just as fast, it vanished. Her mouth tightened to a thin line.

"It's nothing." She started again down the shore. "We have to find Esther. It's getting dark."

"We can look while you tell me why you're lying."

She winced, shook her head, and looked away.

"Please? C'mon, Liza. I'm not the most sensitive guy, but even I can see that it's eating at you."

"Fine." She angled her view down the river as she talked. "I was a sophomore in high school, and yes, it happened pretty much the way I said it. Except I went to an all-girls private art school, and he was from the neighboring high school. We met at a football game—I went with my roommate and some girls she knew. I had just moved from Minneapolis, my mom and stepdad were in the middle of a divorce and... Well, let's say that I wasn't welcome at home."

Wasn't welcome? He didn't remember that part.

But she pushed on. "It was stupid. After the game, we went to a party, and I somehow found myself outside at the bonfire with this cute guy who was more interested in me than the party. He got my number and called the dorm. I was so flattered I didn't stop to think that maybe he wasn't being honest."

Conner balled his fist in his pockets, a new kind of dread in his gut.

"But it didn't take long for me to figure it out. I was young and pretty naive and suddenly..." She shook her head. "Let's just say that when I figured out what he was doing, I didn't know how to stop him."

No! The word is No! He wanted to scream it out for her, but he could hardly breathe with the heat in his chest.

"Thankfully, we were at his dorm and his roommate walked in before..." She blew out a breath. "I ran all the way home—"

"Did you tell anyone?"

"No! I was scared and...devastated. And I had nowhere to go so I just...I just stopped going out. I started spending more time in the art room...it was safe. I never saw him again."

She stood on the shore, scanning the woods. "I don't see her, Conner."

He came up beside her. Called Esther's name. It echoed against the cliff, eaten by the rush of the river.

Please, God, keep Esther safe. Help us find her.

"You should have told someone, Liza." He didn't mean for his words to emerge quite so sharp, but he didn't know what else to do with the roiling in his chest.

She looked at him as if he'd suggested running naked through the school. "Are you kidding me? I was ashamed. I thought he liked me...I should have known better."

Oh, Liza. "That's not how a guy treats a girl he likes."

Her mouth opened, and by the look she gave him, he knew he'd blown it. "Thanks. Thanks for that. I know, Conner. But I was fifteen, and I was a nerdy girl with stringy brown hair and thrift-store clothing who'd been sent to school to get away from my stepbrother's lecherous friend. I didn't know what love or respect was. I just knew that I liked this boy way too much, and he used it against me."

Conner swallowed, not sure where to put his emotions. Or the fact that his brain had stopped on *lecherous friend.* He took in a long breath.

"What?"

"Tell me about the lecherous friend."

She frowned. "No. Listen, we have to find Esther!"

"We will. But once upon a time, we were friends, good friends, and then, suddenly we weren't. And I still can't quite figure out why. When I rewind it, all I see is us sitting together and me thinking about how amazing my life had suddenly turned out after everything I'd been through, and then we kissed. And the next day, you're gone. Except now I'm starting to put the pieces together, and I'm beginning to see that maybe this had *nothing to do with me* and everything to do with some jerk in high school or with some *lecherous friend* of your stepbrother."

She had stopped and now stared at him.

"Fine." Her voice emerged so deadly calm it reached out and took hold of him, a fist around his heart, turning him cold.

"I told you how my mom worked at a camp, as an art teacher, right? Well, that's where she met my stepdad. We'd attended camp for eight years, every summer after my dad died and my one friend was Charlie Bissel. His dad was the director, so he was stuck there all summer, too, and although he was two years older, he took me under his wing. He taught me to fish and ride a bike, and I taught him how to paint and sculpt, and we were inseparable. Until my mom fell in love with his dad and they got married."

She stepped up to the river now and lifted her binoculars. Scanned the bank.

"Mom and I moved back to Minneapolis with Charlie and Doug. I was thirteen, in eighth grade, and just starting to fill out. But you know how middle-school girls are, all knobby-kneed, buck-toothed, and generally terrifying."

"I can't ever imagine you terrifying," he said quietly.

She blinked at him, then her face tightened in a frown. "Stop it."

Huh?

"Charlie started bringing his buddies over after school, and suddenly they started paying more attention to me than to him."

Lecherous, she'd said. He swallowed back a spur of darkness.

"They'd find excuses to hang out with me or invite me to watch television, and Charlie changed. He got angry and sullen, and pretty soon he started ignoring me completely. I was devastated, so I started hanging around him more, hoping he'd pay attention to me. Which only meant that I was hanging around his buddies. I just wanted them to like me. By the time I was in tenth grade, I was one of the guys, or so I thought. Charlie was a senior by then, and, well, I guess I wasn't the gangly middle-schooler anymore."

She gestured to the walkie. "Check in with CJ."

He caught up with CJ on the radio, and no, they hadn't seen Esther or any sign of her.

"Maybe we need to spread out or one of us climb down there—" Liza said.

"Let's keep moving."

She nodded, silent, as if maybe he'd forgotten.

"What happened, Liza?"

She made a face. Sighed. "Charlie had a bunch of his buddies over to the house one night, and they'd stayed up late watching a movie. I sneaked down in my pajamas to get something to eat and..." She sighed again.

Oh no. He couldn't breathe.

"One of his friends came into the kitchen. I think he might have been drinking, I don't know, but he cornered me, put his hands on me—"

A word formed in his brain, and when she frowned at him, he realized he'd said it aloud.

"Sorry—"

"Yeah, well, me too, because Charlie came in, saw us, and lost it. It was awful. Just—I was screaming, and Charlie was slamming his friend against the wall—"

"I suddenly have a great fondness for your brother."

"Stepbrother." She looked away, and he thought he saw her whisk her hand across her cheek. "Charlie did love me, I know it. But by then, it was too late. Mom and Doug were already on the rocks, so Mom called a friend who ran this private school and sent me away. She and Doug separated shortly after."

Liza looked at Conner then, her eyes shiny. "Last thing I remember was Doug hauling Charlie off his friend and Charlie screaming at me like it was my fault. And maybe he was right."

"He *wasn't* right. How on earth was that your fault?"

"I got too cozy with his buddies."

Conner couldn't help it, couldn't rein in his words. "A randy high school boy decides to feel you up because you were his friend?"

She recoiled. "Uh no, because—because—"

"Geez, Liza. You are you *not* to blame for the fact some jerk put his hands on you. You were vulnerable and hurting and, sheesh—" He turned away, his chest tight, his hands clenched. Shook his head.

"If you only knew how amazing and kind and beautiful—I'm *so* sorry that a couple of jerks took advantage of that."

Silence behind him. Finally, he turned back to her.

He wasn't prepared for the anger that lined her face.

"Stop it," she said again, this time quietly.

He frowned.

"Please, just stop it."

"Stop what?"

"Stop acting like you...like you care."

"I do care. I—"

"Fine, you *care.* But stop being nice to me. Because you're...you're acting like you *like* me, and the fact is, it makes me too vulnerable. I wish I was strong, but I'm not. You do that, and I'm not strong enough to stay away from you."

He couldn't move. "I don't *want* you to stay away from me."

"Yes you do, Conner. You're just too nice to say it. And I can't go through that again."

He stared at her. "What are you talking about?"

"I'm talking about the fact that you are who you are."

"And who is that?"

"A great guy. But a guy who doesn't want more than just right now. And I was too clingy."

"You—*what*?"

"I read between the quotes. 'I can't make any promises,' you said, and I was an idiot not to see it, not to figure it out. Especially when you *told* me..."

Now he was really confused, trying to wrap his brain around a conversation he only vaguely remembered having. "Figure out *what*?"

"You didn't want to hurt me by saying good-bye."

From her expression, she was serious.

"But I *didn't* want you to say good-bye. I *liked* you." He swallowed, pushed out the rest. "I still do."

There. He said it, and it felt good, even healing. "We simply miscommunicated."

Which meant, they could fix it. *He* could fix it. Get them back to where they'd left off.

For the first time since her call, the noose around his chest loosened.

He unclenched his hand, the urge to reach for her coursing through him.

Except she didn't respond, her face didn't light up with sweet realization of his uttered feelings.

Instead, she offered him a sad smile. "I know you did. Just not enough."

He gaped at her. Huh?

"See?"

"No, I *don't* see. What does that even mean, *not enough*? Enough for what? To want to spend time with you? To call you every time I got off the fire line, hoping I'd hear your voice? To track you down in Arizona and drive a hundred miles just to take you out for dinner, or go hiking, or even skydiving? Because I did, Liza. I liked you *enough*."

More, actually, than enough. And now he'd taken out his heart, put it right out there for her to see. The truth was, "You didn't like *me* enough. You took off—twice—without telling me—"

"No, Conner. I was just trying to play by your rules. No promises, right?"

His mouth tightened.

"You didn't like me enough to make an entire life with me," she said quietly.

And despite her soft words, they landed sharp, brutal in the soft, still healing places inside. And right behind them, a rush of panic. That sense of having something amazing in his grasp. And, like a year ago when she'd said *Now what?*, the same hand reached up, wrapped around his throat.

An entire life.

And that was the problem. If he promised her a future... well, his profession wasn't exactly safe. He was ever more aware of that now after losing Jock and the team.

Frankly, he simply saw himself letting her down. A final epitaph to a slew of broken promises.

He couldn't dodge that truth even now.

But wasn't she the girl who embraced each new sunrise? He'd sort of thought, out of anyone, Liza was the one who wouldn't expect more than just right now. Had never let on differently, really.

"Aw, Liza. C'mon. You know what I've been through. None of us knows how long that life is. We shouldn't make promises we can't keep—"

"What promises might those be? To live happily ever after?"

"I dunno. Maybe—yeah. Because you know I don't do promises. Isn't it enough to show up every day, one after the next, with you?"

"Maybe it should be. But not for me." Her eyes glistened. "You're right—it wasn't my fault my brother's friend came on to me. Or that the football player took advantage of me. But I didn't do anything to stop them. I just let them, because I was too needy to know how to protect myself. I walked right into the situations, my heart open—and they took that and hurt me."

She turned away. "But—I'm not that girl anymore."

Conner couldn't breathe with the tumult of her words rocking against him and the sheen of tears in her eyes.

"The thing is I wish I *had* misunderstood you. But we communicated perfectly. You can't make me promises...and I can't live without them. The worst part is that I *do* know what you've been through. I shouldn't have expected more. This one really is my fault."

"Liza—"

"So, please, stop saying nice things and calling me beautiful. I panicked. I called you. And yes, I needed you. I might even still be in love with you. But that's my problem, not yours. When this gig is over, you're going to walk out of my life, and I'm going to let you go, okay?"

Not okay.

I might even still be in love with you.

But before he knew what to say, she lifted her shoulders in a shrug, turned, and kept trekking into the forest.

Liza—

Movement from in front of her caught him—forty feet away, a shadow at first, then the outline and a hulking form.

He caught her by the arm, whirled her back to face him.

"Conner, really—"

"Shh. Don't move."

She stilled. "What—"

"Remember what I said about the bear? About being scary and loud?"

Then of course she turned.

He felt, more than heard, the welling of her scream.

And then, because he had suggested it, and because he wasn't sure what else to do, he joined her in an all-out yell at the grizzly, who reared up and roared.

Chapter 10

LIZA DIDN'T KNOW WHICH shook her more—the roar of the grizzly as he scraped the air with his razor claws or Conner's primal shout behind her.

But she didn't have time to sort it out. Not with her screams ripping through the shadowed forest, echoing against the folds of darkness gathering in the gorge.

Spittle cobwebbed from the bear's jaws as it roared at them.

"It's not running!" So much for *scaring* the bear.

Conner's arm snaked around her and yanked her back, against his chest.

Her breaths tumbled, one over another, and she simply held onto Conner's grip, her fingers digging into his forearms as she watched the animal's hoary head swing back and forth.

"Is that—is he warning us? Is it—what did you say about him stalking us?" Sorry, but screaming seemed akin to throwing marshmallows at a charging rhino.

Conner edged her backward, still holding her tight. "Shh. I don't know. Is that the same bear?"

"Maybe. I didn't exactly stick around—"

He made a sound that might have been a harrumph.

The grizzly opened his mouth, roared again. Liza whirled around to face Conner and gripped onto his backpack straps. "What do we do?"

She barely knew a rattled Conner, had never seen him truly untucked, even after the near disaster in Deep Haven, but as he gripped her shoulders, his eyes widened. He glanced into the gorge below, back to the animal.

"Do—should we play dead?" she whispered. Except that would probably lead to them *being* dead.

"If it's the same animal, then he's not spooked, he's hunting us." He grabbed her face in both hands. "Trust me?"

She made a noise—might have been a yes, sounded more to her ears like a yelp of panic. Conner grabbed her hand, turned to the gorge—

"Jump!"

Liza glanced behind her and caught a glimpse of the animal, saliva flinging from its open mouth, teeth bared and—

Her feet left the earth without any help from Conner. Still his hand gripped hers as they flung themselves into space.

Held it as they fell, his grip iron.

She screamed a second before they hit the water. Bracing, but not icy, the shock of the chill stabbed into her skin, swiped her breath as the water sucked her under. Her pack turned to lead, and she fought the current, kicking against the riverbed.

Oh no, she'd let go of his hand. Or maybe he'd let go of her.

She paddled her arms, kicked, her breath leeching out, burning her lungs, aching—

She felt herself rising. She kicked and twisted, lurching for the surface.

Her face broke into the light, and she gulped in air, sputtering as the foam and spray assaulted her nose, her eyes.

Conner held her by her pack straps. "Take this thing off!"

"It's got my first aid equipment!"

"And rocks, apparently."

"It's my mag light and my bear spray!" She worked her hand into his backpack strap, the pot calling the kettle black.

The river had grabbed them and now swallowed them in the fury of the rapids, dragging them into the froth. Conner, still fisting her straps, tried to swim them away from a cauldron of swirling water forming on the backside of a bison-sized boulder. "Kick with me!"

She caught a glimpse of the grizzly overhead, angry.

Then the current slammed her into Conner's arms, and he caught her to himself, one arm around her waist, wedging himself with the current against a boulder, safe in a small eddy.

The water churned around them. For a second, their eyes met. Hers, she imagined, huge and terrified. His blue eyes somehow solid. Calm. And the sense of it slid through her, down to her heart, took a hold. Yes, whatever faults this man had, he showed up when a girl needed him.

And maybe it *should* be enough.

"Hang onto me, Liza. Just hang on." Then Conner pressed a crazy, quick kiss to her forehead and let her go. "I'm going to swim, and you just hold onto my pack. We'll find a way out."

She didn't see how. From here, the walls of the gorge loomed thirty, even fifty feet from the water, with the river tumbling over boulders, into eddies, over ledges, all on its way to yet another roaring waterfall.

The river thundered in the distance, warning.

Conner rearranged her grip to the back of his pack, just above his shoulder, where she could hold on as he towed her.

"Listen, we're going to work our way to the edge of the river, see if we can find a place to climb out. But the current is going to force us downriver. Keep your head up and try and stay behind me."

Then, before she could respond, he pushed off into the current.

It gulped them whole, into the froth and spray. Conner lay on his stomach, trying to swim diagonally toward the shore. She couldn't help but kick with him, landing a couple of blows in his thigh, but he didn't stop.

Her head went under, cold, brackish water doused her nose, blinded her. She came up, gasping, and he grabbed her hand.

"You okay?" he yelled over the flow.

He kicked and fought, reaching for boulders, dragging the two of them closer to the edge.

His breathing heaved with exertion, the current's relentless grasp wringing them out as they tumbled farther downstream.

It occurred to Liza that maybe Esther hadn't escaped the river at all.

Conner finally slammed up against a boulder, his back to it, bracing his legs on some hidden outcropping. He reached out and pulled her to him.

She locked her arms around his neck, breathing hard as his chest rose and fell. She couldn't help but collapse, her forehead against his.

"I just gotta...catch...my breath," he said.

She fought to keep herself from weeping.

He traded positions with her, anchoring her in place with his hands on either side of her.

She couldn't guess how long they'd fought the rapids—it seemed like only a few minutes, but in that time, twilight had sunk deep bruises into the landscape, turning the water nearly black and cutting their chance of finding footholds in the rocky walls razor slim.

"We're never going to—"

He grabbed her backpack, pulling her up, close to him. He put his forehead to hers, breathing, as if trying to conjure up the words. Then he moved his mouth across her cheek, almost like a kiss, and found her ear. "We're getting out of here."

He leaned back and met her eyes. Despite the darkness, a fire lit inside them, something primal and fierce.

She could almost hear the *I promise* on the end of his words.

She nodded.

"Stay here!"

Before she could protest, he launched himself off the rock, back into the current, swimming hard for the edge, aiming toward a low-hanging tree stripped of its branches and lodged in the river. He flung himself toward it, and she could barely make him out in the spray and kaleidoscope of light hazing the canyon.

His silhouette arched out of the water as he pulled himself up on the tree, draping himself over it.

He stayed there a long moment, as if catching his breath. Then he turned. "Float down to me!"

Had he lost his mind?

Apparently he had, because he wrapped his legs around the tree, dropped down, and leaned back, his arms outstretched. "If you kick off the rock on the other side, the current will bring you right to me. I'll catch you."

Now, frankly, she could use some promises.

Lose the pack. The thought—in Conner's tone of voice—swept through her head, and she shrugged it off, let it fall into the current.

It sank as she pushed off, swimming hard for Conner.

She hit a boulder with her shoulder, pushed away, landed her feet on it, and launched herself toward him.

Their hands touched, but the current yanked her beyond the tree, away—

And then something snared her neck, noosing her, choking her. He had her by the collar. She lunged for him again, fighting the burn and praying the shirt wouldn't rip.

His hand caught hers, tightened in a vice grip. Then he was pulling her to himself. "I got you—I *got* you!"

She clung to his strong arms.

He reached for her other hand, moved to a solid branch. "Got it?"

She nodded, and held on as he swung himself up. Then, leaning over the tree, he reached down and grabbed her by her arms, swinging her up onto his lap, across his chest, falling back with her on the tree.

A big tree with just a wide enough trunk for her to collapse beside him, gasping, his arms around her.

She'd forgotten his strength and how she relished it.

How he'd held her when they jumped from the plane, her fear disappearing, the sense of calm that bathed her. Now she clung to his amazingly solid shoulders, feeling his breath in her hair.

He lay with his arms around her waist, securing her

against the long, soggy planes of his body, his chest rising and falling. Maybe he didn't even know that he'd reached one hand up to her head, twining his fingers into her wet hair.

Or gave a hard exhale, as if he'd nearly lost her.

And certainly he didn't know that his touch ignited all the places, all the feelings she'd tried to stamp out.

I might even still be in love with you. Might?

But in this nanosecond, caught between tragedy and the sweet, calming strength of Conner Young, she didn't care.

Yes, she would let him walk away, but right now, she didn't have to. Right now, as the folds of night and the hiss of the jealous river reached for her, she turned her face to Conner's shoulder, tightened her arm around his chest, and held on. He smelled of the wild, his skin clammy and wet, and she closed her eyes and breathed in the feel of him, his heartbeat against her hand, her fear dissipating.

She wouldn't think about tomorrow. Just sink into the now.

It *was* enough.

A crack splintered the moment and with it, a jolt from their perch.

"Are you kidding me?" Conner said as the tree lurched again. Splintering, the air rending with barks and snaps as the earth and rock surrendered to the added weight on the tree.

Liza jerked up as Conner scrambled to his feet, one hand vicing her arm.

"C'mon!" He was scrambling toward the cliff, up the length of the tree trunk, tripping over branches as he yanked her along.

Her shirt caught on a twig—she heard it tear, then a branch speared her in the gut. She cried out, but he wouldn't let go.

The tree sank toward the frothing, dark water. With the sun nearly gone, the river turned into a twisty, deadly roil, heading straight toward the hungry waterfall hidden in the darkness beyond.

"Hurry!"

He still had her arm, but the tree jerked again, and she pitched back. "Liza!"

Her arm windmilled, his grasp tearing away.

He yanked her up toward him, holding her tight against him as he clung now to the roots of the tree with one hand. "Hold on!"

To what? She wrapped her arms around his waist as he let her go and lunged for the cliff, seeking a handhold as the roots snapped, whined.

As he struggled to land his hold, the tree tore away from the cliff, falling from beneath them into the river with a deafening splash.

"Don't let go!"

And wow, she wanted to obey him, but the tree tugged at her. The roots had wrapped around her foot and now yanked as the rapids snared the tree, ramrodding it over boulders to send it downstream.

"My foot's stuck!"

"Liza!" He grabbed her shirt and she wished, then, for her backpack, because the flimsy material ripped again.

He slipped, let go of her, clung to the cliff.

The tree wrestled for ownership.

He reached again for her hand. "Hold on!"

"You can't hold me!"

"We can do this—don't let go!"

But the weight of the tree grabbed her, and he couldn't

last, not with his flimsy grip on the rocky cliff.

If they both went down, no one would be left to find Esther. Or her, for that matter.

"I'm sorry, Conner!"

With the tree tugging at her, his gaze desperate in hers, and the slightest shake of her head, she let go.

~

"Liza!"

Conner clung like a lemur to the rock, dangling out over the spittle of spray and foam, watching as the river engulfed her, hurtling her toward the falls.

No!

Beyond impulse, all the way to sheer panic, Conner launched himself into the river, hitting hard, grateful he didn't faceplant into a hidden boulder. He came up fast, sputtering, and swam hard into the roiling blackness.

In the fragile minutes between twilight and moonrise, the river turned inky, snarled, the cold stinging his bones. He slammed against rocks, letting the river take him, keeping his eyes on the bulk that he hoped was Liza and the tree.

He prayed that the massive boulders en route to the falls would hang up the tree.

"Liza!"

No answering call. The river yanked him under. He bounced off a boulder and came up fighting.

He would not lose her—not this way.

Not after she'd clung to him as they lay on the tree, the way she burrowed her face into his neck. He could still feel the heat of her breath against his skin.

Not to mention her words still pulsing through him, spoken right before they'd cannonballed off the cliff.

I might even still be in love with you.

Still. In love.

Conner rolled over, breathing hard, lying on his back, feet up, arms out, riding the current, kicking off of boulders. If he wanted to save Liza, he had to stay alive, instead of, say, slamming his skull against a boulder hidden in the folds of darkness.

He hoped the bulk he spied was the tree and Liza. Its skeletal branches scrabbled against the deep bruise of the horizon as it careened down the canyon.

The waterfall thundered ahead. And perhaps above that roar, a scream.

Suddenly, the tree jerked, arrested in the water, the bulk of it coming around to lodge at an angle.

Snagged. "Liza! Hold on to the tree!"

He couldn't see her, couldn't hear her anymore. Please, God, don't let the tree have dragged her under.

The river slammed him against the trunk. He held on, and climbed along it, against the current, sputtering as water and foam crashed into his face. The force of the current threatened to wedge him under the tree, drown him. A branch speared him in the shoulder, and he jerked back, held on, gasping.

The depths reached up, tugged at him.

And then the tree shifted, rolling back on him into the grasp of the river. Branches caught him, netted him, dragged him down. Water crested over him, the current twisting him into the wreckage of branch and rock.

Imprisoned, he bucked and thrashed, but the tree had him by his shirt and pants.

He'd lost the surface.

His air began to hemorrhage. His chest turned to fire.

No—not like this. He'd made promises, and more—

He wanted to live. *Really* wanted to live, instead of this half-hearted, gray life—

A hand grabbed his shirt, fisted the fabric, and yanked.

Not enough oomph to pull him up, but it gave him a start. He followed the tug, wrestling past the gnarled branches.

He broke the surface, gasping hard.

Liza was hunched over on the tree, her legs hooked around a branch, reeling him in.

Saving his life.

He draped himself over the trunk, breathing hard.

She knelt next to him, shaking. "I saw you go under—I thought—" She wrapped her hands around his body, holding on, leaning into him. "I thought you were going to drown."

Everything hurt, and he coughed, clearing water from his lungs, his nose.

"Me too." He looked up.

Her eyes were so wide, so luminous, he thought he might lose his breath again. "Thank you for grabbing me."

She backed away and sat in the middle of the tree, curled in a ball, bedraggled and shivering, her eyes huge and dark.

Conner pulled himself the rest of the way onto the tree. "Are you okay? I thought you were caught—"

"I got free when the tree landed."

He felt their life raft shift beneath him. "Oh no."

"It's moving," Liza said, gripping the branches. "We have to get off or we're going over the falls."

Ten yards away the world dropped off into a darkened horizon. Spray hazed the air.

"We're not getting off here," he said. "The rocks are buried, and the branches lodged against them are breaking." He climbed up to her, caught her cold, trembling hands. "We're going over, Liza."

She shook her head, eyes still wide, her gaze in his. "I can't—we—"

"Shh. We can. The current will bring us to the edge and pull the tree over. When it does, we'll jump away from the tree and the falls. As far out as we can. And I've got you. I'm not letting go—"

"But you did before—"

"I swear I won't let you go!" He took her hand, clasped it between his. Cold and wet, she was trembling, and he longed to pull her into his arms. "I promise."

Her jaw tightened and for a second she didn't move.

Then the tree jerked, and she fell against him, her arms around his waist.

"Sorry." She leaned back.

Really?

He reached down to lace her fingers between his. Strong, long, beautiful fingers, used to shaping pottery bowls and pitchers. She tightened her grip, reinforcing it with a hold on his forearm.

He found his feet, leveraging himself on a branch.

"Don't let go!" she said over the roar.

Never. "Make sure your feet are clear of any branches!"

The tree jostled against boulders but otherwise ran a clear path, rocketing toward the edge of the falls, the mist rising over them, sprinkling their skin.

"Ready?"

She might have nodded, he didn't know, but she edged up behind him.

Then the front of the tree shot out over the lip of the falls.

Seconds later, the back end rose with the force of the leverage.

"Jump!"

With everything inside him, he launched himself into space, his hand a death grip in hers, willing them to float, to fly, to soar over the churning cauldron below the falls.

He didn't know how far down it might be, hadn't gotten a good look as the tree climbed, but time lengthened as his feet kicked the air, his arm windmilling to keep them upright.

Liza's scream rent the air.

He splashed down hard, sinking fast, this time without the lethal weight of his backpack to derail him and drag them to their deaths.

Only as he began to kick did he realize that she hadn't let go.

And neither had he. He pulled her up with him, fighting the tempest wanting to drag them back under.

His head broke the surface. He yanked her up a second before the current grabbed them. "Swim!"

He used the combat stroke he'd learned in the military to propel them away from the falls. She kicked valiantly beside him.

He swam them toward shore and parked them in an eddy where his feet could touch. Here, on the far side of the falls, the water calmed, smoothed out in a pool before gathering strength to surge to the next great ledge.

Still in the water, he pulled her against himself, releasing her hand, his arm around her waist, his breaths tumbling over each other.

The moonlight fell against her whitened face, glistening in her hair.

"Are you okay?"

She gave a watery, flimsy smile. A nod.

And he couldn't stop his gaze from tracing over her beautiful face, skimming to her lips.

Couldn't ignore the fact that she was in his arms, hers around his neck, her body pressed against his, clinging to him.

Wow, he'd missed her.

And suddenly, he wasn't cold at all.

A great big piece of him just wanted to lean in, kiss her. Just gulp her whole with a crazy, hot, palpable joy.

He could nearly taste her with the yearning for it.

Because, yeah, he still loved her, too.

And that thought came hot, fast. Brilliant into his head. Loved?

Okay, yes. If love was not being able to forget her, to have the almost insatiable desire to talk to her, the deep need to hear her voice, to see her smile.

If that was love, then he'd probably loved her from the moment he'd found her on the beach in Deep Haven and she'd offered him hope. Breakfast.

The kind of friendship that he should have realized was more, *much* more.

When this gig is over, you're going to walk out of my life…

Oh no he wasn't.

He wrangled his voice free. "Ready to get out of this river?"

Her mouth curved then into a delicious smile. "I dunno. Is there a grizzly waiting to eat us?"

"Oh, that?"

She laughed.

And then, he couldn't take it. The sound of her laughter was like water to his parched heart.

Wow, he'd missed her.

Almost without thinking, he leaned down and pressed his lips against hers.

He meant for it to be quick, something akin to relief or gratefulness. Something that didn't commit either of them to anything but simply relished the fact they'd survived.

But he'd never been able to keep his heart from racing out ahead when it came to Liza. One look, one touch, and he found himself all in, even if his common sense told him otherwise.

And he was fresh out of common sense.

His kiss turned in one rich, blinding second from short and sweet to something primal and needy, something wrought from the fact that he'd had her in his arms, lost her, and found her again. He didn't want to think about anything beyond right now and never letting her go.

So his kiss went deep, diving in to really taste her.

And, hallelujah, she was kissing him back. Not sweetly, not quietly, not tentatively, but her arms around his neck, pressing herself against him, or maybe just holding on—but thank you, river!—reaching for all he could give her.

In fact, he couldn't remember—*ever*—being kissed like this, by her, by anyone. Not quite so thoroughly, without reserve, as if she wanted to inhale him, gulp in all of him.

He'd gotten a taste of the passion behind her reserve back

in Sedona during their first kiss. But he'd forgotten how it could reach in and ignite his own.

Then, before the river could steal her away, he reached down and wrapped her legs around his waist, locking her there.

His arms lifted her, closing around her back, his legs planting, just a little offset, and he twined his fingers into her floating, long silky hair, letting himself explore, taste, relish.

She tasted of fear, relief, the delicious friendship they'd shared, and more.

Healing, and even the hope for tomorrow. He thought his heart just might explode.

Then all at once she jerked back.

What—? "Liza?"

She met his eyes. "Oh no."

"Huh?"

"No, no...oh no." She unlocked her legs, pressed away from his shoulders.

As she floated back, a tiny fist formed in his gut.

"What's *oh no*?" he said stupidly, hating his own words. Because yeah, he knew.

But please, he didn't want her to say it...

"I'm such an idiot. I did it again—I'm sorry. I know you didn't want this—"

"Liza, I kissed you first. Trust me, I *wanted* to."

She shook her head. "No, you didn't."

What—?

He wanted to reach for her again, but she treaded water just out of his reach.

"Listen. We're alive, right? It's just adrenaline." She turned and worked her way toward the dark folds of shore. "We're cold and tired and shaky."

He could admit to shaky, but it had nothing to do with being cold and tired.

"Liza, I—"

"It's okay, Conner." She pulled herself up onto a boulder, her arms around herself, shivering. "Like I said. When this gig is over, you're going to walk away, and I'm going to let you. But..." She smiled then. "I do thank you for keeping your promise to hold on."

His question must have shown on his expression.

"Although I think my fingers might be broken."

He came to sit beside her on the boulder, tamping down the urge to pull her close, to keep her from shivering.

And wished he'd made that promise long ago.

CHAPTER 11

THEY'D BECOME THE ONES needing rescue.

Liza stood at the edge of the river, water running in rivulets down her back as she shivered from her core. A nip of chill laced the night air, raising gooseflesh on her skin.

Overhead the moonlight sparkled against the blackened river, the boulders along the shoreline glinting like steel. Behind her, the wind twined through the forest, hushing, gathering the quiet darkness into dangerous, inky pools where a grizzly—or any other predator—might scent her fear.

Didn't animals prey on the fearful, the weak?

She had half a mind to crouch right here, on shore, and not move.

Or maybe cry.

Conner came up beside her, however, after climbing out of the river and shaking himself off like a dog. He pushed his hair back from his face, his T-shirt plastered to his frame.

A very muscular, solid, safe frame, one that she'd practically had to peel herself away from.

Oh, she was definitely playing with fire now.

"We can't hike out. We'll need to find a place to hunker down." Conner held out his hand.

Liza took it without a pause. Never mind about the kiss, the fact that she'd practically attacked him. Tomorrow, in the light of day, she'd somehow gather up her common sense. Tonight her frayed edges made her cling to him, follow him along the shore.

He led her across rocks then deeper into the forest, as if he knew where he might be going. But with their equipment at the bottom of the river, well—

So much for keeping promises to Shep.

"Do you think the bear will find us?"

"I don't think so," Conner said, not looking at her.

She'd hoped for something more reassuring.

"If it's tracking us, it would have lost our scent when we went in the river," he added, as if reading her mind.

He stopped, let go of her hand, and parked her at the edge of a small clearing. The starlight reflected off the river, adding texture and faint illumination to the night. From what she could see, he'd found them a small alcove in the forest, surrounded by aspen and scraggly pines.

Walking into the middle of the clearing, about fifteen feet of inlet space, he seemed satisfied and began to clear away the earth. He kicked away duff with his boot, scattering twigs and rocks before he bent to root out the spot with his hands.

"What are you doing?"

"We can't bushwhack out of here in the dark—and we're still pretty shaken up. Best to make camp and figure out what to do in the morning. I know it was hot out today, but the mountains cool down quickly at night, and I don't want us to get hypothermia."

He scraped out a small rectangle and rolled stones in two lines, bracketing the patch of earth.

"Are you making a *fire*?"

He was squatting, putting the final stone into place, adding it to one end. "Yep."

With what? Except, yes, he'd been Special Forces—a Green Beret. Of course he knew how to build a fire with his bare hands.

What *couldn't* the man do? He'd saved her from a bear, rescued her from a waterfall...

He could also probably make her forget her promise not to fall for him.

She could still feel his kiss on her mouth, the overwhelming urge to cling to him. In one life-altering moment, he could stop the world, turn her to fire, and make her believe that everything would work out.

They would survive. And find Esther.

She didn't have a prayer of emerging from this with her heart intact.

"What can I do?"

"How about find some kindling? Small twigs, pine cones, and needles. You might find some old wood—anything dry, although right now the entire forest is flammable, so it shouldn't be too hard."

He had his knife out—she hadn't even noticed that he still wore it on his belt—and was using it to cut birch peels from a nearby tree.

She stepped into the forested area and hit her knees, feeling the forest floor for anything on his list. Her hands closed around a nest of pine cones, and she gathered them into her shirt.

He'd created a small pile of kindling and she dumped her cones next to them, then went in search of twigs.

"Look for squaw wood—the branches on the bottom of coniferous trees. They're usually dead, and you can break them off."

She followed his suggestion, found a shaggy pine, and easily broke off an armful of branches.

When she returned, he was shaving birch fiber from a peeled section of bark. Then he took out a metal bar.

She crouched next to him. "What's that?"

"Fire steel. It's part of my knife sheath—a survival kit from the military." He scoured his knife down the edge of the steel, and sparks shot into the birch shavings. In a second, a tiny flame flickered. He set the shavings in the middle of the fire pit and added a handful of peels.

The fire caught, consuming the birch.

"Pine cones?"

She scraped up her pile and dropped them in. They sparked, flamed.

"Pine cones are fantastic fuels," he said, the light flickering across the planes of his face. His hair had dried to a mop of tangles, and his late-afternoon grizzle turned him rough-edged and dangerous. At least to the predators who might want to hurt them. As Liza handed him her offering of sticks, their hands touched, and a wave of emotion swept over her—part gratitude, part relief.

Way too much longing.

"I'll get some bigger branches." With the fire adding illumination to the night, she could pick her way into the folds of the forest, find some dead branches, maybe some downed trees.

"Stay close."

His warning tone raised a shiver. She glanced at him, and he lifted a shoulder, offered a hint of a smile. "I just don't want to lose you."

Huh.

She headed into the woods, the forest undulating under the flickering light. Tripping over a log, she followed it with her hands, found bigger branches, which she broke off and hauled back to the camp.

He had built a firebreak with rocks on one side of the fire. On top of the fire, he'd created a pyramid of sticks and logs, building it up with crisscrossing sections.

He took the branches from her and began to break them with his feet.

"You're a regular MacGyver," she said.

"Six years in Special Forces."

He brought the wood over, finished making the pyramid. "Come closer—we need to get you dried off and raise your core temperature."

Oh, no problem there. But as she crouched near the fire gnawing away at the wood, the heat poured into her hands, her chest. She was colder than she'd thought.

"I'm going to build us a shelter," he said after a moment.

"I can help."

He didn't argue with her, just stood up and motioned to a stand of trees. "We'll use these as our shelter braces. If you can find a suitable ridgepole or cross section to brace the logs, I'll find some spruce roots to lash it to the trees. Then we'll lean trees and brush against it to make a roof thatch. That'll at least give us some shelter."

Nope, Daniel Boone had nothing on Conner Young.

Liza measured out the length between the stand of trees and cast about for something that might serve as a ridgepole—a downed tree, a long branch. Meanwhile, Conner hiked into the woods. She could hear him breaking branches, snapping roots.

Twenty feet from the edge of the forest, she found a poplar as big around as her arm, the casualty of a downed pine. Kicking it, she freed it from the earth and hauled it back to the camp.

Conner held a coil of roots in his grip. "Nice ridgepole."

A crazy pride bloomed inside her.

She held the branch up to the tree about waist high as he looped a root around one side, securing it, then moved over to the other.

"I know you're getting tired, but if we can find some more branches, we can cut off the boughs and make a quick shelter. I think we'll feel safer inside a lean-to."

He didn't allude to the bear, and she didn't follow up. Instead, she followed him into the forest.

To her surprise he reached out and took her hand. Warmth radiated up her arm, back down to her core. She probably didn't need a lean-to to feel safe.

He found branches from a shaggy white pine and cut off the boughs, leaving only the bare poles, and angled them onto the ridgepole, lashing them with more spruce roots. Then he piled on the boughs to make a bushy layer of thatch.

"If we had more light, I'd spread down a layer of moss, then the boughs," he said in a weird sort of apology.

"That'll do, pig," she said quietly.

He looked at her, frowning.

"It's a movie reference."

"I know. *Babe*," he said, and walked over to the fire. "My kid brother loved that movie." He sat down, held his hands out.

For a moment, as the fire flickered against his face, it grooved out lines of fatigue, the wear of fighting for their lives, the sense that so much hung on his shoulders.

Somehow, despite the fact that they'd crash-landed, without food, water, or supplies, on some remote outlet of river in the massive, overgrown Kootenai forest, he'd crafted them a snug, warm homestead.

And she'd nearly forgotten about the bear.

She sat down next to him, her leg bumping against his strong thigh, his shoulder against hers. "Can I borrow your knife?"

He unsheathed the knife and handed it over.

She got up, went over to a nearby birch tree, and cut away another swath of birch bark.

Then she returned to sit beside him, spread out the birch bark, and began to carve away the thin top layer of white.

"What are you doing?"

"I don't only make pots from clay," she said. "My mom was a folk artist—she used to work with birch bark. It was one of the first skills I learned." After removing the top layer, she flattened it on the rock and traced out a pattern with the tip of his knife.

"Birch bark is a bit like leather," she said. "And it's waterproof." She began cutting out the pattern—round in the center, with a T-flap on the top and the bottom.

Conner watched her work in silence.

"Do you have spruce root left?"

He retrieved a small coil.

"Clean it off for me."

He used his fingers to smooth off the length.

She folded the top and bottom of the T together and used the knife to cut a hole through both ends, then she cut holes all the way down. She twined the spruce root through the holes, sewing it together, then folded the rounded edge inside at the bottom and sewed that shut.

She repeated the work on the other side.

It made a sort of flat-bottomed, part-rectangular, part-oval basket.

"Can you cut me a sapling about the size of your finger?"

He regarded her with a strange, enigmatic look, then got up. A few moments later, he returned and she sewed the sapling along the rim of the basket to give it structure.

"You amaze me."

Liza looked up, saw him sitting across from her, his eyes shining. "I can make a fire, but you made us dishes."

She grinned at that. "Now if only we had food. Or water."

"Food I can't do, yet...but water?" He took the container and went over to the river, set the container in to soak. Then he walked past her, into the forest, and in a few moments returned with a handful of rocks. He washed them in the river and set them in the fire. "We'll get the bowl wet, fill it with water, and then add the coals, bring the water to a boil, and it'll be safe to drink."

"With amenities like this, I'll never go home."

She drew up her knees, wrapping her arms around them.

The forest was alive around them, the wind washing through the trees, carrying with it the hoot of an owl, the river at a hush just beyond their alcove. She sat under the cover of the lean-to, her clothing nearly dry.

Finally Liza let her brain settle into the reason they were here. "Do you think Esther survived the falls?"

Conner sat down next to her. He held a stick in his hand, broke it in half. "I don't know, but I think we probably need to head back to camp tomorrow. We're in no shape to keep looking for her, and hopefully Pete will have returned with my drone. I can get a birds-eye view of the river, see if we can spot anything."

"Is it the same drone you showed me in Arizona?"

He tossed the sticks into the fire. "An upgraded prototype, but yes. I made five of them over the past year, but they all have some sort of glitch. I've lost all but one—Pete's retrieving that one. The NFS seems to think that when they crashed, they started fires, but—" He shook his head, the fire casting shadows across his face. "I don't know."

He leaned back on his hands, his forearms bare, sinewed. "I just know that I can't hand over my last drone to the government..."

Something about the way he said it, an edge at the end of his tone— "You never found out what happened to your brother, did you?"

He breathed in, swallowed, and looked away from her, jaw tight. "The worst part about it is that I promised my grandfather—I gave him my word I'd find out. I had high-level security clearance, and still the government slammed the door in my face. Grandpa said it didn't matter, but..." He sighed, ran his thumb over his cheekbone. "It mattered. I should have never promised him something I couldn't deliver. It just got his hopes up."

"It's not your fault, Conner. Sometimes promises get broken. It happens, and it's okay."

His mouth tightened. He looked away from her, the flames flickering against his dark eyes. Then, abruptly, he got up, retrieved the pot from the river, and brought it back, dripping, filled with water. He set it down then picked out the rocks with a couple of sticks and dropped them into the water, one after another.

The water began to steam.

"That's why you left the military, isn't it? To find your brother's killer."

He picked up a stick, began to clean off the bark with his knife. "I just thought, after everything, my grandfather deserved answers. First my parents, then my brother—it just wasn't fair to him."

"Or to you."

Conner glanced over at her, lifted a shoulder in a shrug. "It doesn't matter if it's fair—it's what happened. If I believed in fairness, then—"

"Then you could trust God to work it out."

He frowned at her. "No. I know God's not fair. He's *just*—but He's not fair. If He were, we'd all be doomed. He wasn't fair to Jesus to have Him die for our sins, and yet we benefit. It's because God's *not* fair that we have a chance at salvation."

"All true, but you still want a God you can count on to be fair. And if not that, to at least be on your side. If you knew that God had your back, then it wouldn't be so hard for you to see beyond today and...make a promise to someone."

He sighed. "Liza. I don't make promises not because I don't trust God, but because *I know they don't matter.* A promise doesn't guarantee that everything will work out. We don't know what tomorrow will bring. Believe me, if I could have kept my promise to my grandfather, I would have."

"But a promise means you have hope—and that hope comes from the fact you believe God hears you and is on your side."

"I know God is on my side. That He loves me."

"But you don't believe that He is going to work everything out for good."

He stared at her, and for a second, a rawness entered his

eyes. He looked away as the water in the pot began to bubble. "Of course I do."

"No. You don't. You think that somehow you failed God by not keeping your promise to your grandfather. And then there's the fact that your parents died right before your eyes, and you couldn't save them."

Yes, she went there. Saw her words land in his flinch, the rawness of his expression.

"The result is that you're still trying to find a Romans 8:28 ending, something good that will come out of it, and justify your grief. So you say you believe in a good God, one who loves you, one who is on your side. Problem is, you don't act like it."

"That's not fair, Liza. Just because I didn't tell you that I loved you, that I wanted to spend the rest of my life with you, doesn't mean that I'm a spiritual cripple."

She recoiled. If he had slapped her, it would have hurt less.

Her voice fell, sharpened. "I didn't need you to drop to your knees and propose, Conner. And no one is saying you're a spiritual cripple."

She took a breath, dug around to find compassion behind the ache, the fresh wound. "It's not even about the fact you can't make a promise—frankly, Conner, when you say you'll show up, you do. You're great in the moment."

His jaw tightened. "Then why is it so important?"

"Because a promise, or a vow, means that you hope in something good beyond this moment. That you believe whatever you are promising—and to whom you are promising—is worth that hope."

He reached over, stirred the water with his cleaned stick, releasing more heat.

"But the fact is, deep down inside, you *don't* believe that God will work things out for good. You're so afraid that God won't keep His *own* promises toward you and He'll let you down that you've stopped hoping. Stopped having faith. Stopped believing in happy endings."

With someone like me.

But she left that part off because her eyes smarted.

He added another stone from the fire to the pot, then stared at the boiling steam.

"I don't make promises, Liza, because I know I can't keep them." He got up, stalked to the edge of the river. She traced his outline against the blue-black of the night, the fire illuminating his shoulders, the way he struggled with some unnamed emotion.

Then, suddenly, he turned, a fierceness in his eyes. "But I want to." He took a step toward her. "You have to know that I wanted to believe in us. Like I said, I liked you—I didn't want you to leave. But if I'd started talking about tomorrow, then you would have, too."

She got to her feet, stared at him, stymied. "So?"

"So—what if *you* couldn't keep them? It goes both ways, Liza. You never acted like I was anything more than a friend. *Ever*. As if you were afraid to hold on. And after today's story, I get it. You're afraid of getting too close, afraid of getting hurt."

His voice fell, wretchedly thin. "Don't you think I feel the same thing? You walked out of my life without a word. You didn't take my calls. You cut me off."

And the broken edge of his voice told her just how much that had hurt him.

"I'm sorry, Conner."

He said nothing.

"I thought it was the best for both of us."

His mouth tightened. "It wasn't. You always made everything around me brighter, and...and it got pretty dark after you left. I had an entire team of friends die, and I..."

"Oh, Conner, I'm so sorry—"

"I don't want your pity, Liza. And I don't want your promises, either. Because if you do make me a promise, then you're right—I'm liable to believe it, to depend on you, to *hope*, and then if—*when*—you walk away, it will kill me." His voice dropped, his shoulders rising and falling with his breathing. "Again. It'll kill me *again*."

He stared at her, his eyes dark, riddled with emotion.

Again. A knot formed in her chest, her throat thickening. She hadn't known, had thought—

A root snapped.

Conner stiffened.

A rustling in the woods.

He reached for his knife, crossed over to her.

Then, in one swift move, he pushed her behind him, holding her there with his hand on her hip.

"Whatever happens, stay behind me. And if you have to, run for the river."

Conner planned to go down swinging. Grizzly or no, his fear of tomorrows notwithstanding, he intended to live through this night. Or at least for *Liza* to live through this night.

Because he wasn't going to let someone he loved die when he could stand in the way, give her a chance to survive.

The wind sifted through the trees, and Conner stilled, hoping for a scent, something grimy and foul, but the air only lifted the smoky haze from the fire, the earthy loam from the forest.

Maybe he'd imagined—

A high-pitched scream echoed through the darkness.

Liza's grip tightened on his arm.

"It's a fox," he said.

"Really?"

"I think so."

More snapping, and behind it, the guttural hoots of an owl.

"Something's out there," she hissed.

The blood rushed in his ears.

Then, "Conner!" Light flickered across their camp.

Conner tightened his hold on Liza and searched for the source. "Who's out there?"

"It's CJ! And Skye."

Liza's grip loosened, but Conner didn't release her until he saw the light flash again and this time made out the shadowed outline of CJ St. John entering the ring of firelight.

He looked intact, if not soggy, his green pants grimy and plastered to his body, the sleeves of his shirt rolled up.

Skye came behind him, similarly doused in her cargo pants and T-shirt. She rushed forward toward Liza. "Oh my gosh—we saw you in the water! Did you go over the falls?"

Liza stepped from behind Conner, and he released her to be caught in Skye's embrace. "Yeah," she said. "But Conner saved us."

Then she gave him a look that reached in, twisted his insides. *You're great in the moment.*

Yeah, well that was his superpower. But don't depend on

anything beyond that, apparently.

"We lost sight of you and were trying to figure out a way to get to you when we saw the fire from across the river—we were hoping it belonged to you guys," CJ said.

"Did you swim across?" Conner sheathed his knife.

"Sorta. The river flattens out about five hundred yards downstream. We took boulders across, but—"

"I went in," Skye finished for him. "It wasn't very deep, but CJ went in, too, to pull me out." She grinned at CJ, something extra in it.

Conner noted an accompanying *aw-shucks* grin from his rookie smokejumper. Oh boy.

"The bear found us," Liza said. "So we jumped off the cliff, into the river."

"And went over the falls," Conner added.

"You made quite the digs here," CJ said, hunkering down by the fire, holding out his hands. "Hotel accommodations, romantic fire..." He leaned over, peered into the bowl. "Stone soup?"

"Drinking water," Conner said. He fished out the rocks with his stick and knife, then set them back in the fire to sizzle. "Please tell me you have dinner in there."

"Soggy granola bars and some beef jerky," CJ said as he peeled off his backpack. "But I have better news than that." He gestured with his chin to Skye.

"We found this." She held out a soggy, knit blue cap—no, a backpack with thin straps and a drawstring. "I think it's Esther's."

Liza took it, opened it, and pulled out waterlogged paper, pencils. "Maybe she was going to meet me. Draw the sunrise."

"Or do some writing," Conner said. "Or maybe it was

simply a decoy for their great escape—it doesn't matter. It's hers. Where did you find it?"

"Downstream, near where we forded the river. But it wasn't caught in the river—we found it onshore, hanging from the branches of a willow."

Liza pulled out the papers, flipped through the tablet. "Does that mean she made it over the falls?"

Conner stood up, walked over to the pack, took it from Liza, testing the weight. "I don't think it would have floated. She must have shucked it off when she climbed ashore."

"Or it might have gotten caught as she climbed out," CJ said.

"Which means she's here somewhere," Skye said, plunking down her backpack. She pulled out the granola bars and passed them out.

Conner took his, opened it. Not soggy at all. And his stomach roared to life. He watched Liza dive into hers, clearly ravenous. Standing there in the dim light of the fire, she looked wrung out, her beautiful long brown hair in tangles, a scrape on her cheek, her clothes filthy, albeit mostly dry. And so much hope lit her eyes from CJ's backpack discovery, it made him hurt.

If Esther were in the woods, cold, wet, hungry—

Along with a bear hunting for prey...

This was why he shouldn't make promises. It had nothing to do with not believing in hope but everything to do with *reality*. And maybe he didn't believe that God worked things out for good—but sometimes, yeah, He didn't.

And that thought filled Conner's throat with a slow, aching burn.

He walked over to the fire, knelt by the water bowl. "CJ, do you have your water bottle?"

"Yeah, but I drank it all." CJ handed him the empty bottle.

Conner filled it with the distilled river water. Took a drink of the hot water then passed it to Liza. "It'll warm you up."

She took it without meeting his eyes.

"Tomorrow morning CJ and I will keep looking. Skye, you and Liza will head back to camp."

"Wait a doggone moment. I'm not going back until we find Esther," Liza said, her eyes flashing. "I can't just sit around and wait."

And he got that, really he did. Because it felt like he'd been sitting around and waiting for his life to restart after his brother died. But with her back at the camp, she wouldn't be jumping into any rivers, being chased by a rogue bear.

Conner sighed, not wanting to fight with her, but, "Yeah, actually, you are going to. I told you I couldn't keep you safe. And apparently, I was right. I can't have you getting hurt when I need all of my attention on finding Esther. It'll be easier without my worrying about you."

He ignored her expression, the fury in her eyes, the way her mouth tightened.

Then, suddenly, "Fine. I get it." She capped the water bottle, handed it back to him. "You're right. I'm just in the way."

He frowned. "Liza—"

"No, really, Conner. I don't want to be a burden." She turned to Skye. "Did you bring a blanket?"

Skye looked at CJ, then Conner, but nodded to Liza. She pulled her survival blanket from her pack.

"Do you mind if we share it?" Liza asked, and Skye shook her head.

"Liza, it's not like that," Conner said, not sure why her words raked through him, burned him. "You're not a burden, it's just—"

"Oh, no." She held up her hand to stop him, her voice oddly light. "It's true. You don't need me, and really, with CJ here, it's probably best." She sat down under the shelter. "Do you mind if the girls take the hotel room?"

He shook his head, not sure why he felt like a jerk.

Nor why she'd given up the fight.

Liza curled into the back of the shelter. Draped a portion of the blanket over her, closed her eyes. Skye joined her, sat down with her back to her. Looked at the boys with a shrug.

"C'mon, Conner," CJ said. "You can bunk with me."

"There's a bear out there," Conner said grimly. "I'll take the first watch."

He walked to the river's edge, stared out at the night, the stars falling from the sky like fire. How many times had he returned to Sedona in his memory—sitting out under a starlit night, Liza tucked beside him?

He'd done it again. Pushed her out of his life when all he longed to do was pull her close, hold on.

"Think we'll find Esther?" CJ came to stand by him.

Conner didn't have an answer. Instead, "Maybe you should take the ladies back in the morning. That bear just might be hunting us, and I don't want them alone."

"Skye's pretty savvy."

Conner glanced at him. "You're willing to take that chance?"

"I trust her. She's capable and smart. And we need her—both of them, to find Esther."

Conner stiffened, his hands in his pockets. But CJ was

right—he needed Liza, too, although more than just for this search. Probably since Deep Haven, but definitely today when she'd reached down, grabbing his shirt just as the river tried to take him under.

But Conner saved us. No, they'd saved each other.

And tonight, they'd worked together to keep each other alive, to build something.

He glanced at her, tucked under the dark folds of the shelter.

Deep down inside, you don't believe that God will work things out for good. You're so afraid that God won't keep His own promises toward you and He'll let you down that you've stopped hoping. Stopped having faith.

Maybe, despite his assertions, he didn't have faith. Not really. Not the kind that reached out in hope, knowing God might be at the end of his grasp.

But maybe that's exactly what he needed to do—reach out in hope. Believe that God would help him keep his promises

He turned back to CJ. "Yes," he said. "In answer to your question, we're going to find Esther."

Chapter 12

"I CAN'T SLEEP." LIZA turned onto her back, her shoulder pressed against Skye's as they huddled together under the makeshift shelter. The night arched overhead, pressing through the cracks in the bough-tossed roof. The smell of balsam and pine mingled with the hint of smoke drifting from the still-crackling fire.

She wouldn't have spoken, but Skye had just rolled over onto her side, her back to Liza. With the fire warming their enclave, Skye had shoved off the blanket, wrapping up in her Blue Sky windbreaker.

Near the river, Conner sat on a rock, staring downstream as if he could somehow pinpoint Esther with his x-ray night vision. CJ had curled up next to the fire, emitting the faintest snore.

"I don't see why not," Skye said quietly. "With the roots of the mightiest oak in the forest dissecting our tail bones..."

Liza wanted to smile, but, "I hope Esther has found someplace warm to hole up in." She wouldn't think of the alternatives. The discovery of the backpack lit hope like a bonfire inside her. "We should be out there looking."

"We can't find her in the dark," Skye said, and yes, Liza knew that. "By the way, I'm sure Conner will change his mind in the morning. He was just tired—"

"No, the thing is, he's probably right. We need to be focused on finding Esther—and if that means me staying out of the way..."

Skye rolled over onto her back. "Just so I'm clear—he's the one who suggested going in the river, right?"

"Yeah, but he had climbed out, would have been able to rescue himself if it weren't for me. I couldn't hold on—and because of that, we went over the falls."

She found herself subconsciously fisting her hand, as if he might still be holding it.

"And if you hadn't, we might not have had to cross the river. And we never would have found her backpack. Clearly God has a plan, and you falling into the river was part of it. Who knows what amazing things He's going to do tomorrow? I for one don't want to miss it."

Liza let Skye's words sift through her. "I'm just praying she's okay."

Silence, then, "I got lost once, when I was three years old, at a county fair. I don't remember it, but the short of it is that my mother thought I had walked away with my father to get ice cream. When he returned and I wasn't with him, they realized I'd wandered off. Thousands of people were there, and my parents were frantic. I was gone for over three hours before a woman whom my mother didn't know, but who knew my mother through an acquaintance, came up holding my hand. She'd seen me, recognized me, and somehow found my parents. Later my mom told me that while she didn't know where I was, God did. After all, He had the perfect view. And she simply prayed that He would keep me safe until she found me. That's been my prayer for Esther. God knows where she is, and I'm praying He keeps her safe until we find her."

The perfect view. "I'd take that right now—a view all the

way to the end of the story," Liza said.

Skye laughed. "I used to do that—I'd read a book and flip to the end to make sure the heroine lived happily ever after, and if she did, then I'd read the book."

"That would be nice—a promise that life would end happily."

"A promise doesn't mean it'll work out the way we want, right? In fact, in a way, if we know the ending, it steals from our everyday faith, those baby steps forward. What if we saw the entire path—would we take it? The future is scary enough—maybe we're just supposed to cling to God for today and let Him worry about tomorrow."

Liza rolled over onto her side, her head propped on her arm. "Who are you?"

"My dad's a pastor. But it's true, right? People say, 'God doesn't give us more than we can handle,' but that's not true at all. Those are just words to make us believe we'll survive. But God purposely gives us more than we can handle so we'll turn to Him. We have the promise of God's love, God's presence, even that He'll work out our suffering for good... And maybe that's enough, come what may. Or it should be. The question is—will you trust God today because of who He is, or do you need a promise of a happy ending?"

A happy ending.

Maybe that was her problem. She didn't trust God for a happy ending, either. She wanted His promise.

No faith. In Conner. In God.

But promises didn't stave off trouble. Or broken hearts.

Maybe she and Conner were more alike than she'd thought.

Liza cast her gaze over to him, her voice soft. "I kissed him."

"I knew it!"

"Shh!"

Skye's voice cut low. "I *knew* it. It was the way you two looked at each other when he landed at camp. You broke his heart, didn't you?"

"What? No—he broke mine."

Skye made a little noise of dissent. "Didn't you hear him? He said he couldn't worry about you when he was trying to find Esther—"

"Yeah, because I keep getting in the way."

"No—because he likes you. Maybe even loves you."

It'll kill me, again.

The fire popped, the top of the pyramid collapsing in an explosion of spark and flame. Embers scattered into the night, and across the site Conner turned, as if to check.

Looking over the fire, she could almost feel his eyes on her, holding her.

"I was in love with him, too," she said softly. "He chased me from Minnesota to Arizona, and for the first time, I started to think that maybe God didn't want me to be single. That He'd put a guy into my life that liked me enough to track me down and not push me away when he was done with me."

She knew how that sounded and didn't care. Next to her Skye just nodded, as if she had her own broken places.

Conner got up, stretched, then walked over to the fire.

Liza watched him, the way he crouched, stirred the ashes, resettled the logs, added more. So capable, the kind of man she could trust. "I got scared. He finally kissed me, but—"

"You didn't want to give out your heart without a few guarantees." Skye was looking at CJ, who roused when Conner nudged him with his boot.

"But he couldn't give me guarantees. He lost his parents when he was seventeen, his brother a few years later, and he refuses to let himself hang on to anyone too tightly. Or to let himself look too far into the future."

CJ got up, handed Conner the blanket. Conner draped it over his shoulders like a superhero.

"But that doesn't mean he doesn't put everything he has into the now." Liza watched him hunker down, roll himself into the blanket. "It's what makes him a good smokejumper. He lives from fire to fire."

And had called her in between.

Yeah, she should have trusted him to keep holding on despite his fears. Despite her wounds.

"That's what CJ said. That he doesn't know what fire he'll jump next, so he just fights the one in front of him," Skye said softly. She propped herself up to watch as CJ climbed onto the boulder. "I'll admit it—I feel a little safer with them on guard." She settled back onto the ground.

Me too. Liza watched the firelight flickering over Conner's blanketed body, a wave of tenderness heating her core.

The question is—will you trust God today, because of who He is, or do you need a promise of a happy ending?

Promises or not, she'd never stopped loving him.

And if that meant letting him go, walking away to help him keep his promise to Shep, then that's exactly what she would do.

After nearly twenty years of sleeping on the ground—from sandy draws in Iraq to mountain ledges in Montana—Conner still couldn't figure out how to sleep without knots in his back. Or maybe the knots came from fighting the nightmare images of Liza going over the falls.

Liza screaming at a bear.

Liza with arms and legs wrapped around him, kissing him as if she'd never let go.

And wedged in the crannies of those thoughts, the ever-present worry about Esther.

Please, God, let her be alive.

He stood now at the shore, watching the dawn creep over the river, the rose gold scraping away shadows to reveal the razor-edged rocks cut from the churning water. Just upstream the roar of the falls ate away at the early-morning chirrup of sparrows.

Tracing his and Liza's treacherous escape rendered Conner just a little hollow.

They'd jumped a thirty-foot falls, ridged on each side by jagged, lethal-edged rocks that could have broken legs, smashed skulls. The tree they'd ridden had snagged downriver, a massive skeleton with an eight-foot root base designed to entrap and drown.

A horde of angels, no doubt, had engineered their escape.

The realization bolstered his decision to send Skye and Liza back to camp.

Still, CJ was probably right. They needed all the help they could get. *Today, please, let us find Esther.*

As if to buoy his reach for faith, a glorious sunrise trumpeted into the morning, hope borne on shafts of light that filtered through the forest and glimmered on dark rock. Lavender clouds tufted the sky, edged in rose, shiny with the morning glow.

The air suggested a scorcher of a day, despite the cool mist off the river. An early-morning crow called, soared low, and landed in a nearby aspen.

"I figured you'd be up."

Liza walked up to him, holding a cup of instant coffee. She had drawn her long hair back into a handkerchief, the effect turning her beautiful brown eyes luminous, a familiar sweet jolt of espresso to his system. He fought the crazy urge to reach up, run his thumb along her cheek, wipe away the sleep lines.

Tug her back into his arms.

"Sunrises." He raised a shoulder.

"Agreed. Charlie and I used to sneak down to the dock at camp—he'd bring a fishing pole—and we'd sit and watch the sunrise. Of course he wasn't my stepbrother then, but that was even better. I knew he wanted to spend time with me, rather than being forced to."

Her words made his chest ache.

"Remember the sunset off Doe Mountain? The way the mesa turned practically red, the sky this perfect shade of royal blue? And in the middle, a strip of fire that looked as if the sky was aflame."

"One of the most beautiful sights I'd ever seen," he said, not remembering the sunset at all, but the smell of her hair, the feel of her body tucked into his. And not just the memory of their first kiss, but of a night spent talking in the cover of darkness, cocooned together under a blanket. The deep realization of longing in his heart of something he might have called a happy ending.

It all conspired to tug a grin up his face. "I didn't want the day to end."

"Clearly, judging by the little camping kit you hauled out of your backpack—blanket, your camp stove, cups, and hot cocoa." She took a sip of coffee, peering at him over the rim, her eyes shiny, inviting him into the memory.

"Occasionally I do think ahead to the ending, or at least let myself consider the what-ifs."

"I know you do, Conner."

Her tone dissolved the memory, turned his thoughts back to last night and their argument. You're so afraid that God won't keep His own promises toward you and He'll let you down that you've stopped hoping. Stopped having faith. Stopped believing in happy endings.

"Liza—"

"Listen, I know you're worried about me, especially after the crazy day yesterday." She spoke over him, perhaps not even hearing him.

"It was crazy," he said quietly. The memory of her hand clinging to his—and then that kiss, the one that followed him into his dreams. Yeah, crazy *good*, perhaps.

But perhaps not for her, because she took a breath, then looked at him, her smile falling. "I'll hike back with Skye today if you still want me to. It'll be easier for you if you don't have to worry about me."

He wanted to cringe, the reality of her words like a slap. He'd said that, hadn't he?

And now he wanted to change his mind. Because he might always worry about her—and frankly, he preferred to do that with her by his side.

"I think we can find the way back," she said. "We'll follow the river to where Shep fell, then climb the mountain from there, and we'll end up on the Pine Ridge trail. What do you think—ten miles, maybe?"

His brain scrambled to catch up. "Maybe—"

"Then we'll tell Pete, when he returns, where to find you, and by then maybe we can get reinforcements."

He was nodding but only heard other words suddenly echo-

ing back to him. When this gig is over, you're going to walk away, and I'm going to let you.

Wait—

"I know Esther's out there, Conner. And I believe that you and CJ can find her. She's a tough girl, resilient, resourceful, and we will find her, even if we have to split up to do it."

Split up?

She finished her coffee and turned away.

He caught her arm. More reflex than clear thought, but he swallowed, found his voice, and forced it out. "Don't go."

She stilled, her beautiful brown eyes holding a question, a tiny frown deepening on her face.

"Don't go." This time stronger.

He hesitated and she started to smile. "I...we started this, right?"

The smile fell at his words. "But you don't need me to finish it—"

"I do."

He turned her to face him. "I do need you. And yeah, I don't know what's going to happen, but—okay, it's more than just finding Esther." He turned her to himself, both hands on her arms, wanting her to *hear* him.

"When you called me, it was like I saw a second chance to go back to that moment, that sunset in Sedona, and say the right thing. To fix whatever went wrong between us. I'm not sure I know how, but I *do* know that I'm not ready for you to walk away. Or for you to let *me* walk away." He took a breath. "I've really missed you, Donut Girl."

The old moniker found its place, stirred from her a real smile.

His heart began to beat again.

Conner let go of her arm, pressed his hand to her cheek, and ran his thumb down it. “I don’t know why, but having you around seems like just what I need to believe that it’ll all work out.”

Liza pressed her hand against his on her cheek. And with the gesture, it seemed his entire chest exploded, a sweet, delicious heat pouring through him. She stood in the center of the morning, the sun turning her eyes a deep, golden brown, and it just engulfed him, turned him to fire.

“I have to kiss you,” he said, his voice a whisper. “Please.”

She set her coffee mug down, then lifted herself to her tiptoes and pressed her lips against his.

Coffee. And the taste of the morning, fresh and alive. She smelled slightly of woods and smoke and river, but it only made him want to sink into her, to hold her. To disappear, just for a moment, into a place where time stopped, where people stayed, and to a place where life felt big and whole and bright.

He had his hand cupped around her neck and moved in, his arms around her. Hers slid around his waist as she lifted her head, making a small sound he hoped might be delight.

Desire.

His kiss deepened and he nudged her mouth open, let his tongue taste her, a brush of sensation that lit his chest on fire. His entire body tingled with the sense of her touch, the way she made him feel whole and not at all like a broken guy who couldn’t make—or keep—promises.

Conner wanted to weep with the longing for them to figure out how to put what they could have had back together, for him to have enough faith to believe in an ending that didn’t end in tragedy, in breaking promises. Or both their hearts.

His fingers tangled in her hair, and he pulled away, pressing his forehead to hers, his chest rising and falling with his captured breath. "I love…" Oh. He wanted to say it, felt the word bloom in the center of his chest. Stuck. "…kissing you. Probably too much."

Liza caught her lip in her teeth, but a smile broke through and she nodded. "You are dangerous to a girl's heart, Conner Young."

Oh, but he didn't want to be.

And still the word lodged there. *You. I love you*—and he was trying to figure out how to free them when CJ's walkie, now hooked to his belt, crackled to life.

"Brooks, Young. Are you there, Conner?"

Liza stepped away from him as he turned, scooped up the radio, his heart still ranging about his chest, unhinged.

"I'm here, Pete." Conner cleared his throat, tried to find his moorings, glanced at Liza walking away. He could still feel her curves against him, the smell of her hair, the taste—

"Give us your position. Gilly's going to drop me back in, and I'll hike to you. Please advise."

Right. He'd spent the better part of the last hour sitting in front of the campfire—which he'd worked back into a small blaze—figuring out their position.

"Give me a second." He pulled out the map and guesstimated.

"We're about eight clicks by air from Shep's point of extraction, below the next falls."

Silence over the line. Then, "Gotcha. According to the topo map, there's a clearing about a half click to your northeast." Pete read off coordinates.

Conner found the place on his map. "Roger that."

"We'll leave in ten—I'll meet you there ASAP."

Conner confirmed, clicked off.

He turned back around, found his compatriots standing by the fire, eyes alight.

"Today we find Esther," he said. Then he looked at Liza. "And we find her together."

CHAPTER 13

A WHITE CHUTE OPENED up against the arch of the blue sky, glazed with a thin layer of clouds, and with it blossomed a thrill of hope inside Liza.

Yes, like Conner said, today they'd find Esther. She'd be okay, they'd get back to camp, and then...

She wouldn't think about *then*. Just now and watching Pete drop from the sky. Liza stood with her hand tented over her eyes as the plane dipped a wing and banked to circle for another drop.

Behind her, Conner confirmed Pete's chute opening to the pilot—she recognized Gilly's name—and requested her to drop the gear pack.

"I think I have to be a smokejumper when I grow up," Skye said from behind Liza.

"You're looking at the fun part," said CJ. "Try dropping into a roaring blaze armed with just an ax and a couple of squirt guns."

"And a chain saw," Conner added from a few feet away. About fifty feet wide, the meadow was bordered on all sides by shaggy black pine and stands of aspen. A mountain creek about five feet wide crevassed the middle.

Pete angled his chute perfectly into the drop zone, landed, and rolled. In a slick acrobatic move that reminded Liza of Conner, Pete popped up. He hauled in his parachute, unclipping himself from his harness as Conner watched the metal drone box drop.

CJ and he went to retrieve it.

Pete had pulled off his helmet in favor of a gimme cap shoved into his leg pocket. He'd knotted his golden hair at the nape of his neck and wore a two-day grizzle on his chin. As he shed his jumpsuit, he looked at them and cast a grin that could take most any other girl off her feet. "Hey, ladies."

"Yeah, I definitely need to get into smokejumping," Skye said.

CJ and Conner hauled the gear box to the center of the field.

They set it on the ground and opened it. Inside, cushioned in foam lay a long white cylinder attached to a thin, stainless steel rod, about three feet long. A fixed wing lay alongside it, along with a detached tail assembly. And, nestled beside it, an extra battery pack, a black gear bag, a tablet, and a handgun in a holster.

Pete reached for the gun. "With the rangers still hunting the bear..."

"You're not going to kill it, are you?" Skye asked, her tone identifying exactly where she stood on that idea.

"Not if I don't have to," Conner said, taking the gun from Pete. He clipped it to his belt then knelt beside the box and hauled out the drone.

"Is this bigger than your earlier models?" Liza asked, crouching beside him. "It seems from your pictures those drones were smaller."

"This is big number five, the mama of the tribe. Fifty-one inches long, this baby has seventy-four inches of wingspan."

He pulled out the tail assembly, fixed it to the rod.

"It has GPS, a 3DR radio, and a mile of range. It can fly at twenty-five miles an hour for nearly forty minutes on one rechargeable lithium battery. I have two batteries plus a recharging pack. And this little camera"—he pointed to a tiny lens on the bottom of the drone—"can capture up to two hundred fifty acres in one shot. Then it feeds the data back to this device."

He picked up the tablet. "My software translates the pictures into a 3-D map that we can then stitch together and lay over a topo map to pinpoint Esther's location. It'll also take video if we need it."

"We call it Conner's girl back at the ranch," Pete said, reaching out to touch the drone.

"Hands off, Brooks."

"See?"

Liza laughed.

Conner picked up the drone, moved it over to a bigger space to attach the wings. "I've written a program that not only takes pictures but determines weather conditions, measures flame lengths and heat, and predicts fire behavior." He looked up at Pete, his expression solemn. "My drone might have saved lives."

Pete's grin vanished.

Something passed between the two, and even Skye caught it, because she looked at CJ. His mouth tightened into a grim line.

Conner walked back to the box and retrieved the black bag. He opened the zipper and pulled out a pair of oversized goggles. He put them on, then retrieved the remote control.

"I need to take it for a quick test run, make sure the instruments are working. I don't need a line of sight to fly it—

the goggles act as a dashboard and can tell me where I am. But I've been having some glitches..." He walked away from them, pulled down the goggles, and started fiddling with the remote control.

"What did he mean about it saving lives?" Skye asked quietly.

"He's talking about Jock and the guys who were killed last year," CJ said. He wore a grizzle on his chin this morning—dark blond, a touch of russet red. He, too, wore a baseball cap and had shucked off his yellow shirt for his blue Jude County Smokejumpers tee.

Pete got up, walked away, and stood over Conner, who was making adjustments on the tablet screen. He used his shadow to help to block out the sunlight, offering Conner a better view of the screen.

Liza watched him go, the way he stood, his hands on his hips, his chin taut. And thought about Conner's comment about friends dying.

"Conner, Pete, and Reuben were part of the team. Their crew was spread out and separated from each other when the fire they were working on jumped the line. Jock, their jump boss, had ordered them all out to the safety zone, but there were conflicting orders from another crew boss, and the communication got messed up. Jock went back for the guys down the line, and they all got trapped."

Skye put her hand to her mouth. Liza's breath tightened in her chest.

And she hadn't answered his letters, returned his calls. She wanted to weep.

"Conner's pretty quiet about it. But according to Pete and Rube, he spent the entire winter holed up in his camper working on those drones."

"If I know Conner, he thinks he could have predicted the fire jumping the line," Liza said, looking over at him. The wind ran fingers through Conner's blond hair, ruffling it as he stood to launch the drone. His deft hands worked the controls as the plane bumped down the meadow, then lifted and soared.

Pete had dropped to one knee, was confirming readings on the tablet, answering questions.

And all of that narrowed down to one sharp fact.

She shouldn't have abandoned him. Shouldn't have disconnected her landline, invested in a cell phone. Should have been his friend, despite her broken heart.

Her throat filled, her eyes burning.

I'm not ready for you to walk away.

And she wasn't ready to walk away, either.

Because despite his inability to look beyond today, she could. And maybe that's what he needed—someone to hold on long enough to help him see the future.

And sure, maybe he couldn't promise her anything, but hadn't he been giving her pieces of himself every day since he'd met her? His friendship, when he called from his strike camps or alone at home, preferring her voice to his team's after a fire. And his crazy impulsiveness when he'd tracked her down in Arizona. He gave her his strength when he took her skydiving. When he told her about his brother, he gave her that part of his heart that was still wounded over the death of his family. And he gave her his heroism, his courage when he answered the phone and showed up just because she asked. No, he didn't need to speak his promises.

She saw them.

She walked over to him as the drone landed. It bumped over to Conner and he bent down, his hand on it. "The batteries seem to be cool. I don't see them as the source of a fire."

"Oh, yeah, that's right. Dude, your place is a wreck." Pete held the tablet. "Apparently the Feds came in yesterday after you left and they tore the place apart looking for your drones. They'd broken open your bedside table, but must not have recognized the remote. Jed told me to tell you that you'd better bring the drone back with you or you'll have nothing to exonerate you."

"Exonerate him from what?" Liza asked as Conner shook his head.

"We've had some questionable fires around Ember—looks like arson—and the investigators out of the National Interagency Fire Center have tied Conner's drones to two of them."

"My drones are not causing fires!"

Pete held up his hand in surrender. "I'm just the messenger."

"Are you in trouble?" Liza asked softly.

Conner shook his head as Pete answered, "Yep. The Feds want to question him, but he jumped ship, and now they think he has something to hide."

Liza did the math. "You jumped ship because I called you and asked you for help!"

"You needed me."

"What if you get arrested?" She didn't mean the spark in her voice.

Conner looked at her then, his blue eyes calm, dark. "Let's just worry about Esther."

"I'm worried about you going to jail."

"My drones are not guilty, and neither am I." He offered her a half smile. "But I'm not going to spend time thinking about what could go wrong, rehearse trouble in my mind. Let's find Esther, that's the important thing."

She wanted to live in his world, where he put off worry for another day.

Except someone had to think ahead, right?

"When we find Esther, you are turning yourself in," she said. "And you're going to prove that your drones aren't responsible for the fires."

His eyes widened. "Really?"

"Mmmhmm. Because I'm not interested in living life on the lam. Or lining up outside San Quentin for visiting hours."

Then she held her breath. *Please don't freak out.*

Conner's smile came slowly, a sweet understanding in his eyes, a twinkle in his gaze that lit her entire body afire.

"San Quentin, huh?"

She shrugged. "I'm not well versed in my correctional facilities."

Still wearing his smile, he turned to Pete. "So do you think you can figure out the coordinates from the map? Translate them to CJ?"

Pete nodded, and Conner called CJ over. "Listen. You and Skye head back to the river and work your way down the shore. I'm going to stay here and start working the drone. Pete will call in the coordinates as we clear areas."

"I'm going, too," Liza said, and held up her hand when Conner looked at her. "Listen, Esther is probably spooked, maybe injured, and needs a friendly face."

"Who am I, Frankenstein?" Skye asked.

"Of course not. But Esther and I are friends and, frankly, I want to be there."

Liza looked pointedly at Conner, and after a moment, he

gave her a tight-mouthed nod.

"Did you bring fresh water?" she asked.

"And fresh first-aid and survival packs," Pete said. "The supplies are in my jump pack." He indicated a large backpack next to his folded chute.

She found the canister of water, then opened the survival pack and found the supplies—mag flashlight, whistle, blanket, leather gloves, fire starter, compass, mirror, rope, flare gun. "All I need is a life preserver."

"That's not funny," Conner said, not looking at her, but his mouth tweaked up anyway.

And bear spray. But she left that part out.

Certainly, however, their so-called predator bear had gone looking for other prey by now.

She shouldered the pack as CJ checked his walkie batteries, his connection with Pete, and his SAT phone. Skye headed for the forest, CJ following her.

Liza turned to follow but was stopped by a hand on her arm. "Liza."

Conner stepped in front of her, shielding her from the sunlight, his outline bold and imposing, blocking her way. He reached out to her, cupped her chin in his hand, and raised it. "Please, be careful out there."

The intensity in his blue eyes could lay waste to a girl's lingering resolve to hike out, to leave him behind when this was over. "I'll find her."

"Just..." But he didn't finish. Instead, he bent down and kissed her. Possessive, his hand moving to cup her cheek, his thumb offering a quick caress.

Then he leaned back, his eyes still on hers, filled with so much unshed emotion that it turned her body to flame.

Then he offered a tight, solemn smile.

She heard the words, even if he couldn't say them.

Come back to me.

A little overhead perspective could change everything. The goggles gave Conner a view of the ground as well as a heads-up display revealing altitude, horizon, direction, pitch, and air speed. Behind him, Pete read the data, knitting together the pictures of the terrain acreage as the drone took photos.

Sweat trailed down Conner's back, his neck tight from what felt like peering down over a knotted patchwork of lodgepole pine and towering oak. Their progress seemed achingly slow, with CJ and the girls making better time, moving back to their makeshift camp, then along the shore. He'd worked his way toward the river, snapping so many shots that he'd had to bring the drone home and change batteries by the time Pete scanned them all and they reset their search grid.

Maybe he should call for reinforcements.

In fact, "What do you think about calling Jed, getting the team in here?" he asked Pete.

"I already checked in," Pete said. "Gilly just finished dropping them in at a fire north of Ember about twenty miles. Just a flare-up, but Jed wanted to get a handle on it before it became a conflagration, started threatening the town."

"Another fire."

"And two more in Glacier, one in the Bob and one in Yellowstone. Every jump team in the west is deployed, and Alaska is coming down to help in Idaho."

Which meant that a drone like his could right now be tracking fires, saving lives. If it didn't get confiscated, dissected, and tangled in lethal red tape.

Conner started the drone across another patch in the grid, the river on the far edge, blue and crystalline under the noonday sun. His shoulders burning with holding the remote, he knew he looked crazy with his inability to stand still, his urge to bob, duck, and dodge as he flew the machine lower into the trees. But Esther could be injured, and the closer he got to the ground, the clearer his shot would be.

He dodged a towering lodgepole pine and jerked back, nearly stumbling.

"Whoa, dude, you look a little woozy."

"Nearly got hit by a tree."

No comment from Pete. Until, "Huh. I was thinking it was that kiss you planted on Liza. I'd forgotten that you two hooked up in Arizona."

"We didn't hook up." He flew the plane deeper along the grid, startled a fox, then a deer that ran springing away, her sprawl-legged fawn on her tail. "But, yeah. We sorta, I don't know, had a date, I guess."

"I guess? That wasn't a *date, I guess*, kiss. That was a *come-back-to-me-Scarlett* kind of smackeroo."

Conner smiled, remembering Liza's expression—all wide-eyed and what-just-happened?—and another line of sweat trickled down his back. "Yeah, maybe."

Yeah, *definitely,* it was a come-back-to-me kind of kiss. One full of promise and hope, and maybe he didn't have to say the words. Maybe he could simply show her that he wanted her in his life. It didn't have to be complicated—after all, she was staying here this summer. And after that, well...

After that he'd track her down back to Deep Haven if he had to. Because for the first time in a year, life didn't feel so suffocating. And, if he looked up, past his tiny, dark world where grief lay in wait at every turn, he could spot something on the horizon.

Light.

Healing.

A future.

The battery light on his visor began to blink, and he turned the drone around, directing it back before it dropped and he had to hike to find it.

Conner skimmed the aircraft over the wilderness, scattering birds, then he cleared the forest and soared into the meadow.

He spotted himself and Pete in the heads-up display, a surreal look at the world below, the two men trying to locate a needle in the haystack of the Montana forests. Then he shifted the drone to autopilot, and it landed. He taxied it over to himself then pulled off the goggles, bent, and felt the body of the drone.

Still not hot. Which meant that his lithium batteries weren't going to explode and ignite the under-dry forest.

He turned the drone over, opened the compartment, and pulled out the battery. He changed it out with the first one, fresh off his portable charger, and screwed the compartment shut.

"I've got something." Pete stood up from where he was examining the pictures. Sweat dribbled down his temples. He'd pulled a space blanket over himself to view the screen in darkness, and now held out the tablet, pointed to a square of topography.

The plane could take photos from half a mile up, but Conner had kept his view smaller, under five hundred feet. The images could capture trees, shadows, boulders, bushes, and hopefully a frightened fifteen-year-old girl.

"There. The red dot to the left of the screen. By the river."

Conner peered at it. He couldn't make out a face or body, just the red blotch. Still, it could be something. "Radio the coordinates to CJ."

"It looks to be about a quarter of a mile from their last position," he said. "They're pretty close."

"I'll get the drone back up, see if we can confirm." Conner's pulse thundered as he pulled on the goggles.

The drone lifted off, and he flew it straight for the river. He'd run the length of it until he came to the search point.

Behind him, he heard Pete on the radio and CJ's answering affirmation.

"Anything?" Pete asked, the blanket rustling behind him.

"Not yet..." Except—"Yes!" Conner had slowed the drone as it followed the river, a little afraid of a stall. But as he flew it overhead, he thought he'd spotted a body lying in a pocket of rock along the shore.

"I'm not sure she's moving," he said quietly. He turned the drone for another pass. *Please, God.*

And then, as he soared the drone overhead, the person lifted her head, stared right into his camera.

"I got her! She's alive!" Bedraggled, lying in the fetal position, as if cold, terrified, and clearly hurt, the girl had even lifted her hand to wave.

Smile for the camera, honey.

He turned the drone north, back toward the forest. "Where did you say the team was?"

"About a quarter mile northeast."

Conner just wanted a glimpse, to make sure... He soared the drone over the trees, peering down for the trio, painfully aware that probably he was just wasting batteries, even time.

And then, just where he thought she might be, he found Liza walking—no, running behind CJ.

On fire to find Esther.

Atta, girl.

He turned the plane toward home and noticed the battery light blinking.

It must not have charged to full capacity. *C'mon.*

The battery light shifted to red, the display warning of low capacity.

Still a mile out, but with the wind speed—

The battery went black and with it, his heads-up display.

He tore off the goggles, let them hang around his neck, and searched for the gliding drone.

Nothing. He let out a sound of frustration that had Pete yanking off his blanket.

"What's wrong?"

"The drone crashed. I think. I had it on auto-pilot, but still, with the trees..."

"I probably got a shot of its last position," Pete said. He pulled up the screen, scrolled to the last photo. "Yeah, I think we can probably find it, if we can map it."

"We have to get to Esther."

"Yeah. But CJ and the girls are on their way. And CJ has medical training. We'll call in the PEAK Rescue chopper and pick up the drone on the way."

"I don't know—"

"You need the drone to prove it's not flammable. Like your girlfriend said, she doesn't want to visit you in San Quentin."

Girlfriend. Yeah, that seemed like the right word.

He looked at Pete. "Okay, but let's make it snappy."

Chapter 14

PLEASE LET HER BE ALIVE.

Liza ran over roots, pushing away the slap of tree branches, holding them for Skye so she didn't get smacked. The forest seemed to take on their urgency, birds scattering, squirrels scampering up trees. CJ, for all the cowboy in him, seemed nimble-footed in the forest. And Skye might have been raised by wolves for her ease in the woods.

Liza, however, had barely dodged spearing herself into a tree. And wouldn't Conner love that?

Come back to me. The kiss had felt almost like a promise.

But first, please, *Esther.* She wouldn't think beyond that.

"She seems to be moving," Pete had said to CJ after giving them coordinates. "She's by the river, due west."

CJ had pulled out his compass, turned them the right direction, and headed toward his compass point.

Now he pulled up near a towering oak, stopped, and realigned his compass. Looked out ahead. "That tall black spruce," he said, designating it as an anchor point, and took off again.

Liza didn't know much about using a compass, but he seemed to be hopping from one destination to the next all the way to the river.

She made a comment to that effect to Skye behind her, as she jogged to keep up.

"Orienteering 101. You can't see your destination, but you find a point along the way that lines up with the direction you want to go. That way you stay on course, despite your limited vision."

Her words rattled around in Liza's head as they caught up to CJ, now sighting his next point.

"I think the river can't be that much farther." He pointed to a large boulder, and Liza was still holding her knees, breathing hard, when he took off.

She stood up, taking off after him, careful of her steps as boulders rose to dissect their path.

The question is—will you trust God today because of who He is, or do you need a promise of a happy ending?

She didn't need to know the destination as long as she stayed on course. Walking as far as God's path illuminated, then trusting Him for the next destination.

Wasn't that what faith was anyway?

CJ was climbing up a giant boulder that rose from the earth, jagged edges lined with slick, green moss, tangled bushes growing from the crevices. Liza grabbed his hand and let him drag her to a foothold, then scrambled up beside him.

They stood on an outcropping of rock overlooking the river, ten feet below. A wash of rapids frothed thirty feet upstream where the river cascaded over a sloping run of ledges and boulders.

Below her, it flattened out, eddying around a fallen tree, a lip of ledge rock so close to the surface she could make out the moss and striations of age embedded in the layers. The high sun turned the water to a crystalline blue, deceptively cool and beckoning.

"Do you see her?" Skye asked, coming up beside her. She had braided her blonde hair back into one tight rope held in place with a headband, had her jacket tied about her waist. She was tanned and young, and for a second Liza wished she had Skye's striking confidence.

Maybe then she would have had the courage to stick around, to not run from Conner, to brave him breaking her heart for the chance that he wouldn't.

"Esther!" CJ's voice echoed over the river.

Liza heard only the thunder of her heartbeat.

Then, "Here!"

The voice rose from a place farther downstream, hidden somewhere in the flow of rocks and boulders.

"We're coming to you!" Liza shouted, climbing over the rocky ledge, down along the bouldered shoreline, then up the next outcropping of rock. She stood, scanning the horizon, waiting for Skye to catch up, hearing CJ on the SAT phone calling in their position to Pete.

Then a flash of red—*there*—waving just ten yards downstream in a depression of rock. Esther's jacket. Not the camp-issued blue, but a red Ember High windbreaker.

Liza scrambled across the ledge. "Esther!"

The girl lay in a pocket of rock just outside the reach of the river. She stared up at Liza like she didn't recognize her. Blood smeared her cheekbone where it had been seared against a rock, skin peeled back, and her lip swelled. She held her body as if protecting bruised ribs, one leg pulled up, the other wedged down into the rock.

She shook as Liza climbed down beside her.

"Honey, we're here. You're safe."

Esther's whitened expression trembled, her breath quivering, and then, suddenly, her eyes filled with tears. "I..."

Esther reached out a shaky hand, and Liza caught it, held it, and reached out with her other hand to touch Esther's shoulder, her hair. "It's okay. You're going to be okay."

Esther shook her head, her breath hiccupping. "I...I should have gone back. . ." She pressed a hand to her mouth. "Is he dead?"

He...Shep.

Skye had climbed down beside Liza, was pulling water from her pack. CJ stood looking over the edge, still talking into his radio.

"Shep's okay. We found him and life-flighted him out," Liza said quietly, suppressing the urge to pull the girl into her arms, not sure what might be broken or how she might react.

"I tried to get out." More stumbling breaths. Esther seemed on the edge of breaking. "But I hurt my foot, and then...I should have gone back—"

"Shh," Liza said and then she leaned in, held Esther's head against her shoulder. "Shh. It's okay. You're both alive. That's what's important."

"Let's take a look at that foot," Skye said, moving around Liza.

"Don't touch it!" Esther pushed Liza away, slapped at Skye. "Don't touch..."

Only then did Liza see what Esther protected. Her foot lay as if detached from the bone, floppy and perpendicular to her leg, the ankle clearly smashed.

No wonder the girl looked about to faint.

"I won't touch it," Skye said. She glanced at Liza.

Liza gave her a *just stay calm* look.

Skye stood up. "CJ, we need—" Her breath caught.

Her stuttered breathing made Liza look up at her.

Skye stood without moving, her eyes wide.

"What—?"

Then Liza heard it. The snuffing, the low growl.

No!

She gripped Skye's hand, standing up to confirm.

CJ stood at the edge of the ledge, his walkie in hand, frozen, staring at the grizzly some forty feet away, peering at them.

"What do we do?" Skye asked.

"What's the matter?" Esther's voice shrilled.

"Shh—just..."

"Play dead," CJ whispered.

"Are you *kidding* me?" Skye said. "Run!"

"We can't run," Liza said. "We can't move Esther."

CJ jumped down to the ledge as the bear came out from behind the tree.

The animal let out a bellow, shaking his head from side to side.

"Yes we can!" CJ said. He reached down, shoved his arms under Esther's legs and behind her back.

Esther let out a scream, rending the air with her pain, and for a second the bear startled.

"That's it! CJ, get her out of here!" Liza grabbed Skye's hand. "Get big! Get loud!"

Then she scrambled up on the rock, whipped off her backpack, swung it, and started to scream.

Beside her, Skye jumped up, waving her arms, yelling, wild.

No more running.

Liza advanced on the bear, jumping up and down, still

swinging her backpack, putting everything she had into her voice, her movements.

She was even scaring herself a little.

But no more running.

"Go! Get away!"

Skye had dug out a whistle and blew it, shrill and high.

The bear halted. Snuffed the air. His head swung again from side to side, as if assessing.

"Go!" Liza shouted to CJ.

The bear's pug ears flattened.

"It's not working!" Skye said.

Behind them, Esther was screaming, and Liza guessed that CJ was carrying her away.

"Keep shouting!" Liza screamed. But even she realized their peril as the animal rose on hind legs, swiped the air.

"Okay—run!"

The animal charged. Skye screamed. Liza dove out of the way, swinging her backpack at the grizzly's snout.

She landed on her side, rolled, and saw Skye disappear over the ledge into the river.

Then Liza picked up her pack, found her feet, and fled.

~

"It's got to be around here somewhere," Pete said, behind Conner. They'd been tromping through the forest for far too long, trying to locate the drone.

When, in fact, they should be racing to the riverbank.

Conner estimated they were still half a mile away from Esther, and if he didn't find the drone soon, he'd just have to come back.

He still couldn't believe it had actually worked. He'd used the drone to pinpoint a girl lost in a forest so dense they never would have found her. CJ confirmed it when he'd called in.

"Esther was wedged in the rocks next to the river," Pete said. "But Liza and Skye are taking care of her. CJ thought she had a broken ankle. I'll update PEAK Rescue on their position."

Pete had dropped behind Conner as they hiked along, Conner holding his tablet, searching for the last-known location of the drone. Certainly after he retrieved it—even if it were in pieces—Conner could use it to prove the batteries weren't flammable. And with footage from the tablet, maybe the government would even fund the production of a fleet of drones.

Which meant lives saved.

Lives like CJ and Pete and Jed and Reuben and the rest of the current Jude County Smokejumpers.

Almost a year ago it might have meant that Jock Burns and the six other victims of the Eureka Canyon flare-up would have seen the inevitable entrapment, turned the right direction. Lived.

Conner still sometimes awakened, sweating and shaking, his heart slamming against his chest, hearing their screams.

Yeah, he'd had enough of losing people he loved.

Which meant that if Liza needed promises from him, then he would give them. Not only that, but probably she deserved a promise from him. Not because of her fear but because that's what people did—committed their way to each other.

Promised to keep showing up, every day.

And frankly, he wouldn't mind a promise in his direction, either. Something that might remind her not to run when he blew it, when he said something stupid and made her believe, somehow, that she was too clingy.

Right, as if.

But, please, God, help him not to do that.

But maybe, with her around, he wouldn't always assume the worst, could start believing in that happy ending, even for himself. Because with Liza, he could see beyond his circle of darkness into a crazy light that had her smack dab in the center of it, in something that looked dangerously, amazingly, like happiness.

A bright, family-filled, amazing future that included her waking up in his arms to watch the sunrise. And falling asleep to every beautiful sunset.

They came upon a patch of forest thinned by glacial ledge rock that jutted from the ground in angles, rising from the boreal depths like icebergs. Shrubs and bushes fitted into the nooks and crannies; white pine and balsam grew up in the spongy earthen beds between the slabs. Conner checked the topo map and found a towering black spruce. He turned to locate it from the ground.

"I don't know, Pete. It's probably in pieces—"

Screaming ripped through the air and stopped Conner cold.

Pete toggled the SAT phone. "CJ—you guys okay?"

Static, then, CJ's voice, stiff and sharp. "Bear!"

Conner plowed through the forest, casting a look at the horizon, his instincts heading him westward toward the river. He could hear only the screaming.

Liza's screaming.

And that's when he realized he'd long ago made her promises. He'd just never voiced them. Promises in the way he'd reached out for her, needed her, longed for her. Promises in his broken heart that couldn't scrape her out of his thoughts. Promises that had nothing to do with words and everything to do with the fact that he loved her.

Wow, he loved her. His feet slammed over earth, launched over trees, scrabbled up rocks. Pete kept up, only feet behind him.

Conner stopped for a moment on top of a jutting ledge rock, searching. Saw the break in the trees. "There's the river."

How far upstream from them, he hadn't a clue, but—

"CJ?" Pete said, toggling the walkie. "Come in—!"

Static. Conner took off again, sliding down the backside of the rock.

And although it went against everything he knew about wildlife, about survival, he couldn't help it. No playing dead today.

Run, Liza! Run!

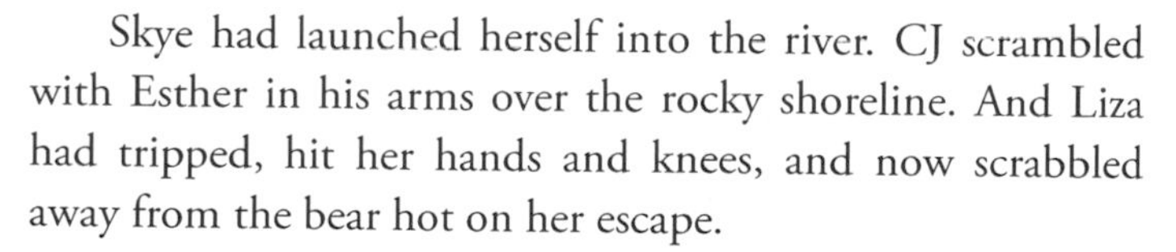

Skye had launched herself into the river. CJ scrambled with Esther in his arms over the rocky shoreline. And Liza had tripped, hit her hands and knees, and now scrabbled away from the bear hot on her escape.

Liza had rounded on the animal, caught up a rock, and slammed it in a wild throw at the bear's face. It grunted and fell back just long enough for her to clamber back to her feet. She didn't look back as she ran.

She knew running was futile. Especially over the bouldered shoreline where a bear could hop huge crevasses. Still, Liza fled with abandon, screaming, turning to throw rocks, fighting the animal as it reached out to swipe her.

It caught her in the leg, ripping her pants, tearing a swath through her calf muscle.

She screamed, heat spurting into her bones. But she didn't stop.

Behind her, she heard CJ calling her name. Skye's shouts also lifted from the river.

Play dead. The mantra resounded in her head, but the thought turned to a rock in her gut.

She wasn't going to just let herself die, let the animal maul her.

Liza found another loose rock, turned, and flung it at the bear's open jaw. The rock cracked it hard, and the animal shook its head, paused.

CJ had stopped at the edge of a cliff, clearly trapped. Now he fumbled with his pack.

She hadn't meant to bring the bear his direction, and now she screamed at him. "Jump, CJ!"

Esther lay at his feet, curled into a ball, screaming.

The bear roared behind Liza, furious.

And that's when Liza knew. She wasn't going to live through this. No amount of fighting or screaming or running—

As if that would solve her problems.

She'd never solved anything by running.

Play dead.

No, that was stupid.

A roar behind her made her leave her skin.

Stop. Trust. Not play dead, but stand firm, hold on to God.

Believing He was enough, come what may.

Liza launched herself at Esther, covering the girl's body

with her own, wrapping her legs around Esther's body, reaching up to cover the injured girl's head with her hands.

Please, oh God, save us.

Esther writhed beneath her, frantic with fear as the animal charged. CJ fell back, going over the edge with a cry.

Liza smelled the animal—feral, rank. A swipe of razor nails raked her side, and she screamed, a thousand knives spearing through her.

Then teeth sank into her shoulder, deep, paralyzing her as the animal's tongue touched her neck, its nose grimy and wet. Pain ripped through her body, curling around her arm, her chest, her breathing.

This was it. He'd shake her, break her neck, and she'd die, right here on this rock in the middle of the forest.

But maybe Esther would live. *Please, God, let Esther live!*

An explosion in her ears. The world turned to fire. Heat, sparks.

The bear roared, dropping Liza back onto a hysterical Esther.

Then the world dimmed around the edges. She used her last strength to hold onto Esther as the blackness closed over her.

Chapter 15

CONNER'S FERAL SCREAM SHOULD have stopped the bear, alerted it, but apparently the animal had no eyes for anyone but his prey. And with Conner still thirty feet away, the scream lifted impotent into the air, drowned out by the roar of the grizzly.

Then the animal dove in, biting Liza's neck with its grimy, powerful jaw. Conner lost all rational thought when the predator lifted her, shaking her.

"No!"

Then the world exploded in a shower of fire and sparks, and the bear reared up in agony, releasing Liza like a rag doll.

CJ stood just behind her, on a ledge below the rock, holding his flare gun.

Almost point-blank, he shot at the bear. The flare landed on the rock at the bear's feet, sparking.

The animal now raged in a furious circle, the flare spitting and sizzling on the rock.

Liza crumpled, unmoving, on the rock, her body still over Esther.

The bear, backed up against the edge of the outcropping, landed on all fours, spittle dangling from its jaws, its dark eyes shiny.

It turned again toward the prone girls, Esther trying to extract herself from Liza's limp body.

Conner had his gun out before he realized it, his instincts kicking in. He dropped to one knee at the apex of the ledge, took aim.

The bear charged the girls.

Conner let out a breath and squeezed the trigger, praying for good aim.

The bear dropped, skidding on its side as the bullet tore through its temple.

It died with a grunt, its razor claws still pawing the ground.

The sulfur of gunshot braised the air, backdropped by the howl of Esther's screams.

He couldn't breathe, her name more of a moan. *"Liza!"*

Pete beat him to her, hovering over her, assessing her wounds. Esther pushed him away, nearly falling off the ledge in her attempts, but CJ caught her, holding the girl in his arms. She clung to him, weeping.

"She's losing a lot of blood." Pete opened up his pack, ripping out gauze pads, as if they might have any effect at stopping the flow of blood pooling into the jagged crannies of the rock.

Conner landed on his knees next to Liza, his hand going to her shoulder where the bear's teeth had left deep punctures in her neck and shoulder, to the razed skin that flopped from her upper arm. Her right hand lay mangled, having taken the brunt of the attack. Probably it saved her from having her carotid artery severed.

Conner grabbed a pad and moved the flesh back over her shoulder wound and held it there, hoping to stem the bleeding.

Pete pressed his gauze pad over the tear in her side where the bear had raked her, wounds that bared bone as they curved around her body.

"How's her breathing? Did he nick a lung?"

Conner leaned over her. "Shallow and fast."

"Okay, we need to slow this bleeding, then get a blanket on her," Pete said, a litany of directions they all knew. Still, Pete's commands were something Conner could cling to in order to keep himself from unraveling.

He pressed a kiss to Liza's cheek. "You're going to be okay."

Pete handed him another gauze pad and a roll of wrap.

Skye had climbed out of the river, pale, her arms around herself, as if trying valiantly not to unravel. She helped CJ lower Esther to the ground and move her away from Liza.

CJ then bent next to Conner, holding the gauze in place as he wrapped Liza's shoulder. The blood streamed around it.

Conner clenched his jaw to keep from whimpering, but wow, he wanted to hurt something, to stand up and scream, to rail at anything—God, nature, even himself for letting her go.

Why hadn't he demanded she return to camp? Although, if she had, she might have run into the bear then, too.

Pete had used up his supply of gauze pads on her side wound, taping the pads over it. "Apply pressure on these, CJ," Conner said and traded places with him to attend to her neck wounds.

Liza started to rouse.

"Shh," Conner said, leaning over her. "I know you're in pain, just relax."

But she stiffened under his hand, and he felt a scream

building.

"He's gone, honey. The bear's dead."

Conner cast it a glance just to confirm. The predator lay in a rank pile, blood and spittle drying around its maw, its claws curled into the rock.

She turned her head then.

"Don't move," Pete said. "I don't think anything is broken, but we don't know for sure."

Conner climbed over her, then down to the ledge where CJ was perched.

It put him just above Liza, nearly face to face. He kept one hand pressed on her shoulder, the other he curled around hers, still extended to protect Esther. He folded it in his, squeezed. "The rescue team is on its way."

Tears filled her beautiful eyes. "I'm sorry. I know I shouldn't have run, but I couldn't help it."

"No, baby, you did the right thing. You fought him, and then—you saved Esther." His eyes burned, filled, and he didn't care that he suddenly started to sob. "Liza, you are so brave. So amazing. And I—I can't lose you. I just can't—"

He pressed his forehead to hers, closed his eyes. "I love you."

He whispered it, then leaned back, met her eyes. "I love you so much. And I should have said that back in Arizona. Because that's the best promise I can give you. I love you so much that I can hardly breathe without you. And if it takes a thousand promises to hold onto you, then you have them. Every day. In as many ways as I can say it. Just—please live."

Her hand tightened in his. "Shh." Then somehow she worked her other hand into his shirt, gripping it. "I don't need promises."

In the distance, thank God, he heard the *whump, whump*

of a chopper's blades dicing the air. He wanted to weep anew.

Her voice fell to a whisper, soft, laced with a layer of pain under her heartbreaking veil of bravery. "I just need you, showing up every day to love me." Tears hung in her eyes. "And I'll do the same, okay?"

The wind lifted around them as the chopper approached, kicking up dust and the odor of death.

Conner shook his head, his gaze holding hers. "No. Because *I'm* going to need a promise. Because you aren't going to die on me, Liza."

She offered a slight smile, and he hiccupped back a sob as he pressed his lips to hers. A grimy, bloody, soft, forever kiss. He didn't move, just held himself there, unable to let her go.

Then, from overhead, "I'm coming down with a litter!"

Jess, the PEAK Rescue EMT, hung out the open door, a blow horn to her lips, her blonde hair tucked up in a helmet.

The roar of the chopper drowned out the rest of her words. Pete and CJ bent their bodies over Liza to protect her from the debris. Conner covered her head with his, one eye on the chopper.

Jess hooked herself, then the litter, to the hoist and swung out over them. The pilot lowered her down onto the rock. She unhooked the litter, then herself.

Her expression was grim as she came over to assess Liza. The chopper moved away, circling to keep the blades from churning up the earth below.

Jess then dragged over her medical pack.

"I think we need a backboard," Pete said.

Jess pressed her fingers to Liza's carotid pulse. "Okay, Pete, help me with the backboard."

They retrieved the board from inside the litter, set it beneath Liza, and rolled her onto it. She sucked in a breath as if trying not to cry out. But her hand tightened around Conner's.

Jess secured Liza's head with the foam mounts, strapping her tight, head to foot, then took her blood pressure.

"Let me take a look at our other victim," Jess said, scrambling over to Esther, who still lay cradled in Skye's arms.

"Glad to meet you, Esther," Jess said to her. "Your boyfriend couldn't stop talking about you."

Conner glanced up and saw a smile lifting one side of Esther's grimy face. "My boyfriend?"

Jess snapped on fresh gloves and took Esther's pulse. "Well, he called you his girlfriend, so I was just assuming."

Girlfriend. Conner looked down at Liza strapped on the backboard. "Wanna be my girlfriend?"

She smiled up at him. "I can't really run away, can I?"

He pressed a kiss to her forehead. Shook his head.

At a cry, Conner looked over and saw that Jess had moved to Esther's destroyed ankle.

"I'm just going to immobilize this so we can get you and your friend to the hospital as soon as possible."

Esther smiled, glanced over at Liza. "She saved my life. She was so brave—"

Skye smoothed Esther's hair back. "I know. We all want to be like Liza when we grow up."

Conner glanced down at Liza, but tears filled her eyes. He kissed her forehead, a sad, crazy smile creeping up his face. "It's true, baby."

Jess retrieved her pack and pulled out a board splint. "This part might hurt."

Esther drew in a breath as Jess moved it under her foot.

Jess secured the ankle and Esther whimpered.

"Pete, CJ, I need help getting Esther into the litter. I'll bring her up first, then come back for Liza."

"No," Conner said. "I worked SAR for a while. You just send the litter back down. I'll load Liza onto it and back up to you."

"There's only room for three in the chopper," Jess said.

He looked at Liza, met her eyes. "Then I'll meet you at the hospital."

I promise.

He mouthed the words and got a return smile.

He watched as Jess and Esther were hoisted into the chopper, as Jess pulled Esther in, and then sent the litter back for Liza.

Conner worked quickly, his face grim as he loaded her for transport, glad for somewhere else to focus his attention than on the fear free-ranging through his chest.

Then, just before he indicated for Jess to lift her, he knelt beside Liza. "I'll be there as soon as I can."

"I know," she said. "Don't forget to bring the drone."

He offered a grim shake of his head. "It's gone, honey. It crashed. But it doesn't matter. I have you, and that's what counts."

Liza's entire body ached, her arm hot with pain, her leg burning, her side raw.

But she was alive.

And Conner was on his way. I'll meet you at the hospital.

"Just sit back and enjoy the ride." Words spoken by Jess, the EMT who sat beside Liza on a bench in the back of the helicopter. Esther sat in the copilot seat, her whimpering eased with a shot of painkiller, an IV attached to her arm.

Tall and blonde, in her blue one-piece uniform and helmet, Jess looked every inch a rescuer. She checked Liza's blood pressure as the chopper banked and turned up the river, lifting out of the canyon.

Then she started an IV in Liza's arm and tucked her in tight with a blanket.

"Someone should alert Esther's mom that we found her," Liza said, her voice drowning under the roar of the chopper.

Just when she thought she might have to repeat herself, Jess leaned over and spoke into her ear. "Her mom already knows! Our chopper pilot, Chet, thought you might need us again, so he parked at camp last night." Then Jess slipped an oxygen mask over Liza's nose and mouth. Cool sweet air rushed into her lungs.

Oh, good. Liza sank into the quiet shadow of painkiller and adrenaline drop.

Jess found her hand, gripped it. Then she leaned over again. "Don't worry—everything will be okay. There were some federal agents waiting for you all to come back. I'm sure they'll get Esther's mom to the hospital."

Jess sat back up, spoke into her headset to the pilot.

Liza closed her eyes.

I'll meet you at the hospital

Wait— She squeezed Jess's hand.

Jess looked down at her.

"The federal guys—why were they there?" Liza said through the mask.

Jess leaned down again. "Stop talking."

But Liza moved the mask aside, raised her voice. "Why

were the feds there?"

Jess shook her head. "I don't know. They were tracking Conner's progress, listening to Pete call in updates. They said they'd meet us at the hospital."

Liza closed her eyes, wincing.

"What hurts?" Jess asked, clearly concerned.

"The feds. They're not here to help—"

Jess heard at least the essential parts, because she backed up, frowned at Liza, clearly confused.

Oh, Conner. "The drone. He needs to bring his drone!"

But Jess replaced the oxygen mask over her face. "Stop talking. Everything is going to be fine."

No. No it wouldn't.

Because it occurred to Liza that if the feds camped outside her door, she'd be bait. Luring him. Trapping him. And if Conner went to the hospital, he'd walk right into the embrace of the feds.

She tried to grab Jess's arm.

Jess leaned down then, clearly realizing it was a losing battle. She moved the oxygen mask away.

"Please. Tell him that he shouldn't come to the hospital. It'll only get him in trouble."

But Jess frowned, shook her head, and reached to replace the mask once again. But Liza shook her head. She'd keep it simple, precise, and unmistakable. "Tell Conner to stay away!"

When Jess nodded, Liza let her replace the mask. Then she closed her eyes and tried not to weep as the shadows settled over her.

CHAPTER 16

JESS'S CALL CAME IN as Conner, Pete, CJ, and Skye hit the Pine Ridge trail, a half-click from Camp Blue Sky. Conner picked up his pace to a jog as he held the SAT phone to his ear.

They'd spent the day tramping through the forest, out to the meadow, then up the mountain, orienteering themselves back to the main trail, cutting their trip in half despite the brutal ascent.

Now a new strength flooded through Conner as Jess updated him on their trip to Kalispell, on Esther, and finally Liza. They'd rushed her into surgery to set her hand and repair her collarbone, which had been shattered by the jaws of the bear.

Jess's final words to him over the SAT phone, however, stopped him cold, right there at the view of Snowshoe Peak.

"What?"

"She said she didn't want you to come to the hospital."

Pete caught up to him, winded, grimy, sweat trickling down his face. They'd washed off in the river, but Pete's hands, his clothes, still bore traces of Liza's blood. Conner imagined he didn't look much better, his T-shirt bloodied, his hands scraped from where he'd scrabbled over rocks and ledges to get to her.

The image of the bear lifting Liza, shaking her, turned him cold.

"What do you mean she doesn't want me to come to the hospital?" Conner asked, his breath heaving. He didn't know whether to attribute that to the climb, or...well, the fact that she *didn't want him to come to the hospital*?

"What she said was, 'Tell Conner to stay away.' It was the last thing she said to me before she slid into unconsciousness."

If he'd had something to hang onto, Conner would have reached for it. As it were, he bent over, working hard to catch his breath—again, mostly from the climb, but yeah, from her words.

Stay away.

Never. Because this time Conner had spoken promises, had bared his heart. Had told her he loved her.

It didn't make sense.

"If it helps, she got upset after I told her the feds were at the camp, listening to your communication. She seemed to think they'd be waiting for you."

Conner stood up. "The feds are at the hospital?"

"They arrived about an hour ago with Esther's mom. And yeah, they're still here."

Waiting for him to show up.

Aw, Liza. No wonder she'd warned him away.

"Roger that, Jess." Conner wanted to tell her to go in, to convey to Liza that no way, no how would he not be at her bedside as soon as his legs could carry him. But yeah, he had to consider the feds.

And how to dodge them.

"What was that all about?" asked Pete as Conner clicked

off.

Conner updated him as he picked up his speed down the path. He looked over his shoulder, spotted CJ and Skye running doggedly after them. Skye might make a decent smoke-jumper, with her teeth-bared determination to keep up and contribute.

Pete's expression darkened with Conner's story. "We'll get you into that hospital room," he said, not elaborating.

They reached the camp and, hallelujah, the truck was waiting for them. Pastor John handed over his keys.

Skye jumped into the backseat of the extended cab. "Someone needs to bring it back."

Right.

Conner drove, trying not to kick up gravel as he took off out of camp, down the mountain, out of the Kootenai forest. But with dusk settling around them and a three-hour drive ahead of them—

He white-knuckled his way down the mountain, onto Highway 53, then south to 200.

Pete, CJ, and Skye had collapsed into slumber, Pete's head knocking on the side of the door. Skye had curled up on the seat, her head on CJ's lap. CJ's head flopped back onto the headrest, his hand on her shoulder.

Sweet.

The stars rose, glittering, watching as Conner drove through Ember. He nudged Pete awake, asked him if Conner should drop him or CJ off, but Pete pushed him ahead to Kalispell, still ninety miles south.

Now that Pete was awake, he fiddled with the radio, stopping the dial on a country tune. "I love this group—Montgomery King. The lead singer, Ben King, grew up with me and my brother, Sam." He hummed along.

Are you dreaming of me, out on your own.

Are you thinking of us, and our own song.

Are you wondering if I miss you too.

Are you hoping that I'm just as blue.

The country twang of the singer only stirred up the past, burned regret through Conner. He reached over, turned it off.

Pete said nothing.

Conner rolled down the window, letting the cool, bracing air keep him awake, his fingers drumming on the steering wheel.

"So, now you have a girlfriend, huh?" Pete asked out of the blue.

Conner glanced at him.

"Just summing up that last conversation. Why don't you just cut to the chase and marry her, dude?"

Marry. The word settled over him, through him. Marry her.

He must have made a sound of dissent, because Pete shook his head.

"Jed told me about your brother, Justin. About how he died working undercover and how you never found his killer."

He'd have to thank Jed personally for revealing that tidbit of information. Conner's mouth tightened into a knot of disapproval.

"You probably don't know this, but my dad died when I was fifteen—a skiing accident. He was skiing with me, something my brother, Sam, can't forgive me for." Pete said it loosely, with a half shrug.

"The thing is about my dad was that he was this great Christian, and while I believe in God, well, I'm nowhere near who my dad was. But you are. I overheard you and Jed talking a couple of weeks ago. You said something about faith, and how it believes that God is on our side, every time, all the time, and that He'll show up. And I want to believe that."

Conner looked at him and Pete sighed.

"I think after this summer I'm headed back home to Mercy Falls," Pete said. "My mom got diagnosed with cancer about a year ago, and I spent the winter there—working at the family lumber company. But I made a lot of mistakes in Mercy Falls, and it's not without the memories, you know? So I guess I need to know—is it true? Does God really forgive us, fix our messes, love us anyway? Or is that a fairy tale? Because I'm thinking if it's up to me to fix my mistakes, I'm in trouble."

Pete made a face that, for the first time, seemed devoid of any Pete-Brooks-Charm, something authentic. "But seriously—do you really believe that, or are you just saying it? Because you always look like you have everything together. But if you don't believe in happy endings, there's not much hope for me."

Conner stared ahead at the shiny black tar, sorting his reply.

He *did* have it all together—at least to the guys. But if he were to take a good look, he preferred to have faith in what he could hold onto, control. And yes, while he believed his words to Jed, maybe he hadn't exactly embraced them for himself.

Liza's words thundered into his head. I don't need promises. I just need you, showing up every day to love me.

And that was the point, wasn't it? In order to trust God, he had to trust God's goodwill toward him, His desire to show up every day to save him.

After all, hadn't He already proved it?

"If God is for us, who can be against us?" Conner said quietly into the night.

A slow smile slid across Pete's face. "There he is. The Reverend Young."

"It's true for you, Pete. And me. Because that's what God does—shows up to save us. Shows up to love us, every day. Nothing can separate us from His love. And that's the hope we need that everything will work out. And yeah, I believe in happy endings, because God says so."

And he would start living like it, too.

The lights of Kalispell turned the night sky to amber as he turned east, headed for the medical center. He topped the hill, found the sprawling complex, and pulled into the front lot.

CJ roused, and Skye lifted her head, sat up.

"So," said Pete. "What's the plan on getting Conner in without him getting arrested?"

"No plan," Conner said. "We're just going to walk in there, and I'm going to make them a deal. I'll surrender myself, my drone plans, and all my information as long as they let me say good-bye to my girl."

"But—" Skye started.

"It'll all work out," Conner said, reaching for the door handle. "I promise."

"I'm sorry, sir, but I can't let you go in there."

The words, in a voice she didn't recognize, roused Liza from the cottony darkness into the dim light of the hospital room. A cannula filtered oxygen into her nose, and fluid burned into her veins from the IV in her hand.

She didn't hurt—much—the woozy, ethereal sense of pain meds turning the room wobbly.

And then—Conner? *Not* wobbly, but smiling down at her, his face grimy with dirt and sweat, a two-day grizzle framing his soft, albeit worried smile, his devastating blue eyes holding hers.

"Hey there, Donut Girl," he said quietly, pressing a kiss to her forehead. He met her eyes again with a shake of his head. "Stay away from you? R*eally?* Hardly."

Liza wanted to shrug, but it hurt so she just nodded. "I didn't want to get you into trouble."

"I can get in trouble all on my own, baby. I don't need your help."

Night pressed against the windows in the private room, the smell of antiseptic and cotton mingling with his woodsy, sweaty, manly aura.

She wanted to leap from the bed and climb into his arms.

More voices outside, shouts, and then again, "Really, but no, sir, I can't allow you to go in there. He'll be out in a minute."

Yep, Pete's voice, and now she frowned, trying to catch up. "Wait—are the feds really out there?"

"Yeah, Pete and CJ are having a discussion with them right now. We thought it would be best if I ducked in here first and said good-bye."

He winced a little when he said it, and she wanted to reach up, touch his face, ease the frown away.

"You didn't find the drone, did you?"

He shook his head. "And it was my last one—but I do have my blueprints..." He offered a feeble smile. "I don't know what's going to happen, Liza. But I do know that—whatever does—"

"I'll be here, Conner." She said it fast, before he could offer up anything brave or even stupid. "I love you, and I don't have to know what tomorrow will bring in order to say that or to promise that I'll wait for you."

He had her hand and now brought it to his lips and kissed it. "I know this is incredibly selfish and that I should probably be saying good-bye, pushing you out of my life—"

"What—?"

"Shh...for your own good. Because on the crazy, wild chance that they find me guilty of something I didn't do, then, yeah, you'll be spending your Saturdays being strip-searched and visiting me on the other side of the glass. But I'm trying to put action to my faith, and I'm believing that somehow God's going to bail us out of this mess. That He's got a future and that it includes me and you, together. Living *happily ever after*. So even though Pete is probably right outside that door wrestling a man named Tex, who's intent on hauling me away in cuffs, here I am on my proverbial knee asking you to—"

"You'd better say *marry me*."

He stopped. Swallowed. Nodded. "I know it's not all that romantic—and I promise you romance and sunrises and a ring—but until then, I just need you to know that I'm all in. Forever. And if you promise not to run, I promise to, well... start making promises."

"I told you that you don't have to make me promises." She let a soft smile tip her lips, added warmth to her eyes.

"I know. But, babe, you deserve a promise—not because you're afraid that I'll walk out on you but because that's what people do. They commit their goodwill, their loyalty to each other. Promise to keep showing up and keep that promise every day."

He brought her hand to his lips. "So," he said softly, "I promise. Everything. All of it. If you'll just—"

"Deal," she said quietly. "I'll marry you."

His blue eyes shone. Then he leaned down and kissed her. Sweetly, the ruff of his whiskers brushing her chin, his lips soft on hers. He lingered there, just settling in, the promise of their future in his touch.

And when he leaned up, met her gaze with his, she saw it there, too.

The door banged open behind them, and Conner jerked around to see Pete backing into the room, his hand on the chest of a man who looked, indeed, like a Tex. Tall, wide shoulders, wearing a Stetson and a get-'er-done expression, he dwarfed Pete by a good two inches.

CJ came tumbling in after them. "Sorry, Conner! He said time's up."

And the look of resolve that tightened in Conner's expression said it was. He squeezed Liza's hand, then lifted his hands in surrender. "It's okay, boys." He turned to Pete. "Thanks."

Tex grabbed him by the shoulder, and Liza wanted to weep when Tex turned Conner, pulling his hands down behind him, cuffing him. "You're not under arrest, but I can't have you running away. This would have been a lot easier if you'd simply come in for questioning two days ago."

But Conner had his gaze on Liza, a smile on his face. "My girl needed me," he said.

Tears burned her eyes.

Tex manhandled him back around, when the door banged open again.

And behold, in the frame stood a big man, sooty from head to steel-toed boots, wearing an ash-streaked yellow shirt, grimy green pants, reverse raccoon eyes, and a crazy white grin. "I found your girlfriend!"

Huh?

Liza scanned her gaze from the man to Conner, then back.

Conner started to laugh. "Seriously?"

"Yep. Hauled her in from the Razor Creek fire while you were out playing Superman." The fireman was holding something blackened and mangled, a twisted plastic body, warped tail, wings curled in on themselves. He produced it like it might be an award for Conner.

A burned drone.

"You can barely make out the orange number four on the tail. Wasn't that the one you were looking for a couple of days ago, when you nearly made us dance around the buffalo?"

For the first time, Liza noticed the man's expression, something of disbelief. Conner nodded. "Yeah. It went down in Browning's field."

"I know. So it's got us wondering how it could have ended up twenty miles to the north of town at the head of the tiny, two-acre wannabe conflagration off of Razor Creek."

The man set the drone on the table at the foot of Liza's bed. Then he glanced at her. "Howdy, ma'am. Reuben Marshall. I work with Conner."

A big man with buffalo shoulders, unruly dark brown, nearly black hair—although that could be the soot—he had the bearings of a guy who stood by his friends.

And right behind him stood another man, one she thought she recognized.

"Jed Ransom?" Liza asked, grinning at the Jude County Smokejumpers crew boss. He looked as fire drenched as Reuben. "Are you jumping fires?"

"Hey there, Donut Girl." Jed came over, touched her toes, tented under the blanket. "I heard you wrestled a grizzly." He winked at her. "And won."

"I had help," she said and shot a look at Conner.

"Yeah, well, when Reuben picked up the drone, I figured we needed to track Conner down." His smile was warm. "Should have figured he'd be here with you. It's about time."

"How about uncuffing the poor guy?" A woman's voice—she came in and stood behind Jed, hooked her grimy arm through his. Tall and sturdy, she wore her auburn hair pulled back, her face looking freshly washed, although soot clung to her ears, her nose, her neck. "He clearly isn't going to run, and you have your drone."

"Kate Burns—this is Liza Beaumont. My *real* girlfriend," Conner said, casting a gimlet look at Reuben, who shrugged.

Tex was working off the cuffs. "We need to have a long and detailed conversation. Tonight."

Conner rubbed his wrists. "Of course." He reached out to pick up his melted drone, turning it over, a sadness in his expression. "If the drones are being refitted with something flammable, then we have a real problem."

Jed came over to inspect the drone. "Right. Because that means someone else has their hands on them and is trying to set you up as an arsonist."

"No," Pete said. "The *real* problem is the fact there is someone setting fires around Ember, knowing we'll jump them."

"In faulty parachutes," Kate added. "We found damaged chutes at the beginning of the season," she said as an aside to Tex. "Which means this is personal. Someone is out to get the Jude County Smokejumpers."

The words settled over them a long moment before Jed finally nodded, then addressed the federal agent. "Listen. Our team is grimy, tired, and hungry. We're hunkering down in a nearby hotel tonight. How about you come with us, and we'll tell you what we know about the fires, where the drones went down, and which of the fires might have been arson. Conner will swing by when he's done tucking in his gal."

He shot Liza another smile.

"I'll meet you for breakfast tomorrow," Conner said, amending Jed's plan. Clearly the man had no intention of hunkering down anywhere but at her bedside.

He came over, took her hand.

Skye had come in with CJ and now sidled over to Liza's bed as the team exited into the hall. She leaned close to her ear. "You were right."

Liza frowned.

"They are *way* too easy to fall for." She grinned and cast a look at CJ.

Oh boy.

Conner pulled up a chair, settled into it.

"How's Esther?" Liza asked, reaching out for his hand.

"She had surgery on her foot. I think they were able to set it, but I'm sure she'll have a long haul. I saw Shep, though. They brought him to see her."

"Oh, I'm sure Dr. and Mrs. Billings loved that."

"I dodged them. But Esther's mother made it to the hospital. I saw her in the lobby on the way in—she said to tell you thank you."

"For what—believing that a girl like Esther can't land the hottest, cutest boy in the school?"

"Yeah, that was pretty silly." He shook his head. "No, I think it was for saving her daughter's life." He raised an eyebrow.

Right. That.

As for the other... "Now that you're not going to jail—"

"You already said yes. It's a done deal. You promised, Donut Girl. Marriage. You and me, living in the trailer." Her mouth opened, and he laughed. "We'll negotiate."

She touched his hair, curly, tousled, grimy. "You need a shower."

"After you go to sleep."

"I don't want to close my eyes."

He leaned over, caught her gaze, and ran his finger down her cheek ever so gently. Then he pressed a kiss to her lips, lingering before he finally pulled away, a gleam in his eyes. "Don't worry. I'll wake you up in time to watch the sun rise."

A Note from the Author

You know those two people who are happily single, but you just know that there is the perfect person out there for them?

Yeah, that was Liza and Conner. Conner Young, my single, brilliant, self-sacrificing hero from Team Hope, and beautiful and wise Liza Beaumont, everyone's friend from the Deep Haven series. When they met on the pages of *Take A Chance On Me*, Christiansen book #1, I just knew they had a story.

I just had to wait for it. As the Christiansen series developed, every once in a while, a reference to Liza and Conner would show up…but it wasn't until Conner walked onto the pages in *Where There's Smoke* that I sat down with him and asked…so, what's the deal with you and Liza?

And he told me. A heartbreaker of a story that I knew I had to tell.

Liza is that girl who really can't see herself and the value she has to everyone around her. She often blames herself for others bad behavior instead of standing up for herself. And, she tells herself that she's happy with her and Conner being "just friends." But of course, she's not…and it takes the very real encounter with her darkest fears to realize that she needs to start seeing herself…and what she wants. But is her happy ending too much to hope for?

And poor Conner has made a promise he can't keep… and he can't forgive himself, or frankly, God, for that. Because Conner is the good guy, the one who does everything right. So, God should be on his side, right?

God is on their sides…and he has more waiting for them

than they can imagine if they are willing to trust him, not just his promises, but the very character of God.

Because God loves to delight his children, and if we could just hold onto that, figure that out, and trust that truth even in the darkest moments of our lives, we might be able to find our footing and even stand strong in the midst of our fears. God loves you, and He is good, all the time, forever and ever…even when life feels out of control, even when it's hard to understand, even when it feels like there is no resolution. Nothing can separate you from His love.

We know this because he's already written the happy ending. You can find it in John 14:3. And Romans 8:31-39.

Look it up and let it fill you with hope.

My deepest gratitude goes to Ellen Tarver, Barbara Curtis, David Warren, Lacy Williams and my parents, MaryAnn and Curt Lund who, through the hard lesson of grief, have sealed the truth of our happy ending in my heart.

I hope you'll continue with *Burnin' For You*, Gilly and Reuben's story. Reuben has loved Gilly for far too long…but it takes nearly losing her to give the big sawyer the courage to give away his heart. But…will it be too late? As for Gilly…it's up to her to save her team from an arsonist…but it just might cost her everything. The exciting conclusion to the Summer of Fire Trilogy!

Until we meet again—**Go in Grace!**

Susie May

Montana Fire

Book Three
Burnin' For You

Sneak Peek

CHAPTER 1

IF THEY STARTED RUNNING now, they just might make the lake before the fire consumed them.

That's what Reuben Marshall's gut told him when the wind shifted and rustled the seared hairs on the back of Reuben's neck, strained and tight from three days of cutting line through a stand of black spruce as thick as night.

After a week, the fire in the Kootenai National Forest had consumed nearly twelve hundred acres, and, as of breakfast this morning, his team of smokejumpers, as well as hotshot and wildland firefighter teams from all over Montana and Idaho, had only nicked it down to sixty percent contained.

Now, the fire turned from a low crackle to a growl behind him, hungry for the forest on the other side of the twenty-foot line that his crew—Pete, CJ, and Hannah—had scratched out of the forest, widening an already-cleared service road. CJ and Hannah were swamping for him as Reuben mowed down trees, clearing brush. Between the two of them, they worked like an entire crew, still proving themselves. Pete worked cleanup, digging the line down to the mineral soil.

Reuben's eyes watered, his throat charred from eating fire as he angled his saw into a towering spruce—one more tree felled and it would keep the fire from jumping the line or candling from treetop to treetop.

Chips hit his safety glasses, pinged against his yellow Nomex shirt, his canvas pants. His shoulders burned, his arms liquid.

In another hour they'd hook up with the other half of their crew—Jed, Conner, Ned, Tucker, and Kate—dragging a line along the lip of forest road that served as their burnout line. They'd light a fire of their own, consume all the fuel between the line and the active fire, and drive the blaze to Fountain Lake.

The dragon would lie down and die.

At least that seemed the ambitious-but-attainable plan that his crew boss, Jed, had outlined this morning over a breakfast of MRE eggs and protein bars. While listening, Reuben had opened three instant coffee packs into one cup of water and drank the sledge down in one gulp.

Still, deep in his gut, Reuben had expected trouble when the wind kicked up quietly, early this morning, rousing the team. They'd been tucked into their coyote camp—a pocket of pre-burned space—their safety zone on the bottom of the canyon near a trickle of river. Already blackened, the zone shouldn't reignite, but it left an ashy debris on Reuben, the soot probably turning his dark brown hair to gray under his orange hardhat. His entire team all resembled extras on *The Walking Dead*.

He felt like it—the walking dead, his bones now one constant vibration, fatigue a lining under his skin. Ash, sawdust, and the fibers of the forest coated his lips despite his efforts to keep his handkerchief over his mouth.

They'd worked in the furnace all day, the flame lengths twenty to thirty feet behind them, climbing up aspen and white pine, settling down into the crackling loam of the forest, consuming bushes in a flare of heat. But with the bombers overhead dropping slurry, the fire sizzled and roared, dying slowly.

He'd watched a few of them—the Russian biplane AN2, which scooped water from the lake in its belly, and the Air-tractor AT, dropping red slurry from its white belly.

Way overhead, the C-130, a loaner from the National Guard, circled for another pass.another pass.

Reuben wondered which one Gilly piloted—a random thought that he shoved away. It did him no good to let his thoughts anchor upon a woman he could barely manage to speak to.

Not that he had any chance with her anyway.

Keep his head down, keep working—wasn't that what his father always said?

Indeed, they all had expected the Fountain Lake fire to fizzle out with their efforts.

Until the wind shifted. Again.

And that's when the fine hairs on Reuben's neck stood on end, his gut began to roil.

He finished the cut, released his blade from the trunk of the tree.

"Clear!" He hollered, then stepped back as the massive tree lurched, crashed into the blazing forest.

The fire roared, a locomotive heading their direction.

It seemed Pete, twenty feet behind, hadn't yet alerted to the shift. Reuben couldn't account for why his gut always seemed to clench as a second sense when he scented danger. The last time he'd felt it, he'd known in his bones that team-mates were going to die.

And they had.

Not again.

Reuben did a quick calculation. They'd completed about

twenty-four chain lengths in the last six hours, about a quarter mile from the safety zone. They could run back to their strike camp in the burned-out section—a theoretical safe zone.

However, he'd known forest to reignite, especially the loam that had been flashed over quickly and hadn't been scorched down to the soil. Plenty of fuel left, if the fire got serious. And air was lethal, too, searing hot in their lungs as it cycloned around the safety zone.

If they turned and ran another hundred yards along the uncleared forest service road, they'd be over halfway to the lake, less than a half mile away. But they'd be running into unburned forest with nowhere to hunker down into safety if the fire overtook them.

Reuben listened for, but couldn't hear the other team's saws.

Through the charred trees, the sun backdropped the hazy gray of the late afternoon, a thin, blood-red line along the far horizon.

Jed's voice crackled over the radio. "Ransom, Brooks. We're battling some flare-ups here, and the fire just kicked up. Sit-rep on your position?"

Reuben watched Pete toggle his radio, standing up to gauge the wind.

"Must be the lake effect. She's still sitting down here," Pete said.

Reuben frowned, nearly reaching for his radio. But despite his instincts, Pete was right. Except for a few flare-ups, the fire *behind* them seemed to be slow moving.

Maybe—

"Right," Jed said, confirming Pete's unspoken conclusion that they were safe. "Just don't turn into heroes. Remember your escape route. To the fire, you're just more fuel. We're going to start bugging out to the lake."

Which probably was what they should be doing.

As if reading his mind, Pete glanced up at Reuben. For a second, memory played in Pete's eyes.

Only he, Pete, and Conner had survived being overrun last fall in a blaze that had killed seven of their team, including their jump boss, Jock Burns.

That had been a case of confusion, conflicting orders, and hotshots and smokejumpers running out of time. Fingers had been pointed, blame assigned.

The what-ifs still simmered in low conversations through their small town of Ember, Montana. Thankfully, this summer had been—well, mostly—injury free.

Reuben wanted to keep it that way. Except if their safety zone was not quite burned to the ground, it could reignite around them, trap them.

If they left now they could probably make the lake. But what if the fire jumped the road, caught them in the middle of a flare-up?

Reuben's low-muttered suggestion could end up getting them all killed. And if he were wrong, God wouldn't exactly show up to rescue them.

Reuben couldn't help, however, shooting a look back at Hannah and CJ still working and unaware of the radio communication.

Embers lifted, spurted out of the forest, across the line, sparking spot fires near the edge of the road. Reuben ran over, stomped one out, threw water from his pack on another.

Pete joined him. "We'll head back to the black."

Reuben glanced up, back along the route. Clear, for now.

"Roger," Reuben said.

Pete yelled to CJ and Hannah as Reuben shouldered his saw, started jogging back along the road to their safety zone. The air swam with billowing dust and smoke. His eyes watered, his nose thick with mucus.

"*Why is being a smokejumper so important to you?*" The words, his brother's disbelief after their father's funeral, smarted in his brain.

Why indeed? He coughed as he ran, a blast of superheated air sideswiping him, peeling a layer of sweat down his face. Sane people had normal jobs—like ranching or even coaching football. They didn't bed down in ash, drink coffee as thick as battery acid, smell like gas and oil and soot, and run *toward* a fire, hoping to find refuge.

If Reuben lived through this, he'd take a serious look at the answer.

Behind him, he heard Pete yelling at CJ and Hannah. "We're not on a scenic hike! Move it!"

Around them, sparks lit the air, the roar of the fire rumbling in the distance.

They should be running the other direction. The thought had claws around his throat.

As if in confirmation, a coal-black cloud rolled down the road, directly from their safety zone, a billow of heat and gas.

Reuben stopped cold.

Jed's voice burst through the radio, choppy, as if he might be running hard. "Pete. The fire's jumped the road. Head to the black *right now.*"

Except their safety zone was engulfed in smoke, embers, and enough trapped poisonous gasses to suffocate them.

Reuben whirled around, and Hannah nearly ran him over. He caught her arm. "Not that way!"

Pete had run back to him. He still held his Pulaski, his

face blackened behind his handkerchief, eyes wide, breathing too hard. "We're trapped."

He knew it—should have said something. But again, he'd kept his mouth shut, and people—*his* people—would die.

He glanced at Pete who was staring down the road, at the flames behind him. He glanced at Reuben and nodded.

The past would not repeat itself today.

Then Reuben toggled his radio, searched the sky. "Gilly? You up there?"

Please. Because though he might not be able to talk to her face-to-face in the open room of the Hotline Bar and Grill, this was a matter of life and death.

"Gilly, it's Rube. Please—"

"Priest, Marshall. I'm here. Starting my last run right now—"

"Belay that. We're making a dash for the lake, and we need you to lay down retardant along the forest road. We're about one click out, but the fire jumped the road about a quarter mile in."

Static. Then, "Roger that, Rube. I'll find you. Start running."

Pete had taken off with CJ, running along the still green fire road, toward the lake, some five hundred yards away.

"You miss this, we're trapped, Gilly." Reuben started running, still holding his saw.

More static, and probably he shouldn't have said that because Hannah, jogging beside him, looked at him, her eyes wide.

He didn't want to scare her, but they couldn't exactly run through a forest engulfed in flame. If Gilly could drop water or retardant on the road, it might settle the fire down enough for them to break through all the way to the lake.

The fire chased them, crowning through the branches, sending limbs airborne, felling trees. Sparks swirled in the air, so hot he thought his lungs might burst.

A black spruce exploded just to his right and with it, a tree arched, thundered to the ground, blocking the road.

Flames ran up the trunk, out to the shaggy arms, igniting the forest on the other side.

Hannah screamed, jerked back just in time.

Pete and CJ had cleared the tree. The flames rippled across it onto the other side of the road, into the forest, a river of fire.

"We're trapped!" Hannah screamed.

Reuben grabbed his water pump, a backpack of water they wore, and began to douse the fire, working his way to the trunk. "C'mon Hannah—let's kill this thing!"

She unhooked her line, added water to the flames. The fire died around the middle, the rest of the tree still burning.

He grabbed his saw, dove into the trunk.

Reuben had once won a chainsaw competition—sawing through a log the size of a tire in less than a minute. He'd have to make this faster.

Sweat beaded down his back, his body straining as he bore down. *Faster!* The saw chewed through the wood, cleared the bottom.

He started another cut a shoulder width away, from the bottom. "More water, Hannah!" The flames crawled up toward him.

He turned his face away, let out a yell against the heat. Heated, blessed water sprinkled his skin as Hannah used the rest of the water to bank the flames.

The saw churned against a branch. "Use my supply!"

She grabbed his hose, leveled it on the fire biting at the branches, the bark.

The fire had doubled back, along the top, relit the branches around him. He gritted his teeth, standing in the furnace, fighting the saw.

Don't get stuck.

He broke free, the wood parting like butter.

The stump fell to the ground, creating an opening through the trunk. Reuben grabbed Hannah and pushed her forward, commandeering the hose and dousing the flames with the last of his water.

Pete and CJ, on the other side, had banked the flames with the last water in their canisters.

Ahead of them, the fire edged the road—beyond, a wall of flame barred their escape.

Reuben dropped his saw. "We can't deploy here. We'll die."

He looked up into the sky, saw nothing but gray, hazy smoke.

He scooped his radio out of his belt. "Gilly, where are you?"

Nothing. He looked at Pete, his eyes blurry from smoke and ash. Hannah was working out her shake-and-bake emergency tent, and he didn't have the heart to repeat himself. CJ had run ahead, as if looking for a way out.

They had a minute, or less, to live.

"Gilly," he said into the walkie, not sure if she could even hear him. His voice came out strangely distant, vacant. Void of the screaming going on inside his head.

"If you don't drop right now, we die."

Made in the USA
Middletown, DE
22 April 2019